the
history
between
us

ASHLEY JAMES

Cover Design: Mel D. Designs
Interior Formatting: Wanderlust Formatting
Editing: Nice Girl Naughty Edits

To the sixteen year old me who was down bad for her dad's best friend. Who was delulu enough to think you guys would fall in love one day and live happily ever after.

Colt is living my teenage dreams, and I love this journey for him.

playlist

Full playlist can be found on Spotify.

One Night Standards by Ashley McBryde
Porch Swing Angel by Muscadine Bloodline
The Fire by Chris Stapleton
Under My Skin by Nate Smith
Complicated by Kip Moore
Sweet Home Alabama by Lynyrd Skynyrd
Worst Way by Riley Green
Snapback by Old Dominion
Craving You by Thomas Rhett, Maren Mooris
Not Good At by Morgan Wallen
Complicated by Josh Ross
Dust on the Bottle by David Lee Murphy
I Remember Everything by Zach Bryan, Kacey Musgraves
Alcohol You Later by Mitchell Tenpenny

Copper Lake Disclaimer

This series takes place in the fictional small town of Copper Lake, Wyoming, and it follows cowboys who compete in the professional rodeo. The use of the Professional Rodeo Cowboy Association (or PRCA as it's frequently referred to as in the books) is a work of fiction. I did my best to keep the organization as accurate as possible with regards to the rules, regulations, circuit schedule, etc., but there are instances where I had to take creative liberties for the sake of the storyline. Names, characters, businesses, places, events, and incidents are either the products of the authors imagination or used in a fictional manner. Any resemblance to actual persons, living or dead, or actual events is purely coincidental.

PROLOGUE

COLT BISHOP

AGE TWENTY-ONE

Sweat drips down into my brow, my heart beating erratically as my hips move from side to side to the beat of the sensual music pulsing from the speakers placed around the room. The body behind mine is hot and hard against my back, and the hand wrapped around me, holding me close, is dangerously low on my stomach. It's gotta be close to last call; I know it's getting late. I've been here for hours now, the liquor diluting my blood, making my head fuzzy and my judgement shotty. I don't even know how much I've had to drink tonight, but I know it's a lot.

All of my nerve endings are on fire, oversensitive to every sound, smell, and touch. Every puff of hot breath on my neck sends a layer of goosebumps all over. Every stroke of his fingers as they inch below the hem of my shirt, teasing the skin there, sending a chill across my overheated body. The rich, mahogany scent of his cologne as it invades my nostrils, and the nostalgia the scent brings—right at the edge of off-limits and forbidden. How my ass grinds against him, rubbing against the hard ridge of his erection. The way my own cock is stiff and throbbing behind my tight Wranglers. *Everything.*

When I came here tonight, it was with the purpose of hooking up. To get my mind off life and get sweaty with a stranger for a few hours. I'm in Seattle for only a few days, and I've always heard how luscious the queer nightlife is here, so of course, I had to check it out. Never in a million years did I expect to see who I did as I walked through the door of the unsuspecting hole-in-the-wall bar-slash-nightclub.

By the time I sat beside him at the bar, my mind was made up. I knew what I wanted, and what I wanted was him. Surprised eyes took me in, and we made polite small talk for a while as we threw back shot after shot. Like me, he, too, was there for a purpose; I could see it in his eyes. And I wasn't blind...I saw the way he looked at me. The way his gaze lingered a little longer than appropriate. The way his body leaned into mine as we spoke. How he got a little more flirty the more we drank. When I asked him to dance earlier after shot number six...or maybe it was seven, he barely even thought about it before he said yes.

And this is where we've been since. The song changes and I chance my luck, turning around in the strong arms wrapped around me. Part of me feels like eye contact will sever the connection. It'll knock some sense into him and he'll shove me off, reminding me how this is *wrong* and shouldn't be happening.

Thankfully, it doesn't. Blame it on the alcohol we've both consumed or the electric way our bodies feel rubbing up against each other, but he looks *gone* for me as I wrap my arms around his neck and begin swaying again. The DJ in this place knows what they're doing with this music, that's for damn sure.

His sapphire eyes pierce into mine, heating me from the

inside out. Standing roughly five or so inches taller than me, he makes me feel small in his hold, which is an interesting—and sexy—feeling. I'm not a short guy by any means, but him... He's a brute. It's one of the things I've always found attractive about him. That, and the eyes paired with thick black hair that I'm dying to drag my fingers through. That combination has always been my kryptonite.

Wetting his lips with his tongue, my eyes track the movement greedily, my mouth watering at the sight. What I would give to taste those plump lips and suck on that sweet pink tongue. Feel it trail across my body, starting up at my throat and working its way down lower...and lower.

The space in here is small and stuffy. Sweaty bodies bump up against us left and right as the dance floor gets more and more crowded. People surround us, grinding, rubbing, kissing, grappling at each other. The energy in here is electric; a thick layer of arousal covering us all like a fog.

My hands are clasped behind his head, while his are holding the small of my back. With every sway of our hips, though, they sink lower. A zap of heat shoots down my spine as he takes a firm hold of my ass, squeezing as a throat-deep groan vibrates out of him. We've been dancing together for a while now, the temptation between us building with each song. I'm going out of my mind, and the need to taste him is growing too strong to ignore. My gaze flits between his piercing eyes and his lips as I wet my own. Every inch of my body lights up, bloodstream infused with liquor and a need so visceral, I can't hardly stand it.

The more packed the dance floor becomes, the closer we're shoved together. He's backed up near a wall now, our bodies flush. My heart drums in my chest, my breathing coming out in harsh pants. The feel of his body plastered against mine is unreal. We're both dripping sweat, the energy, the tension between us sizzling.

I've always been a man who takes what I want. I don't hesitate, I don't get shy, and tonight will be no different. Standing up on my toes, I crash my mouth to his, hoping like hell right now won't be the time he puts a stop to this. I feel his body stiffen against mine for a second before he grips me tighter, holding me as close as possible. Our lips part and our tongues meet in the middle, rolling and tangling together. I can't help the groan that escapes at the flavor of him—whiskey and temptation—as it floods my senses. He tastes better than I ever could've imagined—and I've imagined this *a lot*.

We kiss like we're starving for one another, not a single care in the world about who's watching. We sure as hell aren't the only horny ones in here; a quick glance around the room would prove that.

Ripping my mouth from his, I drag in a deep breath, bringing my lips to the shell of his ear. "Let's get out of here," I say, loud enough for him to hear over the music.

When I pull back to get a good look at him, I bite down on my lip as I watch a smirk tug into place. His eyes darken as he takes me in, looking downright *famished* as he tips his head over to the side and grabs my hand, leading me off the dance floor, over to a set of rickety stairs that leads to a second level I hadn't noticed before.

Each step is another whoosh of blood in my ears. Another heavy thump against my ribcage. Another jolt of electricity down into my groin.

At the top, there's a door that he unlocks with a set of keys retrieved from the pocket on his jeans. As we walk over the threshold, I notice how bare it is up here. It's dark and open, and it looks to be a studio apartment of some sort. There's a small kitchenette in the corner, a couch near where we're standing, and a king-size bed off to the right. A handful of questions pass through my mind, like who's apartment this is, or why it's so empty, but I don't ask any of them.

Shutting the door behind me, he turns the lock until it clicks into place, and then we're both moving. I reach behind me, ripping my shirt over my head, and he does the same. Next, I wiggle out of my jeans, kicking off my boots as I do, and he follows. It's dark in here, but thankfully my eyes have started to adjust so I get to drink him in. And fuck, what a sight it is. He's husky; broad shouldered, with corded arms and defined pecs. His thighs are powerfully built, looking like they could crush my skull. Chest dusted with dark hair that leads down the center of his abdomen. He's *thick* in all the right places, looking good enough to fucking devour.

The booming music downstairs is muted up here, but barely, as the walls shake with the bass.

"Come here," I mutter as I brush past him and pad over to the bed. It's neatly made with a dark comforter and equally dark sheets. I shove him down before crawling on top of him. With his hands planted on my hips, our bodies mold together as I gaze down at him. "Tonight, we're strangers. You don't know me and I don't know you, understand?"

Smirking, he watches me, fingers biting into my flesh. He nods. "Understood."

Soon enough, we lose ourselves to one another, becoming nothing more than sweaty bodies rolling around, gasping breaths, deep, throaty moans, and sweet, forbidden ecstasy. By the time the sun comes up and I peel my eyes open, I'm in the hotel room I don't remember going back to last night. Head throbbing, I roll out of bed and jump in the shower, my mind trying to retrace everything from the night before. The faint outline of fingerprints on my hips and the darkened bruise on my neck are the only evidence that last night wasn't only a figment of my imagination. That it was real.

I wrap a soapy fist around my thickening erection, pumping myself long and slow as broken pictures replay in my mind of slick skin, hungry lips, wandering hands. Beautiful cries of pleasure, the writhing body underneath mine, and how good it felt to play out my teenage fantasy between the sheets.

How it felt to watch William Andino shatter into a million pieces…because of *me*.

CHAPTER 1
COLT BISHOP

PRESENT DAY

"*G*oddamnit!*" Huffing out an aggravated breath, I sit down on the edge of my bed, letting my boot drop to the ground with a clunky *thump*. This is such bullshit. I'm a grown man; putting on my shoes shouldn't be *this* much of a challenge. Yet here I am, unable to do so, and based on the footfalls getting closer outside of my room, I'd say help is on the way—much to my utter annoyance.

"Colt?" my mom calls out before pushing open my door and peeking her head inside. "Are you okay?"

"I'm fine," I lie, out of breath from my failed attempt at getting out the door without assistance.

Her eyes catalog everything, finding the discarded boot on the floor. "Do you need help, honey?" Without waiting for a response, already knowing I need help I'm not going to want to admit to, she enters the room, a red-and-white checkered apron wrapped around her waist and her hair tied up into a messy bun on top of her head. She helps me slip my foot into one boot, and then the other, before sliding my jeans over the top of them. Smiling up at me, she asks, "Do you need a ride?"

Blowing out a breath, I shake my head. "No, I got one already, but thank you."

It's been just over a week since I had shoulder reconstructive surgery for a torn labrum and torn rotator cuff. On top of that, I have a fractured wrist and a few cracked ribs, so moving around isn't as easy as it usually is, and driving myself is completely out of the question.

As if on cue, my phone lights up with a message from my buddy, Whit, letting me know he's about two minutes out. I don't bother responding. It's too much effort. Instead, I stand up and grab an all-black hat off my dresser, putting it firmly on my head before shoving my wallet and keys into my pocket using my non-injured hand. Thankfully, both my shoulder and wrist injuries are all on the same side, but unfortunately, it's my dominant side.

Learning how to do everything I need to do left-handed has been a challenge I haven't quite mastered yet. I keep trying to remind myself that it's only been a week, and it'll probably get easier as time goes on, but I tend to be an instant gratification type of man, so patience isn't necessarily my strong suit. To say the past week has been something straight out of hell would be an understatement.

"Whit's here," I mutter to my mom as I brush past her. "Thank you for your help."

"Of course, honey. Are you coming back here after your appointment?"

Nodding, I say, "I'm grabbing lunch with Whit, but after that, yeah, I'll be back."

My mom grins, and I know she's trying her best to cheer me up. It's what she's been doing all week, and it makes me feel like shit that I can't pretend a little better for her sake. "I'm making your favorite for dinner tonight."

Forcing a smile, I lean in and give her a hug, pressing a kiss to her cheek. "Thanks, Mom. I'll be back."

"Tell Whit I said hello," she calls out from behind me.

Stepping out onto the porch, it's a warm, sunny day. Sweat pricks the back of my neck, and I'm reminded that we're smack dab in the middle of summer in Copper Lake, Wyoming. Had it not been for the accident and subsequent surgery, I'd be somewhere in Colorado with my friends, getting ready to kick some ass on the rodeo circuit. As a professional bull rider, I spend about four months out of the year traveling and competing with the best of the best in my division. All of this shit cut my season short by almost half, and who knows if I'll even be healed enough by the start of next season to compete.

Climbing into Whit's truck, I give him a chin nod. "Hey, man."

"Hey, how're you feeling?"

"Just peachy," I drawl, as that fake smile comes out to play again.

Whit puts the truck into drive. "Seatbelt," he mutters, glancing over at me, not moving even an inch until I'm safely secured in his vehicle.

Thankfully, I'm able to click the belt into place without too much trouble. "Thanks for driving me. I hope you weren't too busy at work."

As Copper Lake's resident veterinarian, Whit is typically up to his ears in furry patients of all shapes and sizes. Our town is your typical cliché small town. We've got one main doctor's office, one dentist, one vet, and only a handful of places to eat on Main Street that include one to-die-for diner, a dive bar, and our version of fine dining, which is really only about one step up from an Applebee's.

"It's no problem," he says, turning onto the main road. "It's a rather slow day, and I was able to schedule around this."

Today's the first day I'm seeing my primary care doctor since my surgery. He has to refer me to a physical therapist, and I'm hoping I can get started on it as soon as possible, so I have the best chance I can at returning to the circuit next spring. Dr. Roger Andino has been my family's doctor since I was little. His clinic is right in town, about three blocks down from the diner Whit and I are going to for lunch afterward. Parking the truck in one of the spots out front, Whit and I both climb out and head inside.

"You don't have to wait here for me if you don't want," I tell him.

He shrugs. "It's this or wait in my truck."

After I check in with the front desk, it's only about ten minutes before I'm brought back into a room. The nurse checks all my vitals and lets me know the doctor will be in soon. In all the downtime I've had over the last week, I've taken to Google to find out how soon I realistically could get back to training. My wrist shouldn't take long to heal; maybe six weeks at most. It's my shoulder that's going to take the longest. There's varying answers; some websites stating I can get back to most activities within six months, but some indicating it could be longer. Six months puts me at around the beginning of the year. We leave for the circuit in mid-May, so if that's the case, I think I could make that work. But honestly, the sooner I can get back to training and working out, the better. The thought of missing out on next season, after already missing half of this one, makes me want to scream.

The door opens, and when I glance up to take in the man walking into the room, my heart sputters in my chest as a familiar pair of sapphire eyes meet mine. Confusion clouds my mind because while Dr. Andino is standing before me…it's a version of him that's about twenty years younger than I was expecting.

"William?" I ask, head cocked to the side.

Jaw clenching, he takes a seat on the round swivel chair in front of the computer in the corner of the room. "Hello, Colt."

Hazy memories of his hot mouth all over my neck flash through my mind before I can stop them. "What are you doing here?"

A crease forms between his thick brows. "My father retired several weeks back," he announces. "The office sent out notice to all the patients letting them know of the switch well over a month ago. Didn't you receive it?"

My eyes widen, and I breathe out a laugh. "I've been on the road since May," I explain. "Wait, so you're telling me *you're* my doctor now?"

About a dozen inappropriate jokes and comments zip through my mind, but I manage to keep them to myself. Based on his narrowed eyes and the hard set of his mouth, I'm willing to bet he's not in the mood to joke with me about our drunken tryst two years back.

"That is correct. I've taken over the practice in my father's absence," he states matter-of-factly before using his key card to unlock the computer. "Now, tell me, Colt. How are you feeling?"

"Like shit," I huff plainly, not bothering to sugarcoat it. This week has been hell. Between the shoulder reconstruction surgery to fix the torn labrum and rotator cuffs, the fracture in my wrist, and the cracked ribs I walked away with after I was bucked off the back of a bull, and then stepped on by said bull, the rest of my year is looking a whole lot different than I thought it would. Being a professional bull rider, it comes with the territory. We all know it's a risk, but nobody ever thinks it'll be them.

Lifting a brow, he glances over at me. "A lot of pain?"

I shake my head. "Not too bad. I've been doing the exercises the physical therapist at the hospital told me to do. You know, to help with stiffness and mobility and all that. It kind of hurts during that, but she said that was to be expected for at least a few weeks."

"Any swelling?"

"Not much," I say. "I've been taking the anti-inflammatories they gave me. How soon can I start physical therapy?"

William raises off his chair and walks over to me, gesturing to my shoulder. "Do you mind if I take a look at it?" he asks, ignoring my question.

"Go for it." I shimmy my arm out of the gown the nurse made me put on, wincing and gritting my teeth as a bolt of pain radiates through my limb.

Stepping into my space, his eyes flick to meet mine for a brief moment before he directs his attention to my incision. A faint mahogany scent reaches my senses, and it makes my heart race a little faster. It's a good smell all on its own, but accompanied by the memories that come along with it make it even more delicious. That night is the very last thing I should be thinking about, especially in this setting, but I can't help it. Especially when he's looking the way he does, all professional and serious.

His facial structure is unreal. I allow myself a moment to admire him while he's preoccupied. There's a furrow to his dark, thick brows as he examines my shoulder, elbow, and wrist with the utmost gentleness. A beauty mark sits below his right eye next to his prominent Grecian nose. His strong jawline is hidden beneath an impressive short, thick beard that's well on its way to being more salt and pepper than just pepper. He's in his mid-forties, but I don't know his exact age, only that he wears it well. William is a strikingly handsome man, and he always has been. If anything, he's aged like fine wine.

"Let me see your range of motion," he mutters, crossing an arm over his chest and resting his elbow on it as he rubs along his jaw with his thumb and forefinger.

I grit my teeth, showing him the small exercises I've been doing every day since leaving the hospital. It's not much, but I know it's helping in the long run. I'm ready for more, though.

"Good," he grunts, then resumes his seat in front of the computer. "That's looking great, Colt."

"When can I start physical therapy?" I ask again, firmer this time, as I readjust the gown to cover my shoulder again. "I know I'm already out the rest of this season, but I'd like to get back to it by the spring."

William's expression hardens. "Colt, this is going to be a process. It takes time to get back to full mobility. Rushing or overexerting yourself can make things worse. This is a marathon, not a sprint, and I need you to understand that."

"I do understand that."

He nods. "I think you'd be okay to start physical therapy right away. There's a physical therapist who is based out of Cheyenne, but once a week, she comes down and she works in this building. I'll send over a referral, and if she has openings here, great, but please keep in mind, you may have to travel to Cheyenne if not."

"Noted," I quip.

"Wonderful." Standing up, he walks over to the door. "I'll get that sent through today, so you should hear from her office this week. I'd like to see you back here in four weeks to check your progress."

"You got it, Doc." A smirk spreads on my lips as I toss him a wink. "I'll be the perfect patient."

His lips purse. "I'll be the judge of that." With a quick check of the time on his watch, he adds, "Four weeks, Colt. In the meantime, do what the physical therapist says. Wear your sling, no heavy lifting, and no activities that force your elbow away from or in front of your body."

Arching a brow, I say, "No activities in front of my body, huh?"

William looks at me, deadpan, and reaches for the doorknob. "Goodbye, Colt."

Well, this could be fun.

CHAPTER 2
WILLIAM ANDINO

A YEAR AND A HALF AGO

Raising my fist to the large door, I knock, waiting a few moments before it's pulled open. The bright, smiling face of my best friend's wife comes into view as she pulls me in for a hug.

"Will, hi! I'm so glad you were able to make it; it's been so long since we've seen you."

"Hi, Trish," I greet as we pull apart and she steps aside, letting me waltz into their beautiful, welcoming home. Notes of cinnamon and nutmeg reach my nostrils, paired with the scent of the turkey surely cooking in the oven. My stomach grumbles, and I inhale a little deeper, loving the warm, comforting smells.

I spot my father sitting on the couch with Max's parents, and it takes him a moment to notice me, but when he does, he stands and crosses the room, wrapping his arms around me in a strong hug. "Happy you came, son," he murmurs in my ear as I hug him back.

This is the first Thanksgiving I've had in Copper Lake since

I moved to Seattle, but it's also my family's first Thanksgiving without my mother, and I couldn't let my dad celebrate by himself, hence why we're here, at my best friend's place instead of at his house. I knew my dad needed to be surrounded by people who love him, and who would lift his spirits. Our families have always been intertwined, even when Max and I were kids. I knew this would be a good place for him today because, even if he won't admit it, I know he's struggling with missing Mom.

Hell, I think we all are. It's only been a few months, but it cuts like it was just yesterday.

"Sorry I'm so late," I say to nobody in particular as my father resumes his spot next to Mr. and Mrs. Bishop. "My flight out of Seattle was delayed, which caused me to miss my connecting flight."

"Oh, don't worry about it," Trish insists. "And you're not even our most tardy today. Colt's over at Jessie's family's house, but should be here soon." Ringing her hands on the apron wrapped around her middle, Trish smiles before turning and strolling back into the kitchen, not even realizing what type of panic she set off inside my mind with that one statement.

A little over six months…that's how long it's been since I woke up alone in an apartment above my buddy's bar with the scent of my best friend's son still on the sheets beside me. A little over six months since my life has effectively been turned upside down. Coming to town for the holiday, I knew I ran the risk of running into Colt, especially given that this is his *parents'* house, but I keep reminding myself that this is for my dad. It's not about Colt, not about me. It's for my dad. My father deserves to be surrounded by happiness and love today, even if that means I will likely spend the entire afternoon uncomfortable.

Colt isn't even here yet, and the sheer mention of his name has my pulse racing like a criminal about to get arrested for their crime. Sweat pricks the back of my neck and along my brows, my shirt suddenly too tight around my throat, and it feels like everybody in the room is privy to this salacious piece of gossip just from looking at me. But that's absurd. I know it's absurd. But so is hooking up with your best friend's son, and I did that, so exactly what does it say about my own mental state?

Setting off to find Max, I stroll through the house and into the kitchen. Trish is putting a salad together at the counter, and when she throws me a look over her shoulder, her lips tug into another warm smile. "He's in the garage," she tells me, already knowing who I'm looking for.

"Thanks."

Max and I have been friends since we were kids. We were thick as thieves growing up, and to this day, we will catch up on the phone at least once every other week, if not more.

A few years back, he renovated the detached garage into a workshop slash man cave, but this is the first time I'm seeing it in person. As I waltz in, he glances up from his current project, giving me a small grin.

"Hey, man. You made it."

"I did, after the flights from hell." I chuckle. "What are you working on?"

"Ah, Trish thrifted this hutch last month, and she asked me to refinish it. Finally getting around to it."

Snickering as I watch him work, I say, "A once world-famous bull rider spends his retirement doing DIY projects."

Max Bishop used to be a household name back in the day. A professional bull rider. One of the best, in fact, until an injury ended his career and nearly killed him.

He huffs out a laugh. "Fuck you, it's relaxing, okay?" Pausing, he glances up. "How're you doing today?"

The sincerity is his tone chokes me up. Clearing my throat, I nod. "I'm good. Just want my dad to have a nice day. I know he misses her, and today has got to be hard for him."

Resuming what he was doing, he nods before quietly adding, "Remember, you can miss her too. She was your mom, and you can be there for your dad while still acknowledging your own grief."

With decades of friendship comes knowledge. Max knows that I all too often will put everybody else's feelings and needs above my own. Especially my father's. I've always been this way, and I couldn't even explain why. Even now, when he's rightfully calling me out, my knee-jerk reaction is to insist that I'm fine again. Instead, I say nothing, and he thankfully lets me.

Nodding his chin behind me, Max mutters, "There's beer in the fridge if you want one."

"Cool, thanks."

"Grab me one while you're at it."

The next half hour or so is spent catching up with my friend and tossing back a cold one. Despite it being years since we've seen each other, it feels like no time has passed at all. It's always been like that with us; a solid friendship that doesn't require a whole lot of maintenance.

Once we finish with our beers, Max tosses his empty can in the trash as I do the same before saying, "Well, we better get inside and socialize before Trish kicks our asses."

I chuckle, but follow him out of the garage and across the yard toward the back door. It's propped open, Trish probably wanting some fresh air while she cooks. As we step inside, I notice she's still in here, along with Max's mother. They're each doing their own thing while they chat. Music is playing from a speaker set up on the counter, and the whole place smells even more delicious.

"About time you boys came back inside," Trish teases as Max lays a kiss on her cheek. Those two are still as in love as they were when we were in high school. "Colt got here a few minutes ago," she tells her husband. "He's in the living room with your dad and Roger."

There goes my racing pulse again.

This is fine. It's for my dad, I tell myself, trying to calm my nerves. It happened months ago, and Colt probably forgot all about it. It was probably an unmemorable night for him. He more than likely has not spent ample time replaying every hazy detail. Heck, he's a hot-shot professional bull rider now, and a popular one, from what I can tell. His drunken romp with an old guy will be the least of his concerns.

Shoulders rolled back, I stroll into the living room with Max, making sure to keep my eyes anywhere *but* on Colt, even though I can see him clearly in my periphery. I don't know what I was thinking at that bar that night. It was careless and stupid and a mistake.

It shouldn't have happened.

And most days, I'm able to push it out of my mind until late at night, but with him in the same room as me? Impossible. The memory rushes back; every feeling, every harsh breath, every touch, every sound, it's right there in the forefront of my mind like it was last night.

Finally, and because I don't want to be rude or raise concern, I let my gaze drift to Colt. He's sitting directly next to my father on the couch, and it looks like he was showing him something on his phone. His bright green eyes meet mine, a twitch of humor tugging on one corner of his lips.

"William, I didn't know you were going to be here," he drawls with that same tone of confidence and swagger he always has.

"Nice to see you, Colt," I say plainly, taking a seat in one of the open recliners. "How have you been?"

His grin is blinding. "Oh, you know, living the dream. How's Seattle?" he asks, with mischief dancing in his eyes. "Staying out of trouble?"

My throat constricts, and I find it hard to swallow as my heart pounds aggressively. "Seattle is great," I grit out.

"I keep telling him to move back to Copper Lake," my father chimes in. "But Will's always been a stubborn one, and he won't listen."

Holding my gaze, Colt's eyes narrow slightly as he says, "What a shame."

Swallowing thickly, I tune in to whatever conversation Max is having with his dad, and spend the rest of the afternoon doing whatever I can to avoid Colt. It's not easy, considering his extroverted, bubbly personality has no issue slipping into conversations. I swear, the entire dinner I don't take a single full breath, scared that if I do, all of my secrets will spill out with the air in my lungs.

We live states away, and it's just one day. It's fine.

It's not like we have to see each other on a regular basis, or at all, really. Surely, I can get through this one day, because *it's for my dad.*

CHAPTER 3
WILLIAM ANDINO

PRESENT DAY

It's a little after five when I lock up the office and head to my truck. Today was interesting, to say the least. Turning on the vehicle, I blast the air conditioning before rolling up the sleeves of my shirt. It's hot as hell out, and it's toasty enough in here to make sweat drip down the back of my neck almost immediately. A vast difference from the coolness that was my office. Reaching into the front pocket of my briefcase on the seat beside me, I pull out my phone and find the contact I'm looking for, hitting call. It only rings a few times before it connects, a deep voice coming through the line.

"Hello?"

"Hey, I'm on my way. Need me to stop at the market on my way and pick anything up?"

"No, got everything here. I'll see you in a bit."

It's been an adjustment being back in Copper Lake. Living in Seattle for the last ten years has gotten me used to the hustle and bustle of the city. Coming back to my roots is such a significant difference. I didn't realize how much I'd missed it.

Not even fifteen minutes later, I'm driving down the long gravel road that leads to Grazing Acres Ranch. Memories from early in my childhood up until college flood my mind as the house and the barn come into view. Many a summer day spent working here, and many nights spent getting into trouble like teenage boys do.

Parking beside an old, beat-up Chevy truck that has to be nearly as old as I am, I turn my truck off and climb out.

"Will," a gruff voice that I'd recognize anywhere says.

I round the truck, finding Conrad Strauss walking out of the barn, a grin on his face. "How the hell are you, friend?" I ask as we give each other a hug and a pat on the back.

"Oh, same old, same," he mutters. "I can't believe you're back in town."

"Me neither." I laugh as we head toward the house.

Conrad and I have been friends since grade school. I remember learning to ride a bike with him and our other friend, staying out and riding up and down the gravel roads as fast as we can until the streetlights came on, and we had to go home. The house I grew up in was about a mile and a half down the road from the ranch, and it didn't have nearly as much land as this place does. So many fond memories. We've kept in touch over the years, catching up every so often if I came into town, but it's nice to be back and be able to do something as simple as a weeknight dinner with an old friend.

Once inside, Conrad grabs us a couple of beers, handing me one before taking a long pull off his own. I do the same, enjoying the crisp, cool taste on my tongue. "Man, it hasn't changed a bit in here," I mutter, glancing around the house that was once like a second home to me. This ranch has been in the Strauss family for generations.

"No, it sure hasn't," he agrees. "I was just going to grill some steaks, if that's okay? I've already got the potatoes in the oven baking."

"Sounds good to me."

Conrad grabs a plate of the seasoned slabs of meat out of the fridge, and I follow him outside to where the grill is. There's a large navy blue and white porch swing that I take a seat in while he gets to work. "How's your dad doing?" he asks.

"He's doing okay," I reply, taking another pull of the beer. "Enjoying retirement."

"He still in that house off Maple?"

"Yeah, he is."

"Are you living with him, or did you get something of your own?"

"With him," I say. "The older he gets, the harder things are for him, and it's just too much house to keep up with on his own. It's not so bad. The house is plenty big enough, and he takes the room on the main level, while I take the upstairs because his knees have gotten so damn bad, he can't go up them all that often."

"I'm sure he appreciates you being there, too." He glances over his shoulder, a smirk shining bright. "Even if Roger would never admit to it."

We both laugh, knowing how stubborn my old man is. If it weren't for my aunt insisting that he finally retire, and keeping me updated on his condition, he probably would've worked himself into the ground. That practice is his pride and joy, and I know it was hard on him to make the decision to leave, but it was the right call. He wasn't fond of the idea of me moving in either, but Conrad's right; I think he appreciates it now that I'm there.

"What else is new with you?" He flips the meat on the grill, the smell already making my mouth water. It's been too long since I've had a nice steak dinner.

Dark brown hair, flirty sea-green eyes, and a slew of inappropriate memories that surround them pop into my head, but I shove them away. There's no way I'm sharing all of *that* with Conrad today, or ever. "Nothing, really. Just settling in."

We spend the next little while talking about how ranch life has been treating him, while he finishes grilling the meat. Once they're finished, we head inside and dish up. It's a nice evening, albeit a little warm, so we opt to eat on the porch. The food tastes damn good, and it's an effort to not inhale it too quickly.

With the crazy work schedule I had in Seattle, I rarely found time to home cook meals for myself like this, and fuck, do I miss it. A goal of mine now that I'm back in Copper Lake and will have a more set schedule at the practice, is to make the time to cook dinner most nights. Sit down and eat without interruption. I don't know how many nights were spent eating in a rush while I was looking over patient files and prepping for the next day.

"How's things with you?" I ask Conrad as we're finishing up our meal. "Doing any dating?"

"Things are good. No dating. I don't have the time or the energy for all that. I'm getting too old."

I chuckle. "I feel you there."

"How's Annie?" he asks, turning his head slightly to look over at me.

"She's good," I murmur. "We grabbed lunch before I left Seattle."

Annie and I met in college. Both of us come from a long line of doctors and wanted to follow in our family's footsteps. We hit it off and got married before going to med school. Since we ended up going to programs at different schools, the first several years of our marriage were spent long distance, which wasn't ideal, but we made it work. About ten years ago, we decided to move to Seattle when we both got an incredible job offer that neither of us could refuse. It was a fresh start I was seeking, and it seemed like it held the answers to all of our problems.

After a few years of opposite shifts, busy schedules, and a lack of any real intimacy, we decided we'd be better off as friends and decided to call it quits. It's probably the most civil and stress-free divorce I've ever heard of, both of us on the same page and wanting nothing but the best for each other.

"She's getting married next spring," I mention as we get up and head back inside. Tossing the plate and my empty beer bottle away, I pad over to the fridge and grab another two.

"Is she?" he asks, looking at me curiously. "Have you met the guy?"

"I have. He's cool, and he's *not* a doctor, which I think is great for Annie."

"That's awesome,"he grunts."Tell her I said congratulations when you talk to her next."

"How's Whit been?"

Conrad's jaw flexes as soon as I say his name, but that's the only outward sign that the question bothers him. Like me, Conrad is divorced. But unlike me, I've always been under the impression that it wasn't something he wholeheartedly wanted. It's too touchy of a subject to bring up with him, so I usually don't, but he brought up my ex-wife first, so it seems like fair game.

"He's good."The response is clipped as he works on putting the condiments away in the fridge.

"He took over his father's clinic a few years back, right?"

"That's right."

"Does that mean you see him quite a bit, what, with the animals here?"

"Yeah, usually a few times a month, give or take."

"You guys at least get along okay?" I ask as I put the leftover food into Tupperware while Conrad gets started loading the dishwasher.

"It's fine. We usually keep it professional." That's all he says for a moment, but then he adds, "He's dating someone."

I glance over at him, his back to me, but I can hear the distaste in his voice. "Is he?"

"Yeah. They've been together for a while now. His name's Reggie."

"Have you met him?"

"A few times." Reaching underneath the sink, he grabs a pod and tosses it in before starting the dishwasher. Conrad dries his hand with the white tea towel on the counter before turning to face me. "Have you seen Max yet?"

I shake my head. "Not yet, but I'm going over to his and Trish's house for dinner on Friday."

"Nice. That'll be fun, and Trish sure knows how to cook a mean dinner."

I laugh. "That she does."

"Did you hear about Colt getting hurt and cutting his season short?"

Inwardly wincing, I nod, remembering how it felt seeing him at the office this morning. "Yeah, I did. Sucks."

I can only imagine the concern Colt has that he'll end up retiring early like his dad, which must be a terrible feeling, given that his career only started a few years ago. Thankfully, his injuries appear much less severe than Max's, but you never know with these types of things.

Conrad and I head back outside where we catch up for a little while longer before we decide to call it a night, making plans to get together again soon. The sun is long gone by the time I'm pulling up in front of the house I now call home, and I'd imagine my dad's already asleep. Like most elderly men, Roger Andino is up with the sun and in bed by eight, no matter what. I don't think he even knows what it means to sleep in; I've never seen him do it a day in his life.

Unlocking the front door, I tiptoe through the house, as quiet as I can be. The house is old, and the floorboards creak despite my best efforts to be light on my feet. My dad's bedroom is near the staircase on the main level. His door is cracked just barely, but I can hear him snoring from inside. I head into the kitchen and grab a glass of water before padding up the stairs.

In the bathroom, I strip down to my boxers, toss my dirty clothes in the hamper, and then brush my teeth before heading to my room. It's still rather early, but I'm exhausted. I've been so busy trying to get settled back at the practice that I completely missed Colt's name on my books until this morning. It left me no time to come up with a game plan, and I'd spent the better part of the day trying to mentally prepare myself to see him, but nothing could've prepared me for how uncomfortable it would be, being alone with him for the first time since that night.

Distorted, fuzzy memories flash through my mind of sweat-slick skin, grappling hands, hot breath dancing across my overheated flesh, our bodies aligned. The pleasure pouring out of us. Then I recall the vehement shame I felt the next morning when I awoke and the recollection of what went on the night before hit me like a ton of bricks.

I can't be Colt's doctor. It's unethical. The entire Bishop

family were my father's patients for decades, but I can't. I make a mental note to speak to my partner tomorrow about taking Colt on as a patient. I don't know what excuse I'll give, but it's for the best. Nobody can ever know what went on between Colt and I in that apartment above the bar two years ago. Like every other time this memory comes back to me, I do my best to shove it far, far away while also trying to ignore the flood of arousal that hits my system at the same time because Colt Bishop, the man who was once the boy I saw grow up, should never, under any circumstances, be on my mind *like that*.

CHAPTER 4
COLT BISHOP

This whole not being able to do any-fucking-thing is getting old, fast. Struggling to get undressed and take a shower is downright annoying. Being chauffeured around like a child is a pain in the ass. I miss being able to run to the store or go for a late-night drive to clear my head.

And what's worse... No sex. Sure, I have no doubt that I can physically do it just fine, albeit with a little discomfort depending on the position, but I'm currently living in my childhood bedroom, unable to drive myself anywhere until my shoulder heals enough for me to go back to my own place. What, am I going to ask my hookup of the night to *pick me up* at my parents' house? I think the fuck not. I've always had a higher-than-average sex drive, and that's normally not an issue. There's no shortage of men or women for me to have a little fun with, especially when I'm on the road.

So, all of this is really cramping my style, and I'm left to taking matters into my own hands, literally, but even jacking off is proving to be quite the challenge too. I'm right-handed, and that's the side that was injured. Go fucking figure.

I'm currently half-lying, half-sitting on the bed when a knock sounds at the door. Pressing pause on the movie I'm watching, I call out, "Come in."

My mom appears in the doorway, an apron around her waist, per usual, and a smile on her face. "Hi, honey." Sitting on the edge of my bed, she rests her hand on my leg. "How're you feeling today?"

"Like I'm going stir crazy," I say with a dry laugh. For the most part, I try not to let my frustrations show around my mom. She's always been a fixer. If she knows someone is sad or hurt or angry, she'll do anything in her power to try to make everyone feel better.

This isn't a situation she can *fix*, nor should she have to. I'm a grown-ass man who has to get over the hand I've been dealt. I'm pissed off that I got injured, and I'm bitter as hell that my season was cut short, but that's not her fault or her responsibility, and both she and my dad are already doing more than enough for me. I don't need to add more stress or worry to her plate.

Glancing over her shoulder toward the TV, she asks, "What are you watching?"

"No clue. It was some movie suggestion Hulu gave me," I murmur. "I'm only really half-watching, but from what I've gathered, it's about a drug lord."

"Well, I wanted to come up here to let you know we're having company for dinner tonight. Maybe get changed and come downstairs?"

"Who's coming over?"

"Will." A bolt of excitement shoots through my bloodstream at the sound of my dad's best friend's name. "He's living back in Copper Lake again."

I nod, schooling my features. "Yeah, I know. I saw him the other day at my doctor's appointment."

Mom's face lights up. "Oh, that's right, Roger retired. I completely forgot about that." She pats my leg before standing. "He'll be here soon, so like I said, get dressed. Maybe splash some water over your face while you're at it."

"Trying to tell me I look like shit, Mom?" I tease, earning me a scowl only a mom could perfect. "Alright, alright, I'll be down in a bit."

She closes the door behind her, and suddenly, my mood got a whole lot better. William has been on my mind a lot since running into him at his clinic. He had moved away from Copper Lake over a decade ago. I never thought I'd run into him here, or anywhere, ever again, so it was quite the pleasant surprise hearing from him that he took over his family's private practice.

I'm not naïve enough to think we could ever have a repeat of that night at the bar in Seattle, but subtly flirting with him when nobody else is around tonight could be fun. Especially since I'm not getting any other type of action these days. It takes much longer than it should, but eventually, I'm dressed in Wranglers and a t-shirt. I skip the socks because that's too much damn work one-handed. I'm already winded just from trying to maneuver my t-shirt over my arm without moving it too much. After I grab my black Powder Ridge baseball cap, I flip it onto my head backwards before I call it good and leave the room.

Low chatter reaches my ears as I descend the stairs. When I reach the bottom, the living room comes into view, as do my dad and William. They've each got a beer, and they're standing in front of the TV. I can tell without even seeing the screen that they're watching the sports center highlights from last night's baseball game. Max Bishop is nothing if not a huge sports buff, and while it's been many years since I've seen William in this house, I recall him being the same.

My dad spots me first, a grin spreading across his lips. "Hey, son. How you feeling?"

William's jaw flexes as he flits his gaze over to me. "Hello, Colt," he offers nicely enough.

"Howdy. I'm feeling alright, Dad."

"How's that shoulder today?" he asks, like he has almost every day since my accident. The support and encouragement I've gotten from both of my parents has been immense.

I drop down into the recliner. "Same as it was yesterday. Sore, but alright."

Both men continue to watch the highlights—I was right—and talk about this play or that one, but I'm finding it hard to pay attention. From where I'm sitting, I have an excellent view of the backside of William, and fuck, is it a glorious one. His raven black hair is longer than I remember, slicked back, but it looks like throughout the day, he's ran his fingers through it a time or two, messing it up. It's clear, based on his white button-up shirt, navy blue Chinos, and a pair of rich brown dress boots, he came here straight from the office.

William and my dad have been friends for as long as I can remember. Pretty sure they went to school together before my dad went pro. I was around fifteen when he moved away from Copper Lake with his wife, who I'm assuming he doesn't have anymore, given the lack of a ring on his finger. Well, that and the liquor-fueled night we spent together two years ago.

I have to bite back a grin at the memory of that night. Much of it is choppy at best, thanks to all the shots I downed, but what slips through my recollection is one for the books. It's been top-tier spank-bank material more than once.

"Dinner's ready!" Mom calls out from the kitchen. Nobody prepares a meal quite as good as my mom, and I'm not just saying that because I'm her son and have to say that. Everybody in town knows that she's an incredible cook.

William is directly across from me, and it's more than obvious he's doing his best to avoid looking at me altogether. It's quite comical. Every time our eyes meet for the briefest of moments, his gaze darts away immediately.

"How is it being back in town, Will?" my mom asks.

William wipes his mouth with the napkin in his lap as he finishes chewing. "It's been nice. Different," he adds. "But I'm happy to be back."

"Do you miss the city living?" she asks.

A deep chuckle rumbles in his throat. "No, I surprisingly don't. If I'm being honest, it's all a bit much for someone like me; I was just too comfortable to realize it until it came time for me to make the decision to come back. The slow and steady of this small town is perfect for me."

My mom smiles. "There is something so charming and comforting about this little town, isn't there?"

The conversation fades a little the more we all eat. Figuring out how to eat left-handed has been a challenge all in its own. You never realize how much your dominant hand does every single day until you aren't able to use it. The easiest, most routine tasks suddenly become a challenge. Using a fork, getting dressed, tying your shoes—it's a damn good thing the only shoes I typically wear are boots—brushing your teeth. Hell, even wiping your ass is difficult.

"Colt," my dad starts, flicking his gaze to me. "When do

you start physical therapy?"

"Wednesday."

With all this downtime, I've had plenty of time to research my injuries and the surgeries I've had, and I have a pretty decent idea of how long it'll realistically take me to get back to a normal use of the limb. According to Dr. Google, I should be able to do easy, normal daily activities within two to three weeks, but it'll be several months before I can get back to training. The latter makes my blood pressure spike. I'm itching to get back on a bull, and knowing that I have to take it easy for *that* long makes me want to scream. It also makes me want to try to beat that recovery time. Surely, there's something I can do to heal faster and get back out there quicker.

After dinner, Dad helps Mom clear the table and put the leftovers away, then he immediately gets started on washing the dishes. It's been this way since I was a little kid; Mom cooks and Dad does the dishes. Granted, during my teenage years, I helped with the cleaning too, but my dad has always been very firm on the fact that my mom shouldn't have to do the dishes if she makes the meals.

William makes himself at home in the living room, watching more game highlights after he offered to help my dad but got shooed away. I grab a water bottle out of the fridge and pad across the floor toward the staircase. It's time to take my meds, and they're upstairs. I pass by William on my way, our eyes meeting briefly, and I can't help the smirk that tugs on my lips as I watch his throat work against a swallow.

"Looking good, William," I murmur quiet enough for only him to hear before I toss him a wink and bound up the stairs. He doesn't respond, nor did I expect him to, but the deer-in-headlights look on his face is enough to make me chuckle. I probably shouldn't find enjoyment out of his clear discomfort, but I do. I'm stuck at my parents' house, unable to compete—or really do *anything*—so I have to find amusement where I can.

Part of me wants to push him to see if he'll acknowledge the history between us or if he's going to keep pretending like it never happened. If it weren't for the way he can't seem to hold my gaze, I'd think maybe he didn't remember it at all. Who knows how much he had to drink that night before I spotted him. But he remembers... I know he remembers, and something about that turns me on something fierce. Maybe it's the secret of it all. Or it's simply the fact that I can't properly jack off, so I'm sexually frustrated as it is. Maybe it's both.

Once in my room, I flip on the light switch and cross the space to my dresser where my meds are. I toss them back quickly before heading back downstairs. Disappointment clouds my mind when the living room comes into view and my mom is sitting on the couch already, talking to William about work. *So much for getting to mess with him.*

I plop down on the opposite end of the couch as my mom and listen to them converse, but I'm barely paying attention. I'm too focused on the way William *owns* that chair he's sitting in. He's such a tall, broad man that he makes nearly everyone and everything in his presence feel small. Legs kicked wide as he relaxes in the recliner, elbow propped on the arm of the chair while his chin rests in his palm, he's focused on my mother and what she's saying as I can't rip my gaze away from him.

My blood heats as memories from that night flash, once again, through my mind. Then the thought of what it would be like to have it happen again. Would he ever let us go there again now that he's back in town? Does he regret it? I have so many questions, and I don't see myself easily getting the answers to any of them any time soon...but that just makes me want to try even more.

After all, I've never been one to step down from a challenge.

CHAPTER 5

WILLIAM ANDINO

The rich, sweet aroma of hazelnut fills my senses as I head out to the porch with a steaming cup of coffee in hand. It's just after sunrise, the morning sun hugging the horizon and splashing the early sky in beautiful pastels. It's going to be a nice, warm day, I can already tell. Taking a seat in one of the two rocking chairs, I bring the mug up to my lips, letting the hot beverage fill my mouth and awaken my senses. It's a quiet Saturday morning, and while I normally don't work on the weekends, I am today.

Powder Ridge Arena is hosting a twice-monthly free clinic starting today until the end of November, and my clinic has donated our services to make it work. This is a great event for low-income families, or families that don't have insurance. The clinic I worked for in Seattle did something similar, but annually, and it always had a great turnout. The cost of basic medical care in this country is outrageous, and I wholeheartedly think that families shouldn't have to go without simply because they don't make enough. I'm honored to get to be a part of something like this.

Checking the time on my phone, I note that I have about a half an hour before I have to leave. Plenty of time to enjoy this cup of coffee and soak in the early morning sun, pushing my loud, obnoxious thoughts about *who* will be there to the back of my mind in the meantime. The doors open at eight-thirty, but since this is the first time we're doing this, I want to make sure to arrive with plenty of time to set up and get organized. There's nothing worse than being scatterbrained while trying to work, especially if we're as busy as I think we'll be until two-thirty. Doug Braylon, the other physician at my practice, will also be there taking patients, so between the both of us, I'm hoping we can get to a decent chunk of families in that time frame.

Doug is a younger doctor; my father hired him a few years back after he graduated from medical school. He's incredibly smart and knowledgeable, and so far, I like the guy. Prior to hiring Doug, my father ran the practice all by himself, with the help of one nurse and a receptionist. I'm glad he expanded because it's a lot for one doctor to handle, especially one at my father's age.

After I finish my cup of coffee, I head back inside. The drive takes no time at all, and before I know it, I'm inside the arena setting up. Meg, the nurse at the clinic, shows up about twenty minutes to opening. She'll be helping with checking patients in and assisting Doug and I during the day.

"Morning, Dr. Andino," she murmurs with a warm smile.

"Good morning, Meg," I respond. "How are you?"

"Oh, I'm good. Excited to see how the turnout is today. Think we'll see a lot of patients?"

Nodding, I say, "I think so."

Spotting the coffee station, I excuse myself and cross the

THE HISTORY BETWEEN US

room. I check my watch, making sure I still have time before loading a couple of doughnuts onto a paper plate and pouring a hot cup of coffee.

Someone steps up to the table beside me, but I don't have a chance to look at who it is before they speak. "Well, would you look who it is."

My shoulders hike up to my ears, and I clench my jaw so tight it pops as I turn in the direction where the rough, gravelly voice came from, my gaze connecting with a familiar pair of emerald eyes. A cocksure grin tips his full lips, and he's wearing his signature backwards hat that I almost never see him without.

"Colt, good morning." I ignore the way my pulse races.

His smile brightens. "Surprised to see me?"

"No, your dad mentioned you had signed up."

Max had informed me a few days ago that Colt was volunteering here. Thinks it'll be good for his spirits to do something meaningful while he's unable to compete. I'd have to agree, but that doesn't make it any less jarring coming face to face with him.

Colt steps closer, crowding me, his fresh citrus and leather scent surrounding me as he lowers his voice and says, "I look forward to working with you, then, *Doc*."

My jaw flexes as I lift my gaze to meet his, not at all surprised to find him smirking. Colt has strikingly handsome features. He's an attractive man, and he knows it. It's clear in the way he carries himself, and in the blatant way he flirts.

Without my permission, a memory of us together on the dance floor flashes through my mind. And even earlier, when we first spotted each other. The brazen way he sauntered over to me, seemingly not at all worried about who I was to him.

Even two years later, I'm unable to pinpoint why I welcomed the flirting, why I accepted his invite to dance when it was more than obvious what he wanted out of it, and why—above all—I took him upstairs to the loft above the bar. The entire evening was inappropriate on so many levels, and I've never been able to figure out how or why I let it happen.

"Look how hard you are, and all for me." His deep, throaty voice echoes in my ears from that night. The unabashed way he spoke to me.

A crashing noise behind me pulls me back to the present, forcing the memory to take a back burner. One thing is for certain... Right now, in this arena, moments before the clinic opens, is not the time to figure it out. Glancing down at my watch and then back up to Colt, I say, "I better get going. They'll be opening the doors any minute."

Colt smirks but says nothing as I hurry away from the breakfast table and busy myself over at my station while I wait for the patients to start fluctuating in.

As expected, as soon as the doors open, we all stay steadily busy for the majority of the day. There are brief moments when I have a little downtime to run to the restroom or grab some water, but for the most part, I'm with patients nearly the entire time the clinic is open. Between Doug and me, we were able to see a great number of patients, and I didn't have any time to focus on how being so close to Colt all morning made me feel.

There was more than one occasion today when our eyes locked from across the room, though, and it felt as if he could read my mind by the look alone. It's absurd, truly. I'm a man in my mid-forties, and I'm getting tongue tied and nervous around a man half my age over a drunken hookup that happened years ago. When I originally made the decision to move back here,

I knew the time would come when we'd run into each other. It was inevitable, but I told myself I'd ignore it. The best plan of action would be to brush it off and avoid being near him as much as possible. Nothing good will come from addressing the elephant in the room.

If the looks and the flirting have told me anything, it's that Colt is not going to allow this to be swept under the rug. Meaning, we're going to have to talk about it, and I'm dreading that. Over the years, I've gotten good at being alone. After Annie and I got a divorce, I didn't go on a hunt to reclaim my singlehood. I didn't hook up just for the sake of doing it. Sure, it happened, but it was very few and far between. What happened that night in Seattle was a one-off. I was in a very weird headspace after finding out my mother was sick, and I desperately needed to blow off some steam and get out of my mind for the night. And while I certainly did just that, it shouldn't have happened with who it did. It's still wrong on so many levels. I've known Colt his whole life. We may not have been close, and I may have moved away when he was a teenager, but I was still there when Max and Trish brought him home from the hospital after he was born. I'm practically a pseudo-uncle to him, and Max would murder me without even thinking twice if he knew. The technicality that Colt is an adult means nothing here.

It can never happen again, and I need to make sure Colt is clear on that. Burying my head in the sand won't work, and it was idiotic of me to ever think it would.

I'm finishing cleaning up my station when, as if he knew I was thinking about him, Colt saunters over to me, that same cocky grin on his face from this morning. "Today was a success," he murmurs, handing me supplies I'm putting away.

"Yes, it was."

"It's nice of you to offer to do this outside of your normal business hours."

Meeting his gaze, I force a smile on my face. "It's not a big deal. I'm more than happy to help where I can."

"I'm sure it's a big deal to a lot of those families."

"Thanks for your help today," I say, wanting to get the focus off of me. "Things ran smoothly because you were here helping Meg with check in. She would've been swamped had you not been here."

"It was kind of fun, actually," he states. "It's been kinda dreadful being cooped up at my parents' house. Getting out and being around people was nice."

"Good, glad to hear that." I finish packing up my stuff before I toss my bag over my shoulder. "Well, have a wonderful rest of your afternoon, Colt."

Before I can escape this conversation, he asks, "Want to grab some lunch?"

Stopping in my tracks, I purse my lips, turning to face him. "I don't think that's such a good idea," I reply, my voice low.

"Why not?" he asks, head cocked to the side. "It's just lunch, *Doc*. Nothing more." That smirk makes my stomach flip before he waggles his brows and adds, "Unless you want it to be."

Biting down on my molars, I huff out a breath through my nose as I try to not let his insinuation get to me. And maybe he's right—at least about some of it. Maybe lunch is the perfect opportunity to have the talk we undoubtably need to have. Set some much-needed boundaries. So, against my better judgement, I nod and say, "Okay, lunch. But *just* lunch, Colt. Nothing more."

Colt looks like the cat that got the canary. "Whatever you

say, Doc."

Lord help me. I'm in trouble.

CHAPTER 6
COLT BISHOP

Lou's Diner is busier than I expected for a Saturday afternoon. Everybody who came to the arena for the free clinic must have had the same idea about grabbing lunch after because it appears all of Copper Lake is inside this small establishment. It takes about twenty minutes, but we're eventually sat in a booth in the back of the restaurant, near the kitchen. William looks like he'd rather be anywhere but here, and I can't help but chuckle to myself.

When my dad told me about the volunteer opportunity, I was already interested. Getting out of the house and being around people will be good for me. I know from watching my dad go through it when I was a kid how easily it can be to slip into a dark place with an injury, so it truly didn't take much convincing. But knowing William was going to be there, and that I could get under his skin, was definitely a nice, shiny added bonus.

There was nothing quite like walking through the front doors this morning and seeing Dr. Hottie grab a couple of doughnuts, looking way too damn good for that early in the morning. Knowing I was going to get to ogle him all day while in his element made me even more excited than I already was.

Our server comes, dropping off our drinks before taking our food order. As soon as she steps away, William glances at me from across the table, his lips pressed into a thin line and his brows furrowed. "Listen, Colt," he starts. "I think we should…talk."

Breathing out a laugh, I bring the glass up to my lips and let the cold water fill my mouth, swallowing and setting it back down on the table slowly before responding. "I'm listening."

"About that night…" He pauses, looking positively uncomfortable as his jaw flexes. "I think we can both agree it was a mistake that never should've happened and can never happen again."

Okay, *ouch*. Not what I was hoping he'd say, but not exactly a shock either. Relaxing into the booth, I shrug it off. "I don't think it was a mistake," I say. "We had fun, like two consenting adults."

William huffs, as if he thinks I'm ridiculous. "Colt, I'm your father's friend. You must know what we did wasn't right."

Arching a brow, I ask, "You're saying you didn't have fun that night?"

His nostrils flare as he exhales heavily, and it's taking everything in me to not laugh. "I did not say that."

"So, you did?"

"Colt, that's not really the point." He sighs, exasperated. "The point is, it can never happen again. Do you understand me?"

A smirk splits my face. "Kind of like it when you go all growly on me, Doc."

"Colt."

"Relax, would you? I'm teasing. Yes, I understand you," I murmur. "I don't agree, but I understand."

William's shoulders relax marginally. "Okay, good."

"That doesn't mean we can't be friends, right?"

"I don't think that's the best idea," he mutters, taking a drink from his water.

"Why not?" I ask innocently.

I'm realizing how much I enjoy the idea of riling him up. William is this ultra-put together, distinguished doctor, and something about knowing that I can make him squirm does it for me. It shouldn't, but it does.

Nostrils flaring on an exhale, he meets my gaze from across the table. "Colt, I have been friends with your father since before you were born. Hell, I held you when you were a baby. A friendship of any sort is severely inappropriate. You must know that."

A smirk tugs on my lips as I watch him from beneath my lashes. "Yeah, but I'm a big boy now, Doc. You must know that," I drawl, throwing his words back at him, insinuation clear as day. "Besides, we're going to be seeing each other at least twice a month at the free clinic," I add. "I don't think it's too out there to suggest being friends."

Brow furrowed and lips pressed into a thin line, William looks thoroughly unamused, which only makes me beam. "Something tells me you're highly incapable of being *just friends* with anybody."

Clutching my chest in mock offense, I gasp. "Are you insinuating that I'm a slut, Doctor Andino?"

"Don't call me that," he scoffs. "And I said no such thing."

I arch a brow. "Why not? You *are* a doctor. What would you rather I call you, then? *Daddy* William?"

He nearly chokes on the sip of his water he just took, and I have to bite the inside of my cheek to hide my laughter. His eyes narrow as he glowers at me from the other side of the table. "Will is just fine."

"Well, that's no fun." I pout as his glare intensifies. His face is turning a shade of red, and I swear I see steam billowing out of his ears.

Our server drops off our food, and despite how annoyed he seemed just a moment ago, it's an oddly comfortable silence while we eat. The food, as always, is incredible. Screw fine dining; some of the best food I've ever eaten has been in this small-town diner.

As if reading my mind, William groans as he takes a bite. "I forgot how good this place is."

"I bet there's some incredible food in Seattle, though, too."

He nods, wiping his mouth with the napkin he keeps in his lap. "There is. I typically cook and eat at home for the most part, but there were some great restaurants I enjoyed going to from time to time."

"Do you miss living there?" I ask in between bites.

"There are aspects that I miss, like the coffee," he says with a deep chuckle. "But Copper Lake is home, and even though I never saw myself moving back, now that I'm here, I'm glad I did."

"Why did you?" I ask. "Move back, that is."

William is quiet for a moment, and I can't help but wonder what's going through his mind. Finally, he says quietly, "The older my father gets, the harder things are for him. His hips are bad, so it pains him to be on his feet for long hours, and he's overall moving a lot slower than he used to. I flew from Seattle to visit him for his birthday a few months ago, and he was in a lot worse shape than he had led on. I knew it was time for him to retire, and he needed somebody around the house to help out with things."

My respect for William just increased tenfold. I've always known he was a good man, but this is admirable. It should be an absolute no-brainer to help your parents when they get older. It's just what you should do, but the reality isn't always that black and white. Sometimes people don't have the means to, or sometimes they just don't care enough. For him to pack up his entire life—a life he'd built for himself over the last however many years—to move back here, seemingly no questions asked, to care for his father and take over the business is almost a rarity in today's world. At least in this country.

"I'm sure he appreciates you being back," I murmur.

William laughs, the sound deep and throaty. "That's debatable," he replies. "Roger Andino is a stubborn, independent man, almost to a fault. It's how his father was, it's how I am. It's the Andino blood; we're a bunch of hard-headed bastards. It took a lot of convincing and a whole hell of a lot of arguments to talk him into this. He's griped about something or other since I've been back."

I chuckle, imagining William getting bitched at by his father. I've known Roger my entire life. He was my doctor up until he retired, and he's the sweetest, most caring man, at least to his patients, so hearing about this side of him is amusing. I'd love to see it for myself, even though that'll probably never happen.

"Even if he sucks at accepting help and doesn't admit it out loud, I'll bet he probably still appreciates having you back."

Popping a French fry in his mouth, William says, "Enough about me. How are you feeling about the injury and the rodeo?"

I bite down on my molars while I drag in a few deep breaths

through my nose before I respond. It's almost impressive how quickly that one small question can sour my entire mood.

"Honestly? I'm angry," I reply.

"That makes sense." He nods, looking at me sympathetically. "This injury has affected your ability to compete. I think anybody in your shoes would feel angry."

"I've worked my ass off to get where I am. I'm constantly compared to my father, which is whatever, it's fine. He's a legend in our world, but I've worked really fucking hard to make my own name for myself outside of the Bishop legacy, only to be forced out of my season because of an injury, like he was."

The words come out in a rush, and I'm surprised at myself for opening up. I've never voiced my feelings about my dad's legacy and what that meant for me as a professional bull rider out loud. I've never wanted to seem ungrateful when that's the furthest thing from the truth, but I have always, *always* wanted to be known as a legend and one of the greats because of *me* and what *I've* done, not because of the way my father paved for me. It can be hard to be taken seriously sometimes in this world, coming from such a big name. I know my buddy, Shooter, a world champ bronc rider, understands where I'm coming from. He also comes from a legacy family, and he's struggled with the weight of that as well. I never want people to think I've gotten to where I'm at because of strings my father pulled for me.

"Colt, your injury and your dad's injuries are nothing alike," William says softly, zero judgement in his tone. "You can come back from this. This doesn't have to define you or your career."

Heaving a sigh, I reply, "Logically, I know this, but my father's injury and speculations that I'll end up just like him have been a hot topic since I first went pro. It feels an awful lot like everyone's predictions of me are coming true, and it's easy to look past logic and wallow in self-pity when I've got nothing but time on my hands."

It's not until the words leave my mouth that I realize where the root of my anger comes from. I've been so caught up feeling sorry for myself while also being pissed at myself to really analyze *why*. I have always strived for perfection; it's both a positive and negative trait I possess, and knowing that I can't rush my recovery, can't put one foot in front of the other and get back on that bull, is fucking hard. I'm angry at myself for getting bucked off that bull. I'm angry at the universe for allowing this to happen. I'm angry at everything because I can't control this situation. I can't fix it with the snap of my fingers.

"Injuries are very common in the rodeo world, especially with bull riders," William states. "You know this, I know this. It's a fact. It could've happened to anybody."

The raw vulnerability I feel talking about this with anybody, let alone someone like William, who is so close to my father, is like being stripped of every layer of clothing I have, and not in a fun way.

"I've spent my entire career, both pro and otherwise, telling myself that I would never end up like my father. I'd convinced myself I was invincible, and then this happened, proving I was very much *not*, and it's been a tough fucking pill to swallow."

His eyes meet mine, face unreadable. "I can understand that, but again, you can come back from this. This doesn't have to be a career-ending injury if you don't let it. This situation isn't like what happened to your dad."

Again, logically, I know he's right, but all of my logic seems to be clouded by anger. I don't know how to clear it or move past it. Still, as we finish up our meal, I can't help but feel lighter than I have since the injury. Getting those thoughts off my chest and having someone listen seems to help. My mom has asked me half a dozen times this week alone how I'm feeling, but I always tell her I'm fine. I don't want to worry her any more than I already have. Not only that, but I also just kind of suck at talking about my feelings, and I don't even know why. It's not like I come from a home where feelings are looked down upon, but I've always been the fun guy. The carefree one who people go to, to have a good time and forget about their responsibilities. I've always kept my shit to myself because I never wanted to ruin that image.

I don't know what it is about William, be it his age and maturity or the simple fact that he's not one of my friends so I don't feel the need to wear the 'fun' mask, but it felt okay to share that with him. And it felt good to get it off my chest.

The conversation drifts, and we get back to eating, but I can't help but smirk as I glance up at William. "You know, for somebody who claims they don't want to be my friend, this feels suspiciously like we're walking into friendship territory, Doc."

With blue eyes narrowing on me from across the table, he stuffs another fry into his mouth, but says nothing.

Yeah, he's full of shit. We both know it.

CHAPTER 7
WILLIAM ANDINO

The last thing I want to do after working all day is be at the hardware store, along with every other person in Copper Lake, apparently, but when my father called me earlier and told me the toilet on the main level was malfunctioning and he was having to go all the way upstairs to use the bathroom, I knew I had no choice. I don't love him having to climb the stairs without me there. He's not necessarily unstable, but it's an older house and the stairs are on the steeper side. It's why when I moved in, we moved him into the room on the main level. He's not getting around like he used to.

It's hard to witness your parents getting older. It's something we all know will happen one day, but knowing it's coming and watching it happen are two very different things. Witnessing my mother's deterioration not that long ago is something I wouldn't wish on my worst enemy. The cancer hit fast; one day, we were learning about her illness, and the next, we were saying goodbye. It was like the blink of an eye, and my father hasn't been the same since. I truly think the death of my mother is the reason for his decline. Not necessarily because he's consciously not taking care of himself, but because his heart is broken and the one woman he's spent his whole life with is gone. Whether he realizes it, I think his light, his reason to live, has withered away without her here with him.

I can't imagine loving someone that fiercely.

Annie and I loved each other; we spent many years loving each other, but it wasn't this time-stands-still, my-world-is-bleak-without-you type of love. I've always admired my parents for the way they so clearly and effortlessly adored one another, and I've, on more than one occasion, wondered if that type of love even exists anymore or if it's just one for the books.

After I grab the items I think I'll need based on the information my father gave me over the phone, I get in line, check out, and head home. It's been raining off and on all day, and now there's a rainbow painted across the sky. I know as a man in his mid-forties, rainbows are silly things to find joy in, but I can't help it. Ever since I was a kid, when my mom told me there was gold at the end of rainbows, I've always loved them. Glancing up toward the sky, where the showery prism shines, I'm reminded of how beautiful the natural world can be when we stop and take the time to notice.

Pulling into the driveway, I park my car in the garage beside my dad's truck. I grab the bag off the seat before climbing out and strolling inside. The door in the garage that leads into the house opens into the laundry room, which is connected to the kitchen. My senses awaken as I toe off my shoes and step farther into the house, a savory and sweet aroma filling the kitchen.

"Hey, this smells great," I say to my father as I empty my pockets into the dish on the counter. "What are you making?"

It's not often my dad does it anymore, but he used to cook for us almost every night. When I was a teenager, my mom went back to work as a nurse—not because we needed the money, but because she loved it so much—and oftentimes, she would work a later shift than my father, so he would get home and start dinner so she had something hot to eat by the time she made it home too.

Growing up, I loved seeing it because, especially during that time, it was common for the women to stay home and do the cooking and cleaning while the men worked. It was refreshing to see them share those roles and do it so willingly. Never once did I hear my dad complain about my mom wanting to go back to work, or the fact that he had to pick up some of the slack she couldn't handle by doing so. They were such a strong team, and I vividly remember always wanting to have that strong team feeling with somebody, and how it never felt quite right with Annie.

"Just some spaghetti," he grunts as he stirs the sauce. "How was your day at the office? Anything fun happen?"

Breathing out a laugh, I say, "If by fun you mean sick babies, then yes. I'll be back. I'm going to take a look at the toilet and see if I can't fix it."

"Don't take too long," he calls out after me. "Dinner will be ready in about fifteen minutes."

"Got it."

I'm in and out in less than five minutes; the lift chain was broken, but that's an easy fix. After I place the lid back on the back of the toilet, I jog up the stairs and squeeze in a quick shower before the food's done. Once I toss my dirty clothes and wet towel in the hamper, I join my dad in the kitchen again, getting a couple of plates down, grabbing the silverware out, and pouring us each a drink. My dad drinks milk with dinner every single night without fail, so after I get him some of that, I pour myself a glass of the pinot noir I picked up at the store this past weekend.

After we dish up our plates, we take a seat across from each other at the table in the dining room and dig in. As I knew it would be, the pasta is incredible, and my taste buds are singing their praises with each bite.

"How are you feeling today?" I ask my dad.

"A bit better," he replies gruffly. "The sore throat and cough I had earlier this week have seemed to subside."

"That's good."

"I think I'd like to get a dog," he says, seemingly out of nowhere.

Brows furrowed, I stop mid-chew to glance over at my dad, confusion swirling around in my mind as he continues to eat. "I'm sorry?"

"I'd like to get a dog," he repeats. "I get bored during the day when you're at work, and I think I'd enjoy having a furry companion around the house. We could watch television together, play fetch in the backyard. We could even go for short walks around the block for some exercise."

Where is this coming from? "You hate dogs."

"I do not."

"Dad, every single time I asked for a dog growing up, you told me they were nothing but nuisances who track mud through the house and get into shit."

He scoffs. "I did not."

I bite down on my molars, not wanting to argue with him about something so menial. "Do you know what type of dog you want?" I instead ask.

Nodding, he brings his napkin up from his lap, patting his

mouth. "I was looking on the shelter website earlier today, and saw they have a cute Dachshund available."

"How old?"

"Only a couple years old."

"You know, that's a big responsibility," I say. "Are you sure you're up for that?"

"Oh, Will, can you not talk to me like I'm a child, please?" he grumbles. "I'm a grown man, and I'm fully aware of what goes into caring for an animal. Just because I'm old doesn't mean I'm decrepit."

Clearly, he's feeling extra spicy tonight. "Would you like me to go down to the shelter with you so we can take a look?" I ask softly. "The free clinic isn't until next weekend, so we could go this Saturday if you'd like."

"Maybe. I'm going to call down there in the morning and see if he has anybody interested in him. I don't want to risk him being adopted before Saturday. That's three days away."

"We'll need to go to the pet store before bringing an animal home, Dad."

"I know that."

Heaving a breath, I say, "Okay, give them a call in the morning, and let me know how it goes. I should be home fairly early tomorrow if we need to drive up there earlier than Saturday."

To be honest, having a dog around the house may be nice. I've always loved the idea of having one, but it's never worked out. When I was younger, my dad refused, and once I got married and moved to Seattle, Annie and I worked entirely too much for it to make sense.

Once we're both finished eating, I clear the table and get started on the dishes while my father heads into the living room to watch the news from his recliner. It's a nightly thing for him; dinner, news, bed. Roger Andino is nothing if not routine. I'm not exactly one to talk, though. I find comfort in my life of structure too. After I finish cleaning the kitchen, I grab my book and stroll out onto the porch, where I sit in the rocking chair and read as the sun sets. Sometimes I'll do crossword puzzles instead of reading, but almost every single night, I enjoy sitting outside as the light of day fades, the same way I enjoy sitting out here with my coffee in the morning and watching the sunrise.

By the time I finish reading a few chapters and head inside, my dad has already gone to bed. I amble up the stairs, going into the bathroom to brush my teeth before climbing into bed for the evening, all while making a mental note of everything I need to do if we really are going to bring a dog home. There're about half a dozen things we'll need to pick up at the store. Maybe I'll stop there on my way home tomorrow.

Grabbing my phone off my nightstand and unlocking it, I scroll through social media. Typically, I try not to mess around on my phone right before bed because I notice those are the nights I find it harder to fall asleep, but I have a handful of emails and messages that I want to get to before the day is done. On Instagram, I see that Max posted a story—something he doesn't ever do. Clicking on his little circle icon, the story pops up, and I can tell it's a reshare of a story Colt posted and tagged him in. It's just a photo of them together that Colt took. The two of them couldn't look more opposite. They share the same bright green eyes, but that's where their similarities end. Colt has thick, dark brown hair, whereas Max is more of a dirty blond. Colt has Trish's full pink lips where Max's are on the thinner side—something I never even noticed until I looked at this photo of them side by side.

Against my better judgement—something I always seem to lack around Colt—I click on his profile, surprised by how many followers he has. Close to a hundred thousand, but I suppose that's not all that wild considering how well known he is in the rodeo world. I may not keep up on the professional rodeo circuit, but I'm not blind; I know what an icon he is. One of the youngest world championship winning bull riders at twenty-three, Colt is practically a household name, just like Max was during his time.

Memories of our conversation we had at the diner come back to me. The way he admitted to feeling compared to his dad, and how hard that is for him. From where I'm at, he's not exactly wrong, but he's not right either. Yes, he's compared to Max. He always will be, that's just a fact. But he isn't *just* Max Bishop's prodigy. Colt's been pro for only a few years now, but he's already made a name for himself, and that's coming from someone like me, who, again, doesn't keep up with this world.

Just from that one conversation, I can tell he's incredibly hard on himself, but he has no reason to be. He's talented, he's committed, he's got what it takes to bring his career even further than his dad did. I meant what I said to him when I told him this injury doesn't have to define him. It's not nearly as severe as Max's was, and I think deep down, he probably knows that, but I'm sure it's easier to give in to the doubt when you're already discouraged.

His Instagram is filled with pictures and videos from the circuit or at the arena when he's training. He has a large social media presence, it looks like. Even now, when he's home and unable to compete, there's at least a dozen stories posted just today. I watch them all, wondering why the hell I'm doing this. Why do I care? Why am I now so curious and intrigued by him? I've known Colt his entire life, and never once did I look at him in any sort of inappropriate way until *that* night.

That night changed everything for me, and I've never quite forgiven myself for it. I was weak and lonely, and he was there and willing, and so damn hard to resist. It could've been anybody that I ended up naked with that night, but it wasn't anybody. It was Colt Bishop, the son of my best friend, and now I can't stop seeing him in that light.

Frustrated with myself, I close out of the app altogether and plug in my phone, setting it back on the nightstand. I'm a strong, mature man who doesn't have to let a few indecent urges change anything, and he's one guy in a world of billions. Who cares if the night was incredible and one of the best I've ever experienced. There will be other men and other nights.

Colt Bishop cannot be on my radar, and I need to figure out how to get off of his. I have enough on my plate now that I'm back in Copper Lake. I don't have time to develop feelings for a man half my age.

CHAPTER 8
COLT BISHOP

Whit: Get your ass dressed. I'll be at your house in five, and I'm picking you up.

Cope: Hey, man. Haven't heard from you in a few days. How you feeling?

Bounding down the stairs, I find both of my parents in the living room, sitting in their respective recliners as they watch the Sunday morning news, coffee mugs in hand, robes tied around their waists, and slippers on their feet.

"Good morning, Colt," my mom says with a smile. "Where are you heading to?"

"Whit'll be here in a minute. I don't know where we're going; he just told me he was picking me up."

"Well, that sounds fun."

"Want me to bring you home anything?" I ask, slipping my feet into my boots that I keep by the door.

I'm still stuck in this damn sling, but I'm hoping I can get rid of it soon enough. I had my first physical therapy appointment earlier this week and it sucked. It hurt, and I was sore for days afterward, but I knew that would happen and expected it. Regardless, I'm over this damn sling. It's too restricting, and I'm ready to get back to being able to do little, normal tasks.

My mom shakes her head. "That's alright, but thank you for asking, honey."

"Okay, I'll be back later," I call out as I unlock and open the front door. Whit's truck is waiting in the driveway as I jog down the steps. Pulling open the passenger side door, I slide inside, tipping my chin at Whit as I do. "Hey, man. Where the hell are you taking me?"

He chuckles. "I got to run to the store to pick up something, and I'm taking you with me."

"You dragged my ass out of the house to run errands with you?"

"Yes," he replies simply. "It's good for you to get out of the house, you know."

"Okay, Mom," I tease, buckling my seatbelt. "Where's Reggie? Couldn't he go with you instead?"

Whit's jaw tenses as he puts the car in reverse and backs out of my parents' driveway. "He's working," he explains. "And besides, he's not the one out of work due to an injury. Like I said, getting out of the house is good for you."

"You guys have been together quite a while now, yeah?" I ask him.

He nods, attention focused straight ahead on the road, hands firmly placed at ten and two on the steering wheel like the good little driver he is. "Yeah, it's been about two years."

"Damn. You guys planning to move in together any time soon?"

His face scrunches up, and I laugh at the way his glasses

shift on his nose as he does. "No, why would we do that?" he asks, like he's appalled I would ever suggest such a thing.

"Oh, I don't know," I deadpan. "Maybe because you're in a serious relationship, and that's typically what couples do after a certain amount of time to take things to the next level."

Whit snorts—a sound completely out of character for him. "What do you know about serious relationships, Mr. I Have A New Body In My Bed Every Night?"

Scoffing, I say, "Hey, I take offense to that. I'll have you know, I haven't slept with anybody in, like, a month!"

"A whole month," Whit replies in mock horror. "I'm surprised your dick hasn't fallen off from loneliness."

"Ha ha. Whit's got jokes today. Somebody woke up on the wrong side of the bed, you old man."

"I'm serious," he goes on. "A month has got to be some sort of record for *the* Colt Bishop."

"I'm not that bad," I groan. "You make me sound like some sort of sex addict."

"Could've fooled me."

"There is nothing wrong with getting a little love while I'm on the road," I reply. "People practically throw themselves at me after the rodeos." Gesturing a hand down my body, I add, "Who am I to deny them all of this?"

Whit pretends to gag, which makes me laugh. "Please, you're just as bad as Shooter. Does it ever get heavy carrying that huge-ass ego around all the time?"

"Fuck off," I choke out between laughter.

Pulling into the parking lot of the home store, Whit murmurs, "Let's go, you sex-deprived sad sack."

I huff as I climb out. "What, did you bring me here to help you pick out new couch pillows?"

"Yeah, right." Whit snorts. "Because out of everybody we know, I would go to *you* about home décor style."

"You're kind of mean today," I grumble.

Glancing over at me as we walk through the automatic doors, he grins almost mischievously. "I think you'll live." Inside the store, Whit leads us toward the back. "I'm picking up an order."

As we're walking past one of the aisles, I spot somebody that makes my lips tip up into a grin as I do a double take. "Morning, Doc," I drawl, coming to a stop. "Fancy running into you here."

William's jaw clenches as he glances over at me. "Hello, Colt."

My eyes flit to the man beside him. "Howdy, Dr. Andino," I say with a grin. "How've you been, sir?"

"Good morning, Colt," Dr. Andino says in the warm, familiar way he always does. "Please, call me Roger. I'm retired now," he goes on. "No need for the honorifics anymore."

"Can do, Roger."

"I heard you were back in town," Whit says to William. "How have you been?"

"I've been well," he replies, voice deep and gruff. "Can't complain. How are you? I heard you took over your dad's clinic."

Whit nods. "I did, yeah. I've been good. Business is doing great."

"We'll be seeing you at the office soon," Roger chimes in.

"Is that right?" Whit asks, a smirk playing on his lips.

Roger nods, looking pleased with himself. "I adopted a dog from the shelter yesterday, a two-year-old wiener dog. Show 'em the pictures," he urges, nudging William with his elbow.

Brows furrowed and lips pressed into a thin line, William reaches into his pocket and pulls out his phone. After a few moments, he turns the screen around for us to see the cutest little blonde, long-haired dog.

"I love that breed," I murmur. "Such sweet dogs. Boy or girl?"

"Girl," William grunts, pocketing his phone.

"What's her name?"

"Winnie," Roger offers. "That's the name she came with, and I don't see a reason to change it now."

"Winnie's cute," Whit chimes in. "The name and the dog. I can't wait to meet her."

"How're you holding up?" Roger asks, directing the question at me. "I'm so sorry to hear about the accident."

"I'm doing fine," I reply. "I'm eager to get the sling off, but I'm not rushing it. I know these things take time."

"Should only be a couple more weeks now, shouldn't it?"

I nod. "Hopefully. Going from being fully independent to not being able to do hardly anything on my own has been a challenge."

"You're young and fit," Roger remarks with a warm smile. "You'll be back to normal in no time, I know it."

"Thank you, sir. I hope so."

William clears his throat. "Well, guess we better let you get back—"

"What're you boys shopping for today?" Roger asks, cutting William off.

I have to bite back a grin at the annoyed expression on his face. The humor is quickly replaced, though, as heat ripples through my veins when I catch him looking at me… again.

Since he's been back in town, I've fantasized about having another taste of him more than once. I've gotten pretty good at jacking off left-handed, and I've come with his name on my lips several nights now. It's one of the most frustrating things I've ever experienced, knowing what it's like to feel someone's body against mine, but also knowing it can never happen again. If it were up to me, we would've been sweaty between sheets half a dozen times already.

I'm not one for repeats. Typically, once I've had someone, I'm good and on to the next. But the way I crave another taste of William is next level, and honestly, it's probably mostly because there can't be a repeat. It's not like that with anybody else. If I wanted a repeat, I could have it from anybody except him. Maybe it's the challenge I crave and not necessarily him.

"Oh, I'm finally getting around to buying a hutch I need for my dining room," Whit responds. "We're picking it up before heading back to my place so I can build it. What about you guys? Getting stuff for Winnie?"

"Yeah, we gotta make her feel at home," Roger replies.

"Alright, Dad," William chimes in. "Let's get going. I don't want to be here all day."

Chuckling, I say, "Somebody is in a mood today, Doc."

He scowls at me, which only makes me laugh harder.

"Okay, okay," Roger murmurs. "We'll let you boys go, but it was nice to see you both."

"You too, Roger." Nudging William's arm as they stroll past us, I add quietly, "See you later, Doc."

Whit throws me a funny look, but doesn't say anything. After William and Roger are out of sight, he leads us back toward customer service. He apparently paid for the hutch ahead of time, and they have it ready for him. An employee brings it out to the truck for him, placing it in the bed. I don't know why he bothered bringing me along for this journey. It's not like I can be of any help to him at all while he brings this giant-ass box inside his house.

As soon as we're inside Whit's truck, he turns toward me.

"What the hell was that about?"

My heart stutters in my chest as I avoid his gaze and put on my seatbelt. "What do you mean?"

Starting the vehicle, he says, "Don't bullshit me, Colt. What was with the tension between you and Will?"

"There was no tension," I lie, trying my best to hide the smirk wanting to come out.

"You're so full of it," he remarks. "I want the tea."

My head snaps in his direction, and I snort. "You want the *tea*? Who are you and what have you done with my crotchety, cardigan-wearing Whittaker?"

That earns me a chilling scowl. "First of all, I am not crotchety," he replies, holding up a finger. "And second of all, sorry." He breathes out a laugh. "One of my new students at the clinic constantly says stuff like that, and I guess some of it stuck."

"I can only imagine how fun that is for you," I tease. Crotchety may have been a stretch, but Whit truly is the grumpiest old man-like thirty-something-year-old I've ever met. I'm not fully convinced he doesn't fill his spare time at home crocheting hats or something for fun.

"It's not bad," he muses. "Do not change the subject. Spill."

He pulls into his driveway, putting the truck in park, clearly not letting this go. Rolling my eyes, I unbuckle my seatbelt before turning to him and saying, "If we're going there, we need to be a lot less sober than we are now."

Whit pins me with an unamused expression. "It's barely noon."

Tossing him a toothy smirk, I shrug. "It's five o'clock somewhere, right?"

Heaving a sigh, he unbuckles his belt. "For fuck's sake. I'm going to regret asking, aren't I?"

"Probably."

CHAPTER 9

COLT BISHOP

"You did *what*?" Whit's eyes widen behind his thick-framed glasses.

We're each a few beers deep, a buzz barely going, but it's enough for me to spill the *tea*, so to speak. My chest rumbles with a chuckle at the absolute aghast look on his face. I've never seen Whit look so scandalized.

"It was only one time," I murmur. "And it was, like, two years ago. It's not a big deal."

"Colt, he is your *father's best friend*." His voice is nothing more than a whisper-yell. "That is *not*, 'not a big deal.'"

"Okay, maybe it was a *big* deal." I hold my hands a decent length apart from one other, wagging my brows at Whit suggestively.

Whit scoffs. "You know what, Colt, I could've gone my entire life not knowing that little piece of information."

"Not little," I chirp.

"You know what I mean," he hisses. "Will is close with Conrad, and when we were married, I got to know him pretty well, and I do *not* need to picture the size of his penis every time I see him."

"It's a nice penis to picture, though."

"I swear to God, you're as bad as Shooter," he grumbles. "How is there two of you?"

Puckering my lips, I blow him an air kiss before chuckling and tossing back another gulp of beer.

Whit miraculously had a dolly in his garage that he used to bring the giant box inside. He's got it opened up, and all of the parts sprawled all over in his living room as he scans the directions with a furrow in his brow.

"Do you want some help?" I offer, setting my beer down on the coaster on the table.

"No," he snaps. "You can't help. I'm not going to be responsible for you injuring yourself more."

"Whit, I've got an injured shoulder and wrist. My eyes still work," I deadpan, ripping the sheet of directions out of his hand. "Let me help."

"How did this even happen?" he asks after he finally gets himself squared away. "What were you doing in Seattle in the first place?"

"A buddy of mine from high school lives out there now, and it was his twenty-first birthday. He invited me out, and I had nothing better to do, so I went."

"Okay, and?" Whit makes a 'get on with it' gesture with his hand. "How did that lead to sleeping with Will?"

"I'd booked my hotel for two nights," I tell him. "The birthday party was the first night I was there, and my plans were wide open the next night. I've always heard how great the queer nightlife is in Seattle, so I decided to check it out for myself. William was at the bar I went to."

"By himself?"

"Yup."

"And then what?"

"I wasn't a hundred percent sure it was him at first. It had been quite a while since I'd seen him; he moved out of Copper Lake when I was in, like, middle school. I tossed back a few shots, got a little closer, and when we made eye contact across the area, I knew it was him."

Whit's looking at me like I've grown a second set of arms. "And there was no point once you realized who he was that you thought maybe you should leave?"

"Fuck no." I laugh. "Are you kidding? Do you know how many times I fantasized about William when I was growing up? He spent so much time at my house because of my dad, and I would drool over him the entire time."

Rolling his eyes, Whit asks, "Who made the first move?"

"Me, of course," I drawl with a smirk.

Whit looks thoroughly unamused, yet the questions keep coming. "What happened?"

"I brought over some shots, and after a few rounds, I asked him to dance."

Brows furrowed behind his glasses, Whit glances up from screwing in one of the wood shelves. "And he just…agreed?"

I nod, finishing off the rest of the beer. "At first, I thought he was going to shut me down. He definitely gave it a second thought, but in the end, yeah, he agreed."

Whit downs the rest of his beverage too. "This is… Wow."

Standing up off the couch, I swipe my empty beer bottle off the table. "Want another?"

"Sure."

"What the fuck is with all of these toy planes all over your dining room table?" I call out to him as I toss the empty bottles into the garbage can before opening the fridge.

"They are not *toy* planes," he responds as I stroll back into the living room, handing him a fresh beer. "They're model planes."

"What is the difference?"

"A toy is for fun," he offers, gaze focused on the task at hand. "These are not for fun. They're for display."

"Uh, okay. But why do you have so many of them? Your table is covered."

"Yeah, there's more on the floor behind the table too." Pausing what he's doing, Whit brushes the hair back from his forehead with his arm as he glances over at me. "I enjoy building them. It's a nice way to fill my free time, and I like how they look when I'm finished."

This is so fucking random. "Okay, but why planes?"

"Honestly, I'm not sure. When I was a kid, my dad would build them from time to time, and eventually, he let me help him. I guess it stuck."

"How did I not know this about you?"

"Uh, I don't know. Maybe because I don't advertise my hobbies on my forehead, and it's never come up? I don't ask you about your hobbies."

"Yeah, but you know mine. Rodeo."

"Why are you asking me so many questions? We're here to talk about you and your smutty affair." Whit mutters, cracking open his beer and taking a sip. "Did you guys go back to his place? Back to your hotel?"

Shaking my head, I say, "Neither. He took me to some apartment above the bar."

"This is wild."

"Wanna know the most fucked-up part?"

"I'm kind of scared to ask," Whit mumbles, making me

chuckle. "But yes, tell me."

"The entire night after we went up to the apartment is so hazy, I barely remember most of it. The next morning, when I woke up in my hotel room, I had to think for a good, long second about what happened the night before."

"Is it possible nothing happened, then?"

I shake my head. "Nah, we hooked up. I didn't fully black out, that much I do remember. And as more time has passed, little bits of the night have come back to me. It's just...I don't know how to explain it. A foggy type of memory, I guess. Like I remember things we did, but I don't necessarily remember what we said during or how we got there."

Whit sits with that for a moment. "Do you think he remembers?"

"Oh, a hundred percent. I knew he remembered from the moment I laid eyes on him when I found out he was back in town."

"Which was when?"

"When I was sitting in one of his patient rooms at the clinic."

His eyes widen. "Your shoulder," he blurts out. "Oh, my gosh, tell me he's not your doctor!"

"He most definitely is," I reply, biting back a grin at the unbelievable expression painted over Whit's face.

"Wow." Blowing out a breath, Whit runs a hand through his hair. "This is...so fucked up."

"I like to think of it as fun," I quip.

Watching me with an arched brow and his lips pressed thin, Whit says, "Of course, *you* would."

"Hey! I'm injured and unable to compete. Gotta pass the time somehow."

As if realization dawns on him, his eyes dart over to mine,

narrowing. "What are you going to do, Colt?"

A smirk splits my face as I give Whit my most innocent look. "Who, me? What makes you think I'm going to do anything?"

"Because you're you, and trouble is your middle name. You cannot pursue him, Colt."

"First of all"—I hold up a finger—"you're not wrong. And secondly, why the hell not? We are two consenting adults."

"Oh my God, you're a moron," he grumbles.

"Okay, ouch, jackass. What about you, then?"

Confusion takes over his expression as he pins me with a stare. "What about me?"

"Earlier, when I asked if you and Reggie were going to move in together, you looked at me like I'd lost my mind. What's up with that?"

He sort of curls in on himself with the question, and I don't even think he realizes he's doing it. Glancing down at his lap, he shrugs. "I know this doesn't make sense to you, since I don't think you've ever been in a serious relationship before, but there's no need to rush, okay? What Reggie and I have is fine the way it is. Why would we mess up a good thing by changing it?"

"Isn't that typically the next step, though?" Whit hits me with a deadpan stare, and I hold my hands up in innocence. "Genuine question."

"Sometimes," he murmurs, looking down at his lap again. "He lives and works out of town, and I live and work here. Neither of us is planning on leaving our jobs, so moving in together would just create a commute for one of us, and frankly, I don't want to move out of Copper Lake. I happen to love it here."

I can't help but smirk at the way he juts out his chin a little at the end. Whit's on the quieter side. He can come off a bit stuffy more often than not, but he can get quite feisty if he needs to be. Though he may be but small, he's mighty, or whatever that Shakespeare quote is.

"It has nothing to do with the fact that the last person you lived with was Conrad, would it?"

That earns me a chilling glare that I can practically *feel*. "No, Colt, my relationship and how we decide to move it forward has nothing to do with my ex-husband."

Laughing, I say, "Oh my gosh, you are *touchy* about this shit. Down, boy."

"I don't know if you realize it, but people are constantly speculating about me and Conrad. People who come into the clinic, all of our friends, even Reggie! Conrad and I split up almost four years ago. We have never given anybody any reason to believe we're getting back together or that there might still be something simmering there. We have moved on; I don't know why everybody else hasn't."

"I'm sorry, man," I say, and I mean it. "I was just messing with you, but I'm sorry. I guess I didn't think about how annoying that must be for you to deal with."

His shoulders relax, and he blows out a breath. "It's fine. I know you're joking around. I'm just...I don't know, sensitive about it sometimes."

Remembering what he said, something stands out to me. "Reggie says stuff about it?"

Eyes flitting to mine, it's like he is just now realizing he let that slip. "Not often, but he has made a comment or two about it in the past."

"Like what?"

Whit chews on the inside of his cheek for a moment. "I think it's natural for him to question it, since Conrad and I still have to work together as often as we do. He's just asked about if the divorce was civil, and if there're still any feelings around on either of our parts. Stuff like that. Nothing too big."

All conversation about hookups, boyfriends, and ex-husbands fades as he gets back to putting together this hutch thing. The directions are confusing as hell to understand, but eventually, we figure it out. Once he's finished, he stands it up, admiring his work.

"This looks nice," I offer, coming to stand beside him. "Where are you going to put it?"

"In the dining room," he murmurs as he picks up the rest of the garbage and spare pieces. "These were all in storage bins in my spare bedroom closet up until a month ago when I got a hankering to do some building. I got them out and put them in my dining room, fully meaning to buy and build this right away, but time got away from me."

"Here, I can help you move it into the dining room."

"Uh, no, the hell you won't," he barks. "I told you, I'm not going to be responsible for you re-injuring yourself."

"Don't be ridiculous," I scoff. "I can use my free hand to lift it."

"No, you will not. Besides, I need to vacuum and move some stuff around in there before I can put it in there, and that's not happening today. I've used all of my energy just building it."

Chuckling, I say, "Fair enough."

"Want to stay for dinner?" he asks. "I don't know what I'm having, but I can whip us up something."

"Nah, I should get home. My mom said she's making my favorite tonight." I grin.

Nodding, Whit asks, "Do you know how long you have to

stay there?"

"At least until my sling can come off." Glancing down at my arm, I say, "I can't do a whole lot for myself, like drive, until that happens, but it should get to come off soon, I would think."

"Think you'll be back on the circuit next year?"

"Shit, I sure as fuck hope so."

The text Cope sent earlier, that I never responded to, comes to mind. It's not the first time one of my buddies has checked in and I left them on read. It makes me feel like shit, because I don't know why it's so hard for me to respond. I appreciate them checking in, but I feel like some sort of… I don't know, wet blanket or something. They're off having the time of their life, competing every weekend, as they should, while I'm home, injured and unable to do shit. I can't face them and see their pity.

I've tried not to think too much about it lately. The circuit and the time I've lost. All it does is pisses off, the fact that I'm at home while all my friends are on the road. I can't help but feel like I've been robbed of my entire season, and then I start to ask myself why it had to happen to me, or why it happened this early in my career? Why couldn't it happen later on when I've had time to make a name for myself?

I can't rush my recovery time, or I risk making everything worse, but I pray like hell that by the time the next season starts, I'm in good enough shape to compete again. I need this. Without bull riding, I don't know who the hell I am.

There is no Colt Bishop without the rodeo.

CHAPTER 10

WILLIAM ANDINO

"Come on, Winnie. Time to go."

I pat my thigh, trying to get Winnie to come to me, but she's rooted happily on my dad's lap where he sits in the recliner in the living room. She's going to the vet this morning for her first check-up—well, first in our care—and I told my dad I would drop her off on my way to work. Grabbing the leash off the hook in the kitchen, I stroll through the house toward the living room. They've been sitting there together as he watches the morning news since I got out of the shower an hour ago.

"Are you sure you're okay to pick her up in a few hours?" I ask my dad as I hook the leash onto the loop on her collar. "If not, I can probably swing by and grab her on my lunch break. We shouldn't be too busy today."

"No, I can do it." He waves me off. "I said I would do it, so I'll do it."

"Okay, well, if you change your mind, just give the office a call."

Grunting his response, he returns his attention to the TV mounted on the wall, and that's that.

With Winnie in hand, I leave the house and climb into my car. The clouds are dark and gray this morning, letting me know it's probably going to rain soon. I much prefer to start my day with some sunshine. When I got in the car, I set Winnie in the passenger seat, but she has since climbed into my lap, standing with her front two paws on the door so she can look out the window as I drive. We haven't even had her for a full week yet, but I have to admit, I'm growing fond of her. She's a sweet girl, and as far as small dogs go, she's not nearly as loud as I expected her to be. She also seems to make my father happy, which is a plus.

Every night when I get home from work, he tells me about what they did during the day. They've gone to the dog park, they play fetch in the backyard, he's even taken her to the trail that runs through town. They can't walk too far because of his hip, but the fresh air and the light exercise are good for his spirits. Maybe he was right about getting the dog, after all. Not that I'd ever admit that to him; I'd never hear the end of it.

Taking a right into the parking lot of the vet's office, I pull into a spot right out front. There are only a few cars here at this time of day, but I believe they just opened. I don't have to be at work for another half an hour, so I'm doing good on time. My first patient is later in the morning than usual, which is a nice change of pace.

A bell sounds as I push open the front door, and Whit looks up from the computer he's typing at as I approach the front counter. "Good morning, Whit. Didn't expect to see you up here."

"Hello, Dr. Andino. Yeah, our receptionist is out today,"

he murmurs, eyes right on Winnie. "Oh my gosh, look at this sweet girl!" Coming into the waiting room, he gives her a few chin scratches, her tail just a wagging at the attention she's receiving. "She's even cuter in person. I saw her on the schedule today, but I figured Roger would be the one bringing her in. What a…nice surprise."

Whit's a bit strange. He speaks monotone for the most part, and he's never been very good with eye contact. At least he hasn't with me, but right now, he's acting even weirder than usual. He hasn't looked me in the eye even once since I walked in, and now, as he scurries back behind the counter to check us in, he's fidgety. He's chewing on his bottom lip as his fingers tap on the keyboard, and there's a line of perspiration shining above his brow, just above the rim of his glasses.

"Are you alright, Whit?" I ask, my brows knit together. The vein in his neck throbs as he continues to type on his computer.

"Yes, of course," he squeaks. "Why do you ask?"

"You seem a bit jumpy."

"Nope, I'm totally fine, Dr. Andino. Thank you for asking." Reaching out of sight, he comes back with a clipboard that he attaches a stack of papers to. Setting it in front of me with a pen, he says, "Please fill everything out, front and back. Anything you don't know the answer to, just leave blank." Still not looking me in the eye, he adds, "I can take Winnie now, and get her situated in the back while you get to work on that."

Handing Winnie over, I take the forms and have a seat in one of the chairs. The forms ask entirely too many questions that I don't know the answer to, considering we only got the dog several days ago. After about fifteen minutes, I finish filling them out to the best of my ability. Back at the counter, I wait a few moments to see if Whit comes back. When he doesn't, I ring the little bell located off to the side.

"All done?" he asks, his voice much higher than it normally is.

"Yes. My dad will be by in an hour or so to pick her up."

He nods, taking the papers from me. "Very well, that sounds good."

"Whit, what's the matter?" I ask again, the words coming out harsher than I intend. "Is something wrong with the dog?"

"What?" Finally, his eyes snap up to meet mine. "No! I haven't examined her yet, but she seems fine from the outside."

"Then why are you behaving so odd?"

Glancing around the office like somebody is going to come save him, or maybe making sure nobody is in earshot, Whit heaves a sigh, meeting my gaze, but only for a moment. His cheeks are bright pink, and he looks severely uncomfortable. "I know," is all he says quietly, sounding dejected.

I stare at him for a moment, expecting him to keep going, my brows furrowing when I realize he's not. "You know... what?" *Is he on drugs? I've never seen him act like this.*

He levels me with a *look*, his face crimson, and suddenly, it hits me what he means by that. *He knows about me and Colt.*

Clearing my throat, I force myself to not outwardly react while my heart pounds more powerfully. "I see." My jaw clenches. "Well, if that'll be all, I really better be getting—"

"I'm sorry," he cuts me off. "I wasn't going to say anything, but I wasn't exactly expecting to come face to face with you this morning."

"Whit, it's fine," I grit out. "But I would appreciate it if you could keep that to yourself. It's something that shouldn't have happened, and it was a long time ago."

Nodding a little harder than necessary, making his glasses slide down his nose, he rushes out, "Of course, Dr. Andino. I would never tell anybody something like that."

"Will, please," I add. "And thank you. Again, my father will be by shortly to pick her up."

"Yes, sir. Have a nice day."

Grunting out a clipped "you too," I hightail it out of the office and into my car, locking the door as soon as my ass is planted in the driver's seat, like maybe the locked door will erase what Whit knows.

Why the hell would Colt tell him?

This *cannot* get out.

Jesus Christ. I should've known this would happen.

What the hell am I going to do? Do I trust that Whit won't open his mouth and tell anybody? I sure hope so.

As my mind rolls through every possible thing that could go wrong if people find out, nausea churns in my gut. It never should've happened in the first place.

What the hell was I thinking? It's a question I've asked myself more times than I can count, and I never can figure it out. And what's worse, is now that I'm back in town, I can't stop myself from replaying the night in my head over and over and fucking over again.

"Fuck!"

CHAPTER 11
COLT BISHOP

Coming to a stop in front of the clinic, my dad doesn't bother putting the car in park. "I'm going to run a few errands, but I'll be back to pick you up by the time you're finished."

I unbuckle my seatbelt with a nod. "Sounds good, thanks." Climbing out of my dad's truck, I offer him a quick wave before I head into the office.

I have a follow-up appointment with William this morning. My first physical therapy session was last week, and this is to check the progress on that, I guess.

Once I'm checked in, I have a seat in one of the chairs in the waiting room. There is one other person in here, but that's it. It's still pretty early, the office having just opened. If I wasn't in such a sour mood, I'd probably be excited, knowing I'm about to see William. It's going to be the first time since I played footsie with him at the diner, and something about messing with him, riling him up even just a little bit, brings me joy.

I'm trying to not let the injury bring me down, but it's hard. I should be well on my way to qualifying for finals again. On to the next stop, the next rodeo. But instead, I'm stuck here, unable to work out, train, or do any-fucking-thing, and I'm sick of it. Why me? Why'd this have to happen to me? Despite knowing I shouldn't, I found the footage of the injury on the internet, and I've started obsessively watching it. Over and over, I'll replay it, pinpointing the exact moment everything went wrong.

Last night, I was scrolling through social media, and I saw some rodeo coverage on a couple of my buddies' pages. It's such a weird juxtaposition; the happiness and pride I feel for them, seeing them work their asses off and do well, while also swallowing down the bitterness that comes from knowing I should be out there too. I wish I hadn't seen those photos because it's done nothing but reignite all the feelings I've been trying to tamp down.

"Colt?" Glancing up, I meet Meg's gaze. She's smiling warmly at me, and I try to return the gesture, but I'm sure it looks forced. "If you want to follow me back," she says.

After she checks my weight, we settle into a room toward the back. I shrug out of my jacket and set it on the chair in the corner before climbing up onto the bed.

"How are we feeling this morning?" Meg asks, taking a seat in the swivel chair in front of the computer. She swipes her card over the reader, unlocking it.

"Fine." My one-word answer comes out clipped. My shoulder is on the sore side this morning, probably from overdoing it on the stretches last night after I saw those pictures, but like hell am I about to tell her that.

"Incision site is looking good?" she asks, clicking away on

the keyboard. "No redness or swelling?"

"Nope. Looking good."

Meg asks me a few more questions before she rises off her chair and crosses the room. We're quiet as she checks my vitals. Finishing up, she inputs all of her responses on the computer before standing once more and glancing over at me. "Okay, Dr. Braylon will be in momentarily."

My brows clash together. "Dr. Braylon?" I repeat. "No, Dr. Andino is my primary care doctor."

Looking as confused as I feel, she walks back over to the computer and scans her card once more. After a few moments, she says, "It looks like care has been transferred over to Dr. Braylon. Were you not notified?"

"Obviously not," I grit out, realizing a little too late how harsh that came out. "Can I speak to Dr. Andino, please?"

"He's not in the office right now," she offers, looking apologetic.

Not wanting to cause a scene when I'm already feeling irritable, I nod. "That's okay. Thanks, Meg."

With a nod, she offers me a small smile before exiting through the door.

Why would he switch me over to Dr. Braylon? And without telling me to boot. Was he really that pissed by me playing a little footsie? *What an asshole.*

A few minutes later, a knock sounds at the door before it's pushed open. Dr. Braylon steps inside, closing the door behind him as he regards me with a warm grin. "Morning, Colt."

I don't know Dr. Braylon all that well; I think he moved here after med school, but he can't be much older than me. He seems like a nice enough guy, but again, I don't know a whole lot about him.

I tip my chin up at him by way of greeting as he sits in the swivel chair and scans his badge to unlock the screen. He's quiet for a moment as he appears to read through my chart, the silence grating my nerves.

"Where's Dr. Andino?" I blurt out.

Gaze darting over to meet mine, he looks confused. "He's not in the office yet."

"He's my doctor." In the back of my mind, I'm aware that I'm behaving like a petulant child who's not getting his way, but something about this entire situation is annoying the fuck out of me.

Dr. Braylon's brows pinch together. "Oh, I'm sorry, Colt. I figured you would've been notified about the switch, but in an effort to lighten Dr. Andino's workload, we moved a couple patients over to me. I thought you knew."

"No, I did not know."

Dr. Braylon glances at the computer screen, then back at me, his lips turned down into a frown. He doesn't say anything for a moment, but his lips open and close a few times like he's trying to find the right words to calm the situation. Not wanting to cause a huge fuss, I blow out a breath.

"It's fine," I finally offer. "Can we get on with it, please?"

His shoulders visibly relax, and the smile returns to his face. "Yes, of course."

From there, the appointment goes smoothly. He advises me to take it easy, to not push myself too hard, but to be sure to keep up with my exercises. I have physical therapy again in a few days, and I'm praying they tell me I can remove the sling after that appointment. As I'm leaving, I schedule my next appointment. It's on the tip of my tongue to ask the receptionist if William is here yet, but I bite it back. I don't want to seem crazy or desperate, but I would like to ask him what his fucking problem is. So what? We hooked up one time years ago. Does he really have to fire me as a patient for that? And without even discussing it with me. What a coward move.

My dad is waiting for me in the parking lot as I exit the building. Aside from asking how the appointment went, the drive home is made in silence. All I want to do is go home and lie down. I'm agitated, but that seems to be the only emotion I'm capable of feeling these days. Dr. Braylon suggested it may be a good idea to talk to someone about all of this, like a therapist. Probably because he could tell how irritated I was, and he probably chalked it up to being about the injury. He's probably right. Yes, I'm annoyed that William got rid of me as a patient, but if I'm honest with myself, had I not been injured and unable to compete, that fact probably wouldn't annoy me as much. I'm on edge, that's all.

Taking the steps up to my parents' house two at a time, I stroll inside, leaving my shoes near the rack by the front door, and just as I'm about to barrel up the stairs in search of my bed, my mom pokes her head around the corner.

"Hi, honey. How was your appointment?"

"Hey, Mom. It was fine."

"Can you come in here, please?"

For fuck's sake. I just want to lie down. "Sure."

"I was hoping you could help me," she says as I step into the kitchen. "I'm baking sugar cookies for Ginny's surprise birthday party, and thought maybe you could cut the dough for me while I roll out the next batch. You can do it with one hand."

Clenching my jaw to ensure I don't bite out that doing anything left-handed is not easy, I nod, taking a seat at the table where she's got a huge thing of dough flattened and ready for me. There's a circle cookie cutter beside it and a couple of cookie sheets lined with parchment paper on the counter behind me.

"Are you planning to go to Ginny's party?" she asks as I get started on my task. It's actually not as challenging as I thought it would be. "I think it'll be fun."

Practically the whole town is getting together at the diner this Sunday to celebrate Ginny's birthday. Her daughter works in the shop next to Whit's clinic, and she's the one who told us about it. Well, told Whit, and Whit told me.

"I don't know, not really in the party mood," I murmur with a shrug.

Glancing over at me, something softens in my mom's eyes as she takes me in. "Honey, I can't imagine how hard this must be for you, to be hurt and not able to ride. I wish I had the magical fix to make you feel better, but I don't. I know I'm just your mom and probably the last person you want to talk to, but please know, I'm always here for you."

My mom is a big talker. She believes in talking about your feelings, getting them out there, and working through it all. She's always been that way, while I tend to take after my dad and hold everything inside. What is talking going to do? Is it going to make my shoulder better? Is it going to get me back on a bull any faster? No. So, what's the point?

A twinge of guilt squeezes at my chest, though. It's not my mom's fault that I'm in this situation, and she doesn't deserve my anger or my poor attitude. With a tight smile, I say, "Thanks, Mom. I appreciate you saying that."

"Know what I think?" she asks, a glint in her eye.

I shake my head.

"I think your shoulder is going to heal nicely, and you'll be back to competing next season. I know it can be easy to wallow right now, when you have nothing but time on your hands, but the body is an incredible thing. You're young and healthy, and I think it'll surprise you how quickly you get back to normal with a little bit of time."

"We don't know that," I mutter.

"A little positive thinking never hurt anybody," she replies with a wink.

My mom isn't the biggest fan of the rodeo, or my bull riding. Considering what happened to her husband when he was a professional bull rider, it's understandable. I'm not dumb; I can admit that his injuries were significantly worse than the ones I'm suffering from. Hell, he was in a coma for a while and nearly died, but I can't imagine the fear that clutched at my mother when she saw me get bucked off that bull and then stepped on.

It was a surprise to nobody when I announced I wanted to be a bull rider when I was younger. For as long as I can remember, I wanted to be just like my dad. I'd go with him to the arena, I'd watch him train, and every summer until sophomore year in high school, I'd travel with him as he competed on the circuit. I was his little shadow for as long as I can remember, bull riding always a dream of mine. I joined the rodeo club in high school, and dedicated all of my free time to learning to be the best I could be. My mom always supported my dreams, rooted for me, even when I knew it terrified her. Even though I know she has always wished I would've taken a different route.

She doesn't say anything else, and neither do I. After I've cut the dough into circles and put them all on the cookie sheet, she puts those in the oven as I get started on the next slab of dough. Working side by side for the next hour or so, I allow myself to enjoy this little moment. I force myself to let go of some of the anger I'm holding on to and appreciate this time spent with my mom that, had the situation been different, I wouldn't be here for.

Once we're done, she fixes us some sandwiches, fruit, and chips, and we eat outside on the porch together. I don't know how she does it, but by the time we're finished eating, I'm feeling better than I have in days.

CHAPTER 12
COLT BISHOP

Fuck. I wince, breathing harshly through my nose as I try to maneuver my shirt over my head without hurting myself. So much for feeling better.

Yesterday, after helping my mom, I went up to my room, drank a handful of beers, and made the mistake of looking up the rodeo stats. More specifically, bull riding stats. It was not my finest moment. Nor my smartest. Especially when I decided a late-night workout in my dad's garage was a good idea. I think I overdid it, and it doesn't help that my father caught me mid-workout. You'd think he caught me rubbing one out with how startled we both were when he walked into the garage and found me.

To say he was irked would be an understatement. I got a very stern talking to like I was a rebellious teenager all over again.

I'm paying the price for it this morning, though, that's for damn sure. My shoulder is throbbing, and I swear it's more swollen than usual, but I could be paranoid. In either case, I'm kind of freaking out. What if I set myself back even more? In the light of day, with a clear mind, I know it was a stupid move. Really fucking stupid. But last night… Fuck, I don't know. I felt hopeless. A voice in the back of my mind kept chirping at me, feeding me my worst fears.

You're never going to recover in time to compete next season.

Your competitors are out there scoring and getting further than you.

They're all going to surpass you while you sit at home and wither away.

You're never going to be good enough.

Why is it that our worst critics are always ourselves?

I'm sitting on my bed with a heating pad on my shoulder when a knock sounds at my door. "Come in," I call out, thinking it's probably my mom checking on me since I haven't left this room at all this morning. Imagine my surprise when the door opens and in walks the last person I ever would've expected. "What the hell are you doing here?"

William leaves the door open as he steps into my room, a broody, bored expression on his face, hands stuffed into the pockets of his slacks. "Your father called me to come check you out."

Huffing out a dry laugh, I say, "Is that right?"

He presses his lips together, probably realizing what he just said. "He said you were working out last night and may have hurt yourself."

Realization dawns on me, and it feels like the wind has been punched out of me. *God-fucking-damnit.* "Why the hell would he call you? You're not even my fucking doctor anymore."

I don't miss the twitch in his jaw or the way his nostrils flare. "Well, I would imagine that, unless you told him, he probably doesn't know I'm not your doctor, Colt. I don't make it a point to discuss my patients with their parents."

"Yeah, well, I'm fine," I scoff. "So you wasted your time

coming over here."

"You're not fine," he argues, stepping farther into the room. "There's a heating pad draped over your shoulder."

"I'm a little cold."

"Right." William rolls the desk chair to the side of my bed, dropping down into it. The rich, mahogany scent of his wafts over to me, and I hate how much that smell excites me. I'm in no mood to see anybody right now, or be told what a fucking idiot I am for going against doctor's orders. "Since I'm already here, how about I take a look at it?"

Biting down on my molars, I glance over at him, and I'm taken aback by the concern etched in his features. "Yeah, okay," I murmur, taking the heating pad off and setting it in my lap.

"Can you take your shirt off for me?" he asks, and the deep baritone of his voice sends a shiver down my spine. Swallowing thickly, I nod, sitting up to maneuver the material up and over my head without agitating my shoulder. I must not do a very good job at concealing my discomfort because William reaches for the hem, stopping me. "Here, let me."

I freeze, hand still gripping the hem of my shirt as my heart thunders in my chest. We hold eye contact for a long, tense moment before he nods, and I drop my hand. With the utmost gentleness, William lifts my shirt, knuckles lightly brushing against my abdomen as he pulls my good arm out first before dragging it over my head until he's able to slide it easily off my injured arm. Setting the shirt in my lap, his eyes find mine again. He pauses, but I don't know why. For permission, maybe? I tuck my chin in a quick nod, and then his fingers are skating over my skin as his gaze averts to my shoulder while he examines the area.

Silence surrounds us as he gently pokes and prods the area,

somehow managing to not hurt me in the process. His fingertips are featherlight against my skin, and my heart is beating so hard I'm certain he can hear it from where he's sitting.

"What kind of exercises were you doing?" he asks. When I don't answer, I feel his gaze on the side of my head. "Colt." My name is a throaty growl that sends goosebumps over my skin.

"I tried lifting a little weight," I mumble.

His blues slice over to mine for half a second before he focuses on my shoulder again. "You know better than that," is all he says, and I'm torn between feeling scolded and being turned on by the tone he's taking with me. Imagining him saying those words in a different setting, with much less clothes on. "Why'd you do it?"

My throat tightens, and I don't bother answering. I can't. There's a gentleness to the question that I wasn't prepared for.

Touch tender, yet firm, the pads of his fingers press into the flesh around my shoulder, massaging lightly. It sends electricity through my body, and it makes my breath come out harsher. It feels good, and I know it's more than just the massage. It's *him*. His hands on my body, his gaze so focused on me.

"Does this hurt at all?" he asks, voice throaty and hoarse all of the sudden. The sound is fire through my veins.

"Nah, it feels good," I reply honestly.

My heart pounds an erratic beat against my rib cage, my skin lit up under his touch. I feel it everywhere. William looks up from where his hands work the muscle, darkened eyes meeting mine again, and I swear he feels it too. It's in the way his throat works as he swallows, in the way his cheeks are flushed, and his lips are parted. And then his fingers stop moving, and somehow he moves a little closer. So close I can feel his hot breath fan my face. So close I can see the way his pupils dilate when they dip down to my mouth.

Time stands still, the entire world fading away as I see the desire swirling in his gaze. He wants to kiss me. "Colt," he whispers, the restraint fading with each passing moment. It's palpable.

"Do it," I breathe, needing this.

A moment passes, and just when I think he may actually lean in and seal his mouth to mine, I hear it.

The heavy thud from feet on the stairs.

In a flash, William rolls back to an appropriate distance, putting some space between us seconds before my dad steps into my doorway. He grins when he sees us. "How's it going in here?" he asks. "How's the shoulder looking?"

Clearing his throat, William looks back at my father. "It's looking good. Thankfully, I don't think he pulled anything or injured himself further." Glancing back at me, he adds, "But you got lucky. I wouldn't suggest doing that again. I don't think I need to tell you that you can't rush a recovery like this. I understand how frustrating this must feel, and how bad you want to get back out there, but you're risking doing more damage the more you push yourself."

I grit my teeth as I look away, nodding. "Got it, Doc."

"I would continue using the heating pad as needed, and take it easy. This is a marathon, Colt. Not a race."

"Thanks for coming out, Will," my dad adds in.

Rising off the chair, William spares me one final glance before he leaves the room. "It's no trouble," he tells my dad as he brushes by him, patting him on the shoulder.

Staring at the spot in the doorway where they just were, I can't help but feel both frustrated and elated at the same time.

He almost fucking kissed me.

CHAPTER 13

WILLIAM ANDINO

Memories flit behind my closed eyelids. A sultry slideshow displaying miles of smooth, toned, bare skin, rough, calloused hands roaming over my flesh, hot breath against my neck, goosebumps blooming along my limbs, and sweet, guttural groans, both mine and his. The feel of his body pressed up against mine, his cock hard and perfectly aligned with mine. His hand wrapped around us tightly, and the spit leaving his mouth to coat our lengths. The slick feel of his palm sliding up and down us both. Electricity pulsing just below the surface, soaring through my veins and invading my mind.

The darkness of the room, only the faint glow of the streetlights, the feel of the barely used bedding beneath my body, the hungry look in his eyes as he alternates his dark gaze between my face and where we slide in and out of his grip. The veins protruding from his forearm, the bulge in his bicep, the sharp point of his dusky nipples. *Everything.* The heavy beating of my heart against my ribs, the heat pooling low in my spine, the tingle through my limbs. All of it is so vivid in my mind, as if it were just yesterday.

"Look at you writhing beneath me," he spoke through gritted teeth. *"Your cock feels so fucking good against mine."*

Soapy and slick, I wrap my fist around my length, squeezing at the base as I slap my other hand against the cool, wet tile on the wall. My head hangs between my shoulders, water streaming over my head and sluicing down my back. I pump my cock the way I remember Colt doing it that night. I'm the one touching myself, but behind my eyes, it's him. It's always him lately. Since getting back into town, Colt plagues my mind, and I don't know how to get him out of there. His cocky smirk, that damn backwards hat he always wears, the deep gruffness of his voice, his tight, tan body. Everything about him drives me wild, and I can't seem to help myself. It's like I'm twenty years younger and can't seem to satiate myself fast enough.

I've made myself come to our time spent together more times than I can count in the weeks since my return. As with most adults, the older and more busy I've become, the lower my sex drive has gotten, but now it's like I can't get enough. I don't understand what's gotten into me.

That's a lie. I absolutely know what's gotten into me... So, here I am, starting my day by stroking my cock at seven in the morning in my shower, fantasizing about the man I shouldn't be. I'm a fiend.

The room was dark; I barely even got a good look at him, but he's burned into my brain. Every sharp line, every muscle and curve, even the filthy way he talked me through it all. Colt took control, and it's something I wasn't used to. All of my previous sexual partners, male and female, have always been on the more submissive side. It was always me making the first moves, calling the shots. Not with him. That night, I was wholly under Colt's spell, and it made the entire experience that much hotter. He wasn't shy, wasn't intimidated. He was sure and steady, and it was sexy to experience.

A bolt of lust shoots down my spine, burying itself low in my groin as I fuck my fist faster. My heart is pounding, my blood is pumping hot, and my chest is heaving with my shallow, desperate breaths. I'm so close, my body's on fire. I need to come. If I had it my way, my fist would be replaced with Colt's lips as he kneeled before me in this shower stall. I allow myself to imagine how it would be to take him right here, knowing someone was downstairs. The risk of potentially being heard sends a molten heat to the base of my spine. Similarly to how I almost kissed him the other day, knowing his dad—my best friend—was just downstairs. The visual has my balls tightening into my body, and before I know it, my dick pulses, spilling my load down the drain. My release seizes my muscles, and I have to clench my jaw tightly to keep from crying out. Wave after wave rolls through me as I pump the last drop from my cock.

Disappointment floods my system almost immediately, like it always does when I allow myself to get swept away by the lust I feel from remembering that night.

Slapping my hand against the wall, I curse out under my breath before finishing up my shower.

I pull into the arena, checking the time on the dash and seeing that I have about a ten minutes before I need to head inside and start setting up. It's the second free clinic this morning, and I'm excited for the most part. The first time was such a success that I can't wait to see what type of turnout we have today. In addition to feeling excited, though, I'm also a little anxious. Assuming Colt comes today like he said he would, this'll be the first time we've seen each other since I reassigned him to Doug. It was a shitty thing to do without notifying Colt first, especially since Meg told me he seemed upset about it when he found out. To make matters worse, I told Meg it had slipped my mind to tell Colt because of how busy I had been this week.

That's a lie; it didn't slip my mind. I purposely avoided telling him because I didn't want to deal with the backlash, and in doing so, my staff has to deal with the brunt of it. The truth is, being near Colt intimidates me, which doesn't make any sense. He's nearly half my age; what he thinks, does, or says should have no effect on me, but it does.

The shower this morning barely took the edge off, and knowing I'm going to be face to face with him soon isn't helping either.

When I can't put it off any longer, I turn off my car and climb out. Once inside, I notice that Doug and Meg aren't here yet, so I begin setting up by myself. I also notice that Colt isn't here. Although, if the first time is anything to go off of, he'll arrive closer to the time the doors open. Probably better that way. The less time we spend alone together, the better.

Over the next ten minutes, volunteers start trickling in, including Meg and Doug. We get set up, and it isn't until a minute before the doors get unlocked that Colt saunters in, steps full of swagger that's all him. It takes me a second to realize what's different about him... It's the sling; he's not wearing it. Sitting behind the check-in desk beside Meg, he turns to her and smiles before they get started checking patients in. It doesn't take long for a line to form, people pouring in as the minutes drag on.

As Colt checks people in, Meg takes them to one of the makeshift designated rooms, which is really just a hospital bed and a chair surrounded by a privacy curtain. It's about five minutes before she steps out and hands the file off to me. Stepping into the room, I'm met with a woman in her early twenties.

"Good morning, Ms. Michaelson," I greet as I take a seat in the chair in front of her. "I'm Dr. Andino, and I'll be taking care of you today.

"Hi."

"Why don't you tell me a little bit about what's going on with you."

"I've had pain in my right ear for a couple days," she explains. "It's only getting worse."

I nod, then glance at her chart. "It looks like when the nurse took your temperature, you had a slight fever. Is that new or did that start when the ear pain did?"

"I'm not sure," she replies softly. "I don't have a thermometer at home, but I think I had a fever last night."

"Alright, let's have a look and see what we find." Placing the otoscope just inside her ear, my suspicions are confirmed when I take in her red, bulging eardrum paired with the pain and the fever.

After getting her a prescription for antibiotics to treat her ear infection, I send her on her way, and once I get the makeshift room sanitized and ready to go for the next patient Meg brings in, I step out and meander toward the front. The line has gotten significantly longer than when I was last up here, and as I wander up to the table Colt is sitting at, and peruse the list of names and symptoms of the checked in patients, I glance over at him, but he remains focused on the task at hand.

"Good morning, Colt," I murmur.

Without even looking at me, he says, "Morning, Dr. Andino."

Dr. Andino. Not *Doc.* Not *William.*

Before I have a chance to reply, Meg calls me back, letting me know my next patient is in "room" number six. From there, the rest of the morning passes in a blur of runny noses and pesky coughs. We're so busy that I don't even have a chance to take a break and eat a snack, but we're somehow able to get through everybody who checked in today, only running over our allotted time by a half an hour. The last patient went to Doug, so I help Meg and Colt break everything down, and he's still not paying me any attention, which is annoying me far more than it should.

The paranoid part of my brain is telling me he's giving me the silent treatment because I switched him over to Doug's care, but even if that is the case, shouldn't that make me relieved? Isn't that exactly what I wanted when I made the decision? It shouldn't be getting under my skin, and I certainly shouldn't be wanting to approach him and start a conversation myself.

Leave it alone, Will.

I'm doing a pretty good job at keeping my distance as we finish putting everything away, but then Meg goes and takes a load of stuff out to her car, and Colt and I are left alone. Like I have zero control over my actions, I find myself walking over to him before my mind has a chance to talk me out of it.

He doesn't look at me as I come to a stop beside him.

"Busy day, huh?" I murmur as I close one of the folding chairs.

"Sure was."

"See your sling is gone. Bet you're happy about that."

What am I doing? Why on earth am I trying so damn hard to

initiate small talk?

Finally, Colt turns his head, bright green eyes meeting mine, and a barely-there smirk slides across his lips. "Sure am."

"Have you gotten any better at doing things left-handed?"

The smirk grows as he regards me. "Some things," he replies before taking a step closer. "Other things I had to…get a little creative with, if you know what I mean."

Heart slamming against my chest at the insinuation that's *very* clear, I swallow thickly, trying to bring moisture back to my mouth as I force a dry laugh through my nose and nod. "I'll bet."

Cocking his head to the side slightly, he asks, "Do you?"

I bite down on my molars as I stare down my nose at him. He's only a few inches shorter than I am, but his energy is about eight feet tall. "Yes, Colt, I think I do."

Gaze dipping down to my lips for a single moment, Colt grins with all his teeth but doesn't reply. We finish breaking down the rest of the chairs, and then the table, by the time Meg walks back inside.

"You two still okay cleaning everything up?" she asks, looking from me to Colt. She must see the confusion on my face because she adds, "Doug and I both have to leave right away, remember? We talked about it earlier this week."

"Right." I nod, the conversation coming back to me. "That's fine. Enjoy the rest of your weekend, Meg."

"Thanks, Will. You too! Doug's still with his patient, but he'll be done any minute," she calls out from over her shoulder. "See you Monday. Bye, Colt!"

Turning my head, I glance over at Colt. Breaking down the table, he's not paying me any mind. It's not something that should aggravate me, but it does. Ethics aside, the entire reason I moved Colt over to Doug's care was to remove myself from the situation, and now, here I am, mere days later, finding reasons to talk to him because he spent the whole morning pretending he didn't know I existed. It's ridiculous.

Clearing my throat, I say, "I'm going to start breaking down one of the patient rooms while Doug finishes up with his patient."

Colt gives me a mock solute before returning his attention to the task at hand. Doesn't bother saying anything.

I spin on my heels with a huffed breath and go back toward the patient rooms. I need to snap out of it.

CHAPTER 14

COLT BISHOP

"Hey, Colt!" William calls out.

Walking down to where he's at, I pop my head around the makeshift wall. "What's up?"

Our eyes meet as he glances up at the sound of my voice. "Can you help me tear this down?" he asks. "It's stuck for some reason, and I can't do it myself."

"Sure thing, Doc."

To say I'm surprised William has made any effort at all to talk to me today would be an understatement. I'm still annoyed that he switched my care over to Dr. Braylon without so much as a heads up, and I mostly intended to not interact with him at all today because of it—which is kind of childish, I know—so, having him come up and talk with me threw me off a bit at first. Now, though, I'm going to enjoy this. Maybe see if I can push a button or two, especially since we're the only ones here.

"How's the new pup doing?" I ask him, after we successfully break down one of the beds.

"She's good," he says, looking more than a little flustered.

"Well behaved and sweet. She's a nice addition to the house."

"Show me some more pictures."

Huffing out a sigh, he brushes his hair off his forehead. "Colt, we're a little busy."

"There's always time for wiener pics."

I'll give it to him; he tries *really* hard to not react to that joke, but I don't miss the twitch to his lips.

"It's okay to laugh, Doc," I tease. "I know I'm funny. Now show me the pics."

"I don't have many pictures of her on my phone."

"Bullshit." I snort. "I'm willing to bet money you have tons of shots of her. Let's see it."

Furrowed brow and a tight jaw, he holds my gaze for a long moment before folding, pulling his phone out. Turning the screen my way, he flips through photo after photo of the small, cute dog.

"Ha! I knew I was right."

"Anybody ever told you how modest you are?" he deadpans, *still* flipping through pictures of Winnie. She seems to thoroughly enjoy cuddling with William. A fact I find positively a-fucking-dorable.

"Once or twice," I retort with a lazy shrug. "And devilishly handsome."

William puts his phone away, looking at me, deadpan, ignoring the last comment altogether. "Speaking of Winnie, I took her to the vet earlier this week."

"Did you now?"

"Yeah. Whit sure had a lot to say."

Uh-oh. "He can get pretty chatty about the animals," I tease. "Try not to hold it against him. We know he's a little weird. You should see how he gets with toy airplanes."

"Colt." My name comes out harsh and growly, and it sends a shiver down my spine. *Oh, fuck, how do I get him to say it like that again?*

"William," I reply softly, innocently, with a smirk.

Placing his hands sassily on his hips, his eyes narrow on me as he asks in a low tone, "Why does Whit know intimate details between you and me?"

Fucking Whit. Big-ass mouth.

"What did he say?"

"That doesn't matter, Colt," he bites out. "Why does he know?"

Fuck, he's hot when he gets mad.

"Wasn't aware it was a secret," I retort, excitement flooding my system at this exchange.

His face screws up. "Oh, don't be an idiot, Colt."

"Relax, Doc," I reply, breathing out a laugh and sitting up. "He got a vibe from us when we ran into you and your dad at the store, and asked me about it afterward. He wouldn't let it go, so that's the only reason I told him. But it's kinda hot when you're mean to me."

Biting down on my bottom lip, I wink at him, to which he completely ignores when he asks, "Does that mean all of your friends know now?"

I shake my head. "No, it's just Whit." *And Boone, but he doesn't need to know that right now.* "We can trust him."

William quirks a brow. "Really? Because he spilled pretty easily when I dropped Winnie off."

"Probably because he got embarrassed picturing you naked," I say, waving a hand dismissively. "I told him you had a really nice dick."

"Colt!"

I scoff. "What? It's true." His cheeks flush, and I have

to bite the inside of my cheek to keep from smiling. I never would've pegged William as the bashful type, but I can't say I hate it. "But honestly, you don't have to worry. Whit wouldn't ever spill somebody else's business."

William regards me quietly as he sits back. Thoughtfully. I can't read his face at all. He rubs a hand over his mouth, scratching at the dark hairs along his jaw. His beard is thick and full, but not too long. It suits him well. It brings out the brightness in his blue eyes and accentuates his full lips.

Continuing to break the equipment down, there's a simmering tension building between us. I know he has more to say, but he's not. Maybe he's working up to it. For once, I'm not going to push him. I'll let him come to it himself, mostly because I'm damn curious as to what's pondering in that brain of his.

Finally, inhaling and exhaling a deep breath, William looks at me and says, "That night we ran into each other in Seattle, I had gone out to let off a little steam. I'd just found out my mother was sick, and I had a lot on my mind."

Heart stuttering in my chest, I swallow thickly, but don't reply. I listen, taken aback by him being vulnerable with me.

"What happened between us," he goes on, "shouldn't have happened. My mind was all over the place, which is no excuse, but it's the truth, and had I taken a step back for even a second, I would've seen how wrong it was of me."

"Of you?" I blurt out, confused. "I'm the one who approached you."

"Yes, but I'm the older one."

"So?" My brows dip as I try to make sense of his train of thought. "I was still an adult, fully capable of making decisions, and I did *exactly* what I wanted to. You didn't force me to do anything."

"Colt," he breathes out, pinching the bridge of his nose. "I can think of several reasons why what we did shouldn't have happened, the biggest one being my relationship with your dad and how long I've known you. I've said it before, and I'll say it again. It's *wrong*."

"Is that why you switched me over to Dr. Braylon?" I ask, arching a brow. It's the question that's been on my mind all week.

William heaves a sigh, meeting my gaze. "No, I did that because it was the ethical thing to do. It is a conflict of interest being your doctor, given our intimate history, albeit short."

"Yeah, well, you could've told me ahead of time," I murmur. "And if you think it's never going to happen again, why would it matter?"

He raises his brows, eye contact never faltering. "I don't 'think' it's never going to happen again," he mutters. "I *know*. And it's still unethical, even if it only happened once. I can't be your doctor, Colt. End of discussion."

The way he thinks he can call the shots without a say from me grates my nerves like nothing else, and I find myself grinding down on my molars as I take him in.

A humorless laugh leaves my lips as I take a step in his direction and lower my voice. "Listen, Doc, I'm sure you're plenty used to being the boss in your world, both at work and in your professional life, but I'm going to let you in on a little secret." I pause, never taking my eyes off him. "Right here, between you and me, you're not the boss. You don't get to treat me like some petulant child who needs to be put in my place simply because your conscience can't handle the fact that I rocked your fucking world at one point. You don't get to dismiss me and tell me *end of discussion*, and expect me to just roll with it. I don't play like that."

William's lips press into a tight line, and there's a flash of heat in his eyes, be it from anger or arousal, I'm unsure. Maybe both. It may have been a guess that he's used to being the boss in his world, but I think it's a pretty solid one. The energy with which he carries himself tells me as much, never mind his tall, imposing frame and the deep baritone of his voice.

Taking a step toward me of his own and matching my stance, William grits out, "If you think throwing a little fucking temper tantrum is going to get your way with me, you're sorely mistaken, Colt."

I laugh, rubbing a hand over my mouth. "If you say so, Doc."

His jaw flexes as he bites down, but he doesn't reply. Instead, he resumes packing up, and I do the same. The tension between us is nearly suffocating, but I can't help but find humor in it. I have no way of knowing for sure, but something about the way William looks at me, and the way he acts when we're near each other, tells me I'm on his mind a lot more than he wants to let on and, if I had to guess, it's probably filthy thoughts from that night and how good I made him feel. He's probably dying for a repeat, but can't allow himself to admit that.

As sexy as he is, William has always been a very by-the-book type of man. He's a solid guy with strong morals. A rule follower. Hooking up with me, I'm sure, broke dozens of his rules. It was probably the one and only thing he's ever let himself do strictly for him, and that's fucking with his head. Fucking with what he believes to be right and wrong. I'm his best friend's son, and I'm also nearly half his age. According to society standards, what we did should be *wrong*.

I don't see it that way. Neither should he.

Blame it on my competitive nature or the fact that I really,

really hate being told I can't do something, but every single atom in my body is *dying* to watch William unravel. Watch him bend and twist his morals when he can't hold on any longer. Watch him give in to what he really wants. And as I finish eating my lunch, with him across from me, I decide I'm going to do anything in my power to make him break. To watch the stuffy, professional, do-good doctor give in to his darkest desires.

And I'm going to fucking relish when it eventually happens.

CHAPTER 15

WILLIAM ANDINO

I'm just finishing the breakfast dishes when my phone rings on the counter. Drying my hands with a tea towel, I reach for it, smiling when I see Trish's name flash on the screen. I hit accept, bringing the phone up to my ear.

"Hello?"

"Hey, Will." Her voice is as cheerful as always. "How's it going?"

"Oh, not too bad," I murmur as I close the door to the dishwasher and turn it on. "Just finishing up some cleaning around the house. How're you guys over here?"

"Good, good," she states. "Look, I whipped up some homemade cinnamon rolls this morning. I've got a ton left over, and I know how much you enjoy them. Can I drop some off with you?"

Despite having eaten not even an hour ago, my stomach rumbles at the thought of devouring a couple of Trish's famous cinnamon rolls. "Of course, you can," I say with a chuckle. "I know what I'm having for lunch now."

She laughs. "Wonderful. I'm packaging them up now, and I'll send Colt over in a bit."

"Colt?" As soon as his name leaves my lips, I realize how panicked it sounded, so I add, "I didn't realize he was able to drive again."

"Yeah, now that he doesn't have to wear the sling, he's cleared to drive. His physical therapist gave the okay at their last appointment. Isn't that nice?"

Shit. "Uh, yeah, that's awesome. Bet he's thrilled."

"He is," Trish confirms. "Between you and me, I think he's going a little stir crazy being here all the time."

"Yeah, I'd imagine," I murmur, rubbing the back of my neck.

"Anyway, I won't keep you. Colt should be by within the hour with those goodies. I hope you enjoy." The smile is evident in her voice, and it brings one to my own lips.

"Thank you, Trish. You spoil me."

Hanging up, I toss the phone onto the counter and pinch the bridge of my nose. The last thing I need is Colt in my house after our tense lunch yesterday after the clinic. I saw a side of him that I haven't seen before. Sure, the night we hooked up, he was confident and sure of himself, but yesterday was... different. He was cocky and focused and, if I'm being honest, it turned me on a little. Seeing his eyes darken and narrow as they took me in. The way his voice was deep and low as he told me I wasn't the boss. It reminded me of the way he took control that night we hooked up, but times ten. I'm not used to being treated like that, and I hate how much my body seems *very* into it.

I'm not some big, rough, dominant man by any means, but with all my sexual partners in the past, I have been the one more in control, and I've always preferred that. It worked with the dynamic I had between them. With Colt, though, he throws me off my axis. He makes me question my sanity, and I'm afraid the longer I'm around him, the more he's going to break down those walls. What happened before *cannot* happen again, yet I find myself imagining what it would be like if we did.

I'm startled out of the lewd fantasy playing in my mind when my phone buzzes on the counter. I notice a text from an unknown number. Swiping to unlock, I freeze when I read the message.

Unknown: Hey, Doc. My mom gave me your number so I could let you know I'm on my way. See you soon. ;)

Dammit. Not bothering with a response, I shove the phone into my pocket and leave the kitchen. Bounding up the stairs, I hang a right into the bathroom, locking myself inside as I stare at my own reflection. My hair is a mess, I haven't done anything to it since I woke up. Turning on the faucet, I run my hand underneath it before bringing it up to my hair, trying to tame the unruly cowlick. Once I've gotten my hair a little damp and mostly flat, I lather some product in my hands, running my fingers through and coating the strands.

Then I'm reaching for my toothbrush, questioning why I'm going through all this trouble. I shouldn't give a shit what I look like in front of Colt, but the delusional part of my brain tells me that I'd do this regardless of who was coming over. I don't want *anybody* seeing me unkempt.

Yeah, let's go with that.

I stroll down the hall to my bedroom, needing to change out of my plaid pajama pants. I find a pair of black athletic pants and slip them on. Reaching behind me and pulling my sleep shirt over my head, I switch it out for a clean Andino Family Medicine shirt instead. That'll have to be good enough, because he should be here any minute. The Bishops don't live that far from here, and he did say he was on his way when the text came through.

Back downstairs, I find myself pacing back and forth in the kitchen, my heart racing a mile a minute. What the hell is wrong with me, and how does he have this kind of pull over me? Needing something to do, I put on a pot of coffee. Because that's exactly what I need right now, more caffeine. As soon as I start the machine, a knock sounds at the door, and a shiver races down my spine.

I blow out a deep breath and pad across the floor, unlocking and opening the front door. Colt's standing on the other side, a rather large tray covered with aluminum foil in his hands. His black hat is turned backwards, and he's wearing his signature smirk as our gaze connects.

"Howdy."

"Hello, Colt." Stepping to the side, I gesture with my arm. "Come on in."

Walking past me, he pauses and murmurs over his shoulder, "You smell delicious, Doc."

I flex my jaw as I close the door. Ignoring the compliment entirely, I say, "Kitchen is to the left. You can set the tray down on the counter."

"Was that the door?" my dad asks as he appears in the hallway. He and Winnie have been out back most of the morning.

"Yeah, Dad." My blood pressure is rising by the second. "Colt's here, dropping off some of Trish's homemade cinnamon rolls."

Coming to a stop in front of the entrance to the kitchen, a wide smile spreads on his face. "Well, hello, Colt. How are you?"

"I'm doing well, Roger," Colt says, his tone friendly and bright, unlike when he speaks to me. "How're you doing this fine Sunday morning?"

"Oh, can't complain," my dad replies. "Enjoying the sun and the cool breeze on the porch out back with Winnie. Will made eggs benedict for breakfast."

Colt's gaze drags over to mine, that cocky smirk sliding into place again. "I love French toast," he drawls. "Looks like I'll be coming over for breakfast next weekend."

I frown. "Eh, I—"

I'm cut off mid-sentence by my father. "That's a wonderful idea! Will always makes entirely too much anyway, and we'd love the company. How about next Saturday?"

"Dad, I don't think—"

"I'd love to, Roger." Humor dances in Colt's eyes as I'm cut off yet *again*. "With my injury, I have a lot of downtime, and it can get pretty boring."

"Oh, I know what that's like," my dad murmurs. "Not being injured, of course, but having a lot of downtime. Now that I'm retired, all I've got is time on my hands."

Winnie prances into the kitchen, probably wanting to see what all the fuss is about, and Colt's eyes light up as he glances down and takes her in. "Oh my gosh. You must be sweet Winnie girl," he gushes in a baby voice. "Aren't you just the cutest little girl I have ever seen. Look at you."

Picking her up, he pets her while she licks everywhere she can, soaking up the attention.

Colt glances up from Winnie to look at my dad. "How's she adjusting to being here?"

"Very well," he replies with a nod and a smile. "She's quite spoiled between the two of us, and I think she's adjusting just fine."

"Are you spoiled?" Colt coos, patting Winnie on the butt, something she loves. "Are you a pretty, spoiled girl?"

"Well, let's go out onto the back porch," my dad says, turning to glance at me. "Will, can you heat up some of those cinnamon rolls and bring them outside with some coffee?"

My lips press into a thin line as I glance over at Colt, finding him already looking at me, a faint smirk fixed on his face. "I like cream in my coffee, Doc," he murmurs, and something about his completely innocent statement sends a lick of flames down my spine.

My dad and Colt don't bother waiting for confirmation that I'll act as their server before they stroll through the house side by side. Colt's still holding Winnie like a baby as they go. *For fuck's sake.*

By the time I meet them outside, they're in the middle of a conversation about the game that was on last night. We all dish up our plates with the now-warm cinnamon rolls, and I have to bite back a groan when I take a bite. It's so damn good. I need to get this recipe from Trish.

For the most part, I sit back and eat, watching the two of them converse. I don't know why it's so surprising to me to see how well they get along. My dad practically has stars in his eyes as he listens to Colt talk rodeo.

"Are you going to compete next season?" he asks.

Colt nods, finishing chewing. "I'm definitely going to try, but I won't push myself to get back out there before I'm ready.

"Smart man," my dad murmurs. "What do you got going on to fill your time currently?"

"Honestly, not a whole lot." Colt huffs out a chuckle. "But now that I can use my arm a little bit more, I'm trying to keep myself busy. I'm volunteering at the free clinic every other Saturday, and then with school starting back up soon at the high school, I'm going to mentor a rodeo club kid like I did last year."

"Oh, what's that entail?"

"It's a lot of teaching them things that I've learned, taking them under my wing, building their confidence in the arena. Stuff like that," Colt explains. "I had a mentor when I was in high school, and I credit a lot of my skill from him. He was an amazing role model, and he made me believe achieving my dreams was possible."

"Surely, you had the support from your dad too," I murmur. "To help with confidence and see that it was possible."

Colt flits his gaze over to me. "Yes and no," he replies. "I'm sure you can understand what it's like following in a parent's footsteps. I never wanted people to think I got to where I am today because I rode my father's coattails. Yes, Max Bishop was a phenomenal bull rider, and yes, he broke records, but I am more than a prodigal son. From the very beginning, I fought tooth and nail to earn my place in the rodeo world, and it was refreshing and motivating to hear somebody in it tell me I had potential when I was in high school."

Listening to Colt talk so passionately about this world of his has a newfound respect for him blooming inside of me, because the truth is, I *do* know what it's like following in the footsteps of a successful parent. The medical field may be exponentially different from the rodeo scene, but the fear and the doubt are the same. That voice is always there in the very back of your mind telling you that the only reason you got to where you are is because of who your parents are and not any actual talent or skill. Each success, it's there to tell you that everyone knows you made it because of who you are, and every failure, it's there to remind you that the world is watching, and this loss is only proving to them what they already know.

So, on some deeper level, unbeknownst to me, I relate to Colt. I respect him for his passion, and I can't help but think maybe we aren't that different, after all.

My dad asks Colt a few more random questions about the rodeo and his experience before announcing that he's tired and going to lie down for an afternoon nap. Winnie goes with him, the same way she does every single day. Afternoon naps are a regular thing with them, like clockwork. Once my dad disappears into the house, a charged silence settles over Colt and I. Suddenly, my pulse is racing and a tingly type of chill rolls through my veins.

One leg crossed over the other, Colt's hand is wrapped around his ankle, index finger tapping away at the leather of his boot. It's a rhythmic sound that almost feels in sync with the beat of my erratic heart. We hold eye contact for a moment, neither of us saying a word. It should feel awkward... but it doesn't. It's comfortable.

Rubbing a hand over my mouth, I fully take Colt in. From the dark brown hair peeking out from underneath his backwards hat, to the vibrancy of his emerald eyes, and the short, dark scruff that lines his chiseled jaw. His white Marlboro shirt is form fitting, as are the Wranglers that are tucked into his well-worn brown boots. It would look ridiculous on anybody else, but for Colt, it somehow works. He's all country, unapologetically so. He's got a pretty face and a witty personality that seem to make up for the fact that he rarely appears to put any effort into his clothes. He regularly looks like he just got finished mucking out horse stalls, and right now is no exception.

"What are you thinking about over there, Doc?" Colt asks with a devilish smirk, and it's only then I realize he probably thinks I was checking him out.

Obviously, I wasn't.

"What you said earlier," I start, clearing my throat. "About following in your father's footsteps. I can relate."

His gaze softens. "Figured you might."

"It's a big part of why I decided to take the job on the West Coast," I admit, surprising myself. "To be somewhere where nobody knew Roger Andino; they only knew me and what I brought to the table. I wasn't a successful doctor because of who my dad was, but because of my skill and my dedication to medicine."

"Does he know that?" Colt asks, tipping his chin toward the house.

Blowing out a breath, I say, "Maybe. I've never outright told him, but I'm sure he gets it. His father was a physician too."

"Are you glad you did it?" Colt questions. "Moved away."

I've never really thought about it. "Yeah, I think so," I finally murmur. "It was good for me, and it showed me a lot."

"You happy to be home again?"

The question hits me right in the chest. "You know what? I am."

I meet Colt's gaze, and I can't decipher the expression on his face. It makes my pulse kick up all over again. And then he mutters two words that effectively knock me off my axis.

"Me too."

There's no cockiness in his words. No flirtation, just warmth.

Swallowing thickly, I hold his stare. This moment is electric, and it's dangerous territory. It would seem everything with Colt is dangerous territory. A road less traveled that I can't help but want to veer toward despite the logic trying to steer me toward the correct one.

Colt sits up, patting his hands on top of his thighs. "Well, I better get back," he announces before rising off the chair, and

I do the same.

I do the same, even though I feel disappointed for some reason, wanting him to stay. "Thanks for stopping by, and tell your mom thank you for the treats."

Smirking, Colt takes a step in my direction, and I freeze. The door to inside the house is right behind me, so it makes sense that he's coming this way, but something about the wild look in his eyes has me halting. It has me frozen in place. This close to him, I catch his scent and wish I couldn't. Smelling like leather and sandalwood and something else entirely... something sweet, my mouth waters. Eyes dipping down to my mouth, Colt swipes his tongue across his lips, and I have to actively bite back the groan burying itself in my throat.

"I'll be sure to tell her you said that, *Doc.*" The sultry lilt to his tone when he hits me with that nickname sends a shiver down my spine. "You have a nice day."

With that, he brushes past me, and I don't bother following. I don't walk him to the door; I can't. My breath comes out in harsh pants as I try to slow my heart rate. How does Colt have the ability to rile me up so much by doing so little?

CHAPTER 16
COLT BISHOP

Every year, without fail, my dad celebrates his birthday by going over to Conrad's ranch for a barbecue slash bonfire. It's a yearly thing that's gone on for as long as I can remember, but the last few years I've missed it due to the rodeo schedule. Well, this year is a little different. This year, I get to help my dad celebrate another year older, and I'm pumped about it. Most of my friends are gone, but Whit should be there tonight, and I'm kind of wanting to drink. It's been a minute since I've let loose and allowed myself to have some fun. After the accident, I couldn't drink all that much because of the meds I was on, but now that I'm mostly off them, I see no reason why I can't go a little crazy.

To avoid being stuck at Conrad's or having to drink and drive home, I decided to carpool with my folks. My dad will throw back a few cold ones, but my mom has never been much of a drinker, aside from the occasional glass of wine with dinner or a mimosa at brunch with her friends. There's also a big likelihood that William will be there tonight, given how close he is with my dad, and I'm giddy thinking about getting to see him. It's been almost a week since I brought cinnamon rolls over to his house, and we haven't seen each other since. I have his phone number now, thanks to my unsuspecting mother, and I considered texting him a couple of times, but in the end, decided it would be silly to do that.

Whether he wants to admit it or not, there's something between us. I don't know what exactly, but it's something. A connection, chemistry, fire. It's there even if he's blissfully ignorant. I'm not blind; I see the way he looks at me. The memories are in the forefront of his mind the same way they are mine. I know it.

Taking a left, my dad pulls onto the long, winding gravel road that leads to Conrad's place. Over sixty thousand acres, his ranch is one of the largest in the state. As a matter of fact, I think it may be the largest in all of the Rocky Mountains too. It's been in his family for generations. As a teenager, I remember working most of my summers here. At the time, it belonged to Conrad's parents who have since passed away, but I have memories of many long, hot, summer days doing whatever it was that Mr. Strauss needed around here. No two days were ever the same, but he made sure to work us all hard and tired by the end of the day. Mrs. Strauss frequently made dinner for everybody working, and we'd all gather round the long picnic tables in the backyard and eat like a family.

Those summers taught me so much, about myself and about the value of hard work. I wouldn't be who I am today if it weren't for this ranch, and I know almost every single one of my friends would agree. This ranch holds so many memories; good, bad, funny, embarrassing, you name it.

Dad parks the truck beside another rig in front of the barn.

Based on the people mulling around, it's safe to say that we aren't the first to arrive. Birthday streamers hang along the expanse of the barn doors, and I just know that's my mother's doing. She left earlier this morning to get a manicure, and I'm willing to bet she made a pit stop here.

Climbing out of the truck, I spot Whit and his boyfriend, Reggie, immediately. They're over by the coolers. Noticing me, Whit offers an awkward-looking smile and nods his chin by way of greeting as I approach them.

"What's up, guys?" I murmur as I grab an ice-cold beer out of the cooler. "How long have you been here?"

"Not long," Whit offers. "Maybe twenty minutes."

"You guys eaten yet? I'm starving."

"Nah, not yet."

"Well then, let's go," I say as I start in the direction of where the food's at. There're a couple of long tables covered in birthday table cloths that have enough food to feed an army. Chips, dips, fruit, cheese, meats, buns and, of course, the grilled hamburgers and hot dogs. There's something for everyone, and I waste no time piling way too much onto a paper plate.

Once all three of us have some food, we amble across the yard and sit on the porch. It's the best spot because it allows us to people watch, just the way I like it. Looking around, I spot William over by where Conrad's grilling. My stomach dips, and I can't help but smirk at seeing him over there. Dressed casually in a pair of sage green Chino shorts and a white short-sleeve button-up shirt, William looks good enough to eat. His hair is styled back, and his ocean eyes are hidden behind a pair of black shades.

My goal for the night is to get him alone somehow. To mess with him and rile him up. It's so fun to do, and I know

Colt after a few beers will greatly agree.

"You're staring," Whit murmurs, low enough that I don't think Reggie heard him. I turn my head, meeting his gaze as a grin splits my face. Being this close to him, I can see the dark circles under his eyes that aren't easy to spot, considering he wears glasses all the time.

"Mind your business," I tease.

"Behave," he throws back, arching a brow.

Chuckling, I shrug. "We'll see."

I dig into my food, starting with the burger I loaded up high. It tastes as good as it smells, and I already know I'll be having at least one more before the night ends.

Movement catches ahead, and when I glance up, I spot my dad over with William and Conrad now. They're laughing about something, and my dad throws an arm around William's shoulders, and for the first time, a pang of guilt sucker punches me right in the gut. I watch them interact for a moment, their closeness, and it's like I finally understand William's hesitancy. What would my father say if he knew I slept with one of his best friends? What does that say about me?

"You okay?"

My head snaps toward Whit, and I nod. "Yeah, I'm good."

Once we finish eating, the three of us grab another drink before we make ourselves comfortable in front of the firepit. It's not lit yet, but it will be as soon as the sun starts to set.

"Do you remember all the bonfires we had here during the summers when I was in high school?" I ask Whit.

He nods. "How could I forget?"

Whit's older than me by nearly ten years. By the time I was in high school, he was already married to Conrad, but even then, they both lived here. They stayed in the loft above the barn until Conrad's folks died, then they moved into the house.

"God, there were some good fucking times we had here."

"Do you remember that time Shooter bought that moonshine off old man River?" Whit laughs.

"Fuck, I forgot about that." I huff out a laugh at the memory. "What was that man's real name? I know it wasn't River."

Whit thinks for a moment. "Albert, if I'm not mistaken."

I don't know why that makes me laugh as hard as it does. "Why the fuck did we call him old man River, then?"

"Beats me," Whit huffs. "The song, maybe?"

"He had no business selling moonshine to teenagers, though." I chuckle.

"You guys got so drunk in the middle of the day when you should've been working, and Conrad had to cover for you guys."

"I never understood why he covered for us in the first place," I say. "That shit was *strong*."

"Cope nearly drowned in the creek, and you puked all over the side of the barn when you guys got back."

I shake my head, laughing. "The one and only time I ever drank moonshine. And, of fucking course, Shooter found the entire thing hilarious. It was his life's mission to get me as drunk as possible whenever he could."

"And Conrad covered for you jackasses because he knew his dad was fed up with you guys and would fire you if he found out," Whit admits. "And then all that extra work would fall on mine and Conrad's shoulders."

"Mr. Strauss would not have fired us," I argue. "He loved me."

Whit snorts. "Yeah, that's what you think."

"Ahh, the good old days." I can't help but smile as I remember everything that went on here. "You know, my first kiss happened here."

Whit eyes me from beneath his dark-framed glasses. "With whom?"

"Jill Donovan." I laugh as I watch Whit's expression shift from confused to surprised.

"Conrad's cousin from Michigan?" he asks incredulously.

"Yup." I finish off the rest of my beer. "She was fun."

"Why am I not surprised to find this out?" Whit groans as I stand up and stretch my arms over my head.

"Because I'm too sexy for anybody to ignore." Waggling my brows, I stand up and ask him and Reggie, "Want another?"

"Yeah, I will," Whit says.

"Not me," Reggie murmurs, holding his hands up. "I've got to leave for work in a couple hours."

"Suit yourself."

Over at the coolers, I spot William getting himself a beverage. The guilt because of my dad is still there, but I can't help but smirk to myself as I step up beside him. His relation to my father aside, he's still fun as hell to mess with. "Fancy running into you here," I drawl, turning my head to the side and meeting his gaze.

"Hello, Colt." So formal.

Grabbing two cans out, one for me and one for Whit, I ask, "Having fun, Doc?"

"I am." He nods. "And you?"

"You know it." A grin spreads across my face, and I don't miss the way his eyes dip down for a moment. "Although, I'd have more fun if you stopped talking to me like I'm a patient at your clinic."

William's brows furrow, the sight quite adorable. "I'm not talking to you any differently than I talk to anybody else."

Scanning the area and making sure nobody is watching,

I lean in, like I just can't help myself, and whisper in his ear, "That's the problem." He stands up straighter as I pull back and meet his gaze. Offering a mock solute, I leave him there, and stroll back over to where I left Whit and Reggie.

We all decide to play corn hole with a couple of Whit's friends from his office after we've tossed back a few more beers. I'm feeling pretty good by the time we all gather around and sing Happy Birthday to my dad. The cake is huge, and I gladly take a piece, enjoying every last bite. Every so often, I'll feel William's gaze on me; sometimes I'll meet and hold it as if I'm challenging him to look away first, but other times, I pretend I don't notice. Part of me likes to think it drives him nuts.

A little while later, I spot him heading toward the house. Probably going inside to use the restroom because a man like William is too good to piss outside like the rest of us. Huffing out a laugh, I nudge Whit. "Hey, I'll be right back."

I don't wait for a response, but I hear him call out after me, "Behave, Colt."

Throwing him a glance over my shoulder, I flash him a toothy grin. As I approach the house, I jog up the few steps that lead up to the porch and stroll through the backdoor. The house is quiet and mostly dark, nobody but William in here, I'm sure. I know this house like the back of my hand, and as I turn down the hallway that leads to the main floor bathroom, I scan all the photos on the wall, making myself look busy while I wait for him to exit.

It doesn't take but a minute before I hear the toilet flush and the sink turn on, and another moment later, the door opens. Keeping my eyes trained on the wall in front of me, the decade's worth of picture frames decorating it, I bite back the grin wanting to break free as I see William freeze in my periphery. Standing in place for a few moments, presumably figuring out what he's going to do next, he eventually comes to stand beside me.

"What are you doing in here, Colt?" he asks, voice deep and hushed.

"Same as you," I offer, the smirk evident in my words.

"I don't believe that."

That has me turning my head to look toward him, but he isn't looking at me. Like I was, his gaze is trained on the wall before us like it's the most interesting thing he's ever seen. Like the wall will be his saving grace. Like it'll somehow keep him from giving into what he wants. Too bad for him.

"Yeah? And why is that?"

"Because everything with you is calculated," he growls, shifting his body until he's facing me. Hands stuffed into the pockets of his shorts, lips pressed into a thin line, he watches me with an expression I can't place.

"That's not very fair," I huff, poking my lip out into a pout as I turn and match his stance. Dragging my gaze down his body shamelessly, I add, "By the way, you're looking mighty fine tonight, Doc."

William's jaw flexes. "Whatever you're thinking is going to happen here tonight won't be happening, Colt."

Holding my hands up in innocence, I huff out a chuckle. "I'm just in here to take a leak, just like you. I don't know what you're talking about."

He nods tersely. "Right, well, then you better get to it."

We remain looking at each other for another tense, quiet moment. It feels like a standoff of sorts. Finally, he takes a step to walk around me, but I stop him with an arm across his middle. Head darting to the side, ocean eyes locked on mine,

William swallows but says nothing.

My eyes flit down to his lips, and as if subconsciously, his tongue pokes out to wet them. A bolt of heat flares inside of me at the sight. "Curious, what did you think I wanted to happen?" I sidestep to the right, putting me now directly in front of him. His breath hitches, and a splash of color appears on the apples of his cheeks.

Taking a step toward him, he takes one back. I do it again, and he follows. Then one more time for good measure, putting us directly in front of the open door that he came out of not even five minutes ago. The air around us is thick and charged, and with my pulse racing and my heart in my throat, I reach out and take William's hand, leading him into the bathroom. There's zero resistance from him, which makes me smile as I close the door behind us, flicking the lock into place.

My back against the door, I peer over at William. He's about an arm's length away from me, and it's too damn far. "C'mere," I murmur as my blood heats, taking in the way his chest heaves and his eyes have darkened substantially.

"We shouldn't be in here," he husks, nostrils flaring.

"Yeah, but it's fun to do things we shouldn't," I tease. "Surely, you remember how much fun we had the first time."

He swallows audibly. "Colt." My name is spoken on a rumbly growl that sends goosebumps all over my flesh. Being in here with him makes me feel more intoxicated than from the beer I've drunk tonight. Maybe that's why it's so easy for me to forget why I really shouldn't be instigating this.

Arching a brow, the corners of my lips curve into a grin. "William."

Brazenly, I reach out and hook my finger through one of his belt loops, tugging until he steps closer to me. Close enough that I can smell the beer on his breath and see the way his pupils dilate at our proximity.

"We shouldn't," he whispers, a pained look crossing his face.

"Tell me you don't want to," I rasp. "Tell me you don't want me to kiss you right now, and I'll walk out of here."

He's silent.

"Tell me, William, or I'm going to do it."

His furrow deepens, and he parts his lips. For a moment, I think he may really tell me no, but instead, he breathes two words that light me up inside. "I can't."

My lips twitch, lust and need coursing through me. Wrapping a hand around the back of his neck, I murmur, "Yeah, that's what I fucking thought," before crashing my mouth against his.

There's no freezing, no panic, from William. No moment to catch up to what is happening. As soon as our lips fuse together, his hands find my hips, and they grip me *hard*. The kiss doesn't start out slow or gentle; it's high speed from the gate. His tongue slips past my lips, caressing mine, and fuck me, does he taste good. Better than I remember. Fireworks go off inside my mind, and an inferno floods my veins with the roll of his tongue.

William's lips mold to mine in a way that makes me think they're meant to be there. They're so damn soft and full, and he certainly knows how to use them. Kissing him isn't awkward or clumsy; it's heated and messy, just the way I like it. I'm dying for him to press his body to mine, but he doesn't. My cock is hard and throbbing, and I'd give just about anything for him to brush up against it, even if only for a second. I need him, but all too soon, he pulls away. Eyes wild, hair tousled, and cheeks flushed, he brushes his two fingers across his swollen lips, as if feeling them to make sure it wasn't all a fantasy.

"Fuck," he growls under his breath. "Colt, we *can't*."

I drag my gaze down his body, pleased to find the obvious bulge in his pants. "Yeah, but you can't deny you want to," I throw back.

He doesn't bother trying to lie. "Let me out of here," he requests, tone firm and clear. The moment we shared is *done*.

Unlocking the door, I turn around and walk out, leaving him to follow me. Irritation tightens my chest, yet I don't know why. I got what I wanted, so why does his dismissal grate my nerves so damn much?

I blow through the back door, jogging down the steps on the porch, just as I hear William behind me. Not bothering to look over my shoulder at him, I stroll across the yard, wanting to get back to Whit. Maybe drink some more and shake off this irritation.

"There you are!" A familiar voice has my head turning as I watch with my heart in my throat as my dad steps up to me. "And Will, I was looking for you too."

"Was just taking a leak," I tell him with a chuckle. "Ran into William. Great minds think alike."

Hooking an arm over my shoulder, my father does the same thing to William. "I want to have a shot with my son and my best friend for my birthday," he drawls. "Come on."

My pulse is through the roof, the realization hitting me square in the chest at how close we were to getting caught. The guilt from earlier, that I so easily shoved to the far recesses of my mind in favor of getting my hands on William, comes back in full force, and I can't even find it in me to look at William to see if he's feeling the same.

Fuck, that was careless of me. And selfish. *Could I be any more of a shitty son?*

CHAPTER 17

WILLIAM ANDINO

Today was one of those days that I wanted to be over before it even began. Truthfully, that's how my entire week has gone. Sleep isn't coming easily to me, work is chaotic and busy—one of my nurses is out with the flu—and I'm more ready for the weekend than I have been in a long time. Tomorrow is Friday, and it couldn't come soon enough. The only upside to today is the fact that I got out of the office by four-thirty, and I'll be able to sit down and eat dinner at a reasonable hour. After dinner, I plan to take a piping hot shower and relax in front of the television with a pint of mint and cookies ice cream. It's practically calling my name from the freezer.

Pulling onto my street, I spot a familiar truck parked in my driveway, right beside where I'm supposed to park, and stomach bottoms out. *Why the hell is Colt at my house?* It's been several days since my run-in with him at Max's birthday party, but I knew that my avoidance would only last so long, especially with the free clinic this Saturday—something I'd rather not do, but that's not an option. I made commitments, and I can't get out of them simply because I'm more exhausted than usual and wanting to avoid a certain somebody.

I put my car in park and climb out, huffing a sigh. Maybe Colt stopped by quickly with some more dessert from Trish, and he's about to be on his way. Although, I would think Trish would've called ahead to let me know, like she did last time. The front door is already open, so once I open the screen door, I step inside, listening for any chatter. Frowning when I don't hear anything, I toe off my shoes, placing them on the shoe rack in the entrance before setting my briefcase on the kitchen counter, and I head off in search of where everybody is.

Since I don't hear anybody, I don't think they're in the living room, so my guess is they're both out back on the patio. A guess that is proven right as soon as I enter the living room, and I spot the sliding glass door open. Quiet chatter reaches my ears the closer I get, and I can't deny the flutters in my stomach. Something about Colt being in my house, especially after that kiss, has me uneasy. Stepping outside, the sight before me isn't one I was expecting.

Sitting across from each other at the table out here, a chessboard between them, Colt and my father appear to be in an intense game of chess. So intense that neither of them even notices me for a moment, not until Winnie perks her head up from where she's lounging on Colt's lap.

Colt glances up first, gaze meeting mine as a smirk curls on his lips. His signature hat is facing forward this time, and he tips the bill by way of greeting. Only then does my dad spot me, glancing up from the chessboard, a furrow in his brow.

"Oh, hello, son. I didn't hear you come in."

Well, you're outside. "Just got home," I grunt, still watching them with bemusement. "What is going on?"

Gesturing at the table, my dad states the fucking obvious. "Colt and I are playing chess."

"I see that." Eyes meeting Colt's, I ask, "What are you doing here?"

I hate how I notice what he's wearing, and how it affects me. Dressed in full cowboy getup, he's got on a pair of dark wash Wranglers, a plain white V-neck t-shirt underneath a powder blue and white flannel with the sleeves rolled up to his elbows, showing off his tan, corded forearms, and the same dark brown boots I always see him wear. He looks ridiculously sexy, and it infuriates me.

Flashing me a cocky little grin, I already know whatever is about to come out of his mouth is going to irritate me. "Your dad and I ran into each other at the grocery store," he says. "He invited me over for a game of chess and for dinner." *Dinner?!* "He said you were making my favorite, and who am I to deny myself a little chess and my favorite food?"

"Is that right?" I deadpan, dragging my gaze over to my father, who grins at me in a way that makes my blood pressure raise. "And what exactly am I making for dinner, *Dad?*"

"I pulled out some ground beef," he explains, bringing his attention back to the board as he calculates his next move. "Figured you could whip us up some of your million-dollar spaghetti."

Confused, I glance at Colt. "Your favorite food is spaghetti?"

Shrugging, he says, "What can I say? I'm a simple man."

Oh, for fuck's sake.

"And son," my dad murmurs, flicking his gaze up to me. "If you could start it soon, that would be lovely. I'm rather famished."

"Me too, Doc," Colt adds in, amusement dancing in his eyes.

I bite down on my molars so hard, I'm surprised they don't

crack. "Coming right up, Your Majesties," I grunt, turning on my heel and heading back into the house.

What the hell is my father up to?

In the kitchen, I turn on some music before washing my hands. In terms of difficulty and time, this is an easy dish to make. After I cook the noodles and prepare the meat sauce, I layer it all in a casserole dish with a ricotta, mozzarella, parmesan, and egg mixture before tossing it in the pre-heated oven. Then I grab the loaf of French bread off the counter behind me, slice it open, and lather it in a garlic butter spread. Once that's done, I wrap it in aluminum foil, and stick it in the oven next to the spaghetti.

Rinsing the dishes, I put them each in the dishwasher as I wait for the food to be done. About halfway through, Colt strolls inside, his eyes somehow immediately finding mine. Holding my gaze as he walks toward the kitchen, my chest tightens, and something like a thrill shoots through my body the closer he gets. He looks like a hunter stalking his prey, with the heated look in his eyes.

"Food will be done in about ten minutes," I say, continuing to rinse the dishes.

As he waltzes into the kitchen, he doesn't respond right away. Coming up behind me, I feel his firm chest as he steps up behind me, and I drag in his rich, masculine scent through my nostrils, flexing my jaw as I try not to outwardly react to his closeness. He's practically flush with my back, and it's maddening.

Instinctively, my gaze darts to the back door, and even though he can't see my line of sight from where he's standing behind me, he must know what I'm thinking because he brings his lips beside my ear as he whispers, "Don't worry, Doc, he ain't coming in here any time soon."

His breath is hot as it brushes across my skin, goosebumps raising and covering the flesh. "How do you know?"

"Because he asked me if I'd get him a fresh glass of lemonade while I was in here," he explains, voice deep and husky. "He's busy with Winnie, which means I've got you all to myself."

That knowledge shouldn't send a thrill down my spine. It shouldn't excite me. But it does, and he knows it.

"You know," he husks, maintaining his too close proximity, "I'm still a little hurt by how quickly you wanted to run off last weekend after we shared that kiss."

Even the mention of that steamy bathroom make-out has sweat pricking the back of my neck and my heart racing a little faster. My breath gets caught in my throat as I feel his hand grab hold of my hip. It's possessive, and I hate how much I like it. How much I want to relax into his touch. I hate how long it's been since I've been able to relax into *anybody's* touch. I crave it, and I think that's why I'm always weak around Colt. I'm touch starved, and I'm unable to deny him.

Yeah, that's it.

"Have you thought about it?" Colt asks, his mouth much closer to my neck than it should be. "The kiss."

Clearing my throat, needing this to come out clearly, I say, "Can't say that I have."

His dark chuckle tells me he doesn't buy my lie. "Right," he murmurs. "Let's play it that way, Doc."

In an instant, the pressure of his body behind mine is gone, replaced with an icy chill. I tell myself I don't miss the contact, but that, too, would be a lie. The sound of the fridge opening reaches my ears, and I force myself to finish rinsing the dishes. After he refills the glass and puts the pitcher back in the fridge, Colt strolls out of the kitchen without another word, not giving me another glance until he's about to exit through the back sliding door. A smirk tugs at his lips as he winks at me, and as soon as he's out of sight, I let out the breath I'd been holding.

Colt Bishop is nothing but trouble, and the hard ridge in my pants would suggest that his cocky, flirty nature turns me on more than anything. *What the fuck is wrong with me?*

Shortly after I finish the dishes, the spaghetti and bread are done. I toss together a quick salad, placing it on the dining room table, along with the butter. Letting both of them know dinner is ready, we all dish up, each taking a seat around the table. Colt sits directly across from me, and while he, thankfully, doesn't play footsie with me tonight, I do feel the weight of his stare on me as I try to eat. After what happened in the kitchen, I'm entirely too riled up to enjoy my food, so I mostly shove it around my plate like a picky child.

After we finish eating, I'm the first out of my seat. As I'm about to start cleaning up, my dad stops me. "How about you boys take Winnie for her evening walk while I clean the kitchen?"

Colt stays silent as my heart stutters. "You don't have to do that, Dad. I don't mind doing the dishes."

"Nonsense," he grunts. "It's a nice evening, you two enjoy the walk. Besides, my hip is rather sore today, so this is the easier task for me anyway."

Huffing, I pinch the bridge of my nose. "Okay, I'll take Winnie, but I'm sure Colt has better things to do than take your dog for an evening stroll."

"Nonsense," Colt parrots my father, spiking my blood pressure again. *These fucking two, I swear to God.* "Your dad is right, Doc. It's a nice day. Let's do it together."

Let's. Do. It. Together.

If I didn't know any better, I'd think these two were joining forces to see who could drive me crazier faster. "Fine, let's go, then," I grit out.

Grabbing Winnie's harness and leash, I put them both on her before slipping my shoes on by the front door. We step out onto the porch, and my father is right; it's a beautiful evening. Sunsets in Seattle are great, don't get me wrong, but there's something about a Copper Lake sunset that really takes my breath away. I can't explain it.

"Surely, you have better ways to spend your time than with two old guys," I mutter to Colt after about a minute of walking.

Snorting, he replies, "I'd hardly call you old, Doc."

"You're nearly half my age."

"How could I forget? You love reminding me." In my periphery, I spot him turning his head and glancing at me. I don't look. "But I don't give a shit about that," he chirps. "There is nothing *old* about you in my eyes. Distinguished, mature? Sure. But not old."

That oddly makes my chest swell, and I have to bite the inside of my cheek to keep from smiling. "Regardless," I murmur, clearing my throat. "You don't have to humor my father. He won't be offended if you tell him no."

"I don't want to."

Finally, I allow myself to peer over at him. He's already watching me with curious eyes and a boyish grin. I don't know what to say back to that, so I just... don't.

Walking for about a mile, we come up to an open field. It's one Winnie very much enjoys running laps around every night. There's a bench off to the side, and after I unhook her leash, I take a seat on one side, while Colt occupies the other.

"How's your shoulder?" I ask him as we both watch Winnie run out her newfound zoomies.

"It's better." Elbows propped on his knees, his hands are clasped in front of him. "Hoping to be able to start training soon."

"Did your physical therapist indicate as much?"

Colt huffs out a breath. "No. I'm aware it's naïve, but I'm still holding out hope that I'll be the exception, you know?" He glances over at me, and the intensity in his gaze is enough to punch the air out of my lungs. "The sooner I can get back to training, the better chance I'll have at competing next season."

"You can't rush it, Colt."

"I know that," he scoffs, looking back into the field. "It's hard, really fucking hard, to not be able to do the one thing you enjoy the most. This isn't just my career, Doc. It's my passion. It's what I'm made to do, and as ridiculous as it is, I can't help but be furious that I can't do it."

"It's not ridiculous." I'm hit with the urge to reach out and rub a hand over Colt's back. Comfort him. But I don't do that. "I can understand the way you're feeling," I say softly. "But you couldn't have prevented this. It's a risk I know you're aware of every single time you climb on the back of one of them beasts. It could've happened to anybody."

His fierce gaze flits to mine. "Yeah, but it didn't happen to anybody. It happened to *me*, and I'm allowed to be pissed about it."

"Of course, you are. Nobody is saying otherwise."

Sitting back, he blows out a frustrated breath, kicking his legs wide. The new position has our thighs brushing ever-so slightly. I should move my leg, but I don't.

I don't want to.

"I... struggle with things that are outside of my control."

Chuckling, I mutter, "You don't say?"

Colt jabs me with his elbow, a smirk gracing his lips, and

something inside of me settles seeing him smile again.

"You saw how much my dad's injury fucked with him," he says. "I don't want to end up like he did."

"You won't," I reply before I can stop myself. "Nobody can predict the future, but your injury is vastly different from what your dad went through. It makes sense that you're comparing the two, but from an outsider perspective, they are not the same."

He nods, glancing at me. "Yeah, logically, I know you're right. Just wish it was easier to convince the irrational side of my brain."

"You'll get there, give yourself some grace. The accident really wasn't all that long ago."

Winnie runs around for another fifteen minutes while the conversation between Colt and I keeps going. It's easy and comfortable, there's no flirting or inappropriate comments. The simmering tension that seems to always be present with us is there, but still, it's not a big deal. Colt heads home as soon as we get back to my place, and by the time I'm back inside, my dad already appears to be in his room for the night. Bounding up the steps, I wash my face and brush my teeth, slipping into a pair of pajamas, before retiring to my room too. I'd like to say I don't spend the rest of the night replaying my evening, but I do. And not only that, but the kiss is on a loop in my mind as well.

As I fall asleep, I can't help but wonder if it's possible to make it through all of this unscathed.

CHAPTER 18

COLT BISHOP

It's Friday night, and the free clinic is in the morning, which means I probably shouldn't be out at the bar, but I am. My friends are finally home from the circuit, and we're celebrating everyone being back home again. It's something we do every year.

My buddy, Cope, just got us all a round of beer, and we're crowded around the pool tables, about to play a couple of games. There's not a whole lot to do in this town as far as nightlife goes. This bar is pretty much the only place we go when we want to get out, aside from Conrad's ranch. When we were all teenagers, we'd head down to the lake late at night when we were supposed to be spending the night at each other's houses. Bonfires and getting wasted down there are some of my core adolescent memories.

"So, how've you been, man?" Shooter asks. "You've been one tough fucker to get ahold of lately."

Arching a brow, he hits me with a look that has me filling with guilt immediately. How do I tell him it was easier to dodge their calls and texts than pretend everything was peachy?

"Oh, you know, hanging in there." I shrug, trying to be cool about it. "My shoulder's doing a lot better now than it was."

"I'm glad to hear that." His sincerity never fails to take me back. Shooter and I have been friends for years now, but like me, he tends to lean more toward the cocky, fun side of his personality rather than tapping into his emotions. I know he cares about me, but it's an odd feeling hearing him express that. "Although, you don't have to deal with all of this shit alone, you know. We're all here for you."

"Thanks, bud. I know that and appreciate it." Taking a long pull from my beer, I ask, "How'd the season go? Sterling kick your ass again?"

If I was a better friend instead of wallowing in my self-pity, I would know how his season was going. It shouldn't be a question I have to ask him. Thankfully, he doesn't seem to notice or mind. I can't help the chuckle that comes out of me as Shooter scoffs loudly. He and his boyfriend, Sterling, are bareback bronc riders. They started out as rivals who couldn't stand each other, but that quickly changed. For how overly competitive Shooter is, they seem to have a playfulness to them when it comes to competing against one another now. They both very much want to win, but in the same breath, it's clear to anybody who pays attention that they're also fiercely rooting for the other as well. It's kind of a beautiful thing to witness.

"Psh, he wishes," Shooter drawls, downing some of his drink. "More like I kicked his ass."

"Ha! Keep telling yourself that, baby!" Sterling hollers from the other pool table.

Shooter flips him off, and I can't help but laugh.

"We missed you on the road," Cope says as he and his

boyfriend, Xander, sidle up beside Shooter and me. Cope's a saddle bronc rider, and the only one in our friend group.

"Aww, you missed me?" I tease, throwing him a smirk.

Rolling his eyes, he chuckles. "I take it all back."

We dive into a couple of very heated games of pool, the conversation staying light and fun, and the drinks continuing to pour. The more beer we throw back, the louder we all get. Right here, in this bar, we're the definition of rowdy cowboys, but I fucking love it.

It's nearing eleven o'clock, and my head is feeling the right amount of fuzzy to want to stir up some shit. Placing my drink down on the edge of the pool table, I reach into my pocket and grab my phone. After I find the number, I know I probably shouldn't message, but I can't help myself. I open up a text thread, smirking to myself as I type out a message,

Me: Question… do doctors stay up this late?

Much to my surprise, it doesn't take but a moment for the message to show read.

William: Yes, Colt. I would imagine some of us do, indeed, stay up past our bedtimes.

I chuckle, picturing his bored expression. The way his jaw tightens when I do something that really annoys him, or the slight way his eyes narrow. After the close call with my dad on his birthday, I told myself I'd back off—and I did, for a little bit—but there's something about William that makes it impossible to stay away. He's sexy as fuck, especially when he's feigning annoyance with me, but more than that, I'm intrigued by him. I enjoy his attention. Yeah, I shouldn't go there because of my dad, but we've already crossed the line, so what's the harm in crossing it again?

At least that's what I tell myself as I thumb out a response to William.

Me: Yeah? And what's this doctor doing up on this fine Friday night?

William: Not anything as exciting as you're thinking.

Me: And what exactly do you think I'm thinking, Doc?

William: With you, you never know. Your mind always seems to be in the gutter.

Me: Only with you. ;)

William: I find that hard to believe.

"Who's got you smiling at your phone like that?"

Locking the screen, I glance up, meeting Shooter's questioning gaze. "Nobody."

"Fucking liar." He laughs.

I shrug innocently, raising my glass up to my lips, and downing the rest of the beer inside. I'm sure at some point, I'll spill to Shooter about my hookup with William, but for right now, I'm enjoying keeping it to myself. The only one of my friends who knows about it, aside from Whit, is Boone, the other bull rider in my group, and that's only because he was struggling with his feelings for his now boyfriend, Grady, because at the time he was his brother-in-law. I admitted my secret to him in an effort to make him feel better about his. Maybe not the healthiest method of cheering my friend up, but hey, pretty sure it helped.

"Next round's on me," I mutter, holding up the empty glass and smirking at him. He knows I'm dodging the question, but as he empties his glass, he doesn't press any further.

Up at the bar, I pull my text thread with William back up as I wait for the bartender to finish pouring the next round, my heart pounding in my chest as I notice he sent a second text when I didn't reply to the first.

William: I'm just at home, having a glass of whiskey and reading. What are you up to?

Me: I'm out with some friends. They got home from the circuit this week.

Me: ...What are you wearing?

I chuckle when he sends back an eye rolling emoji. Testing my luck with him tonight, I thumb out another message, pressing send before I can talk myself out of it.

Me: That night in Seattle, you had whiskey on your breath, just like I bet you do now. Tasted so good. What I would give to indulge in it again...

William: You never quit, do you?

Me: Why would I quit when I know you enjoy it so much?

William: Who said I enjoyed it?

Me: Oh, come on, Doc. I'm not blind. I've seen the way you look at me, the way your breath hitches when I get close. The way your body reacts to mine. You may not want to admit it, but you want me just as badly as I want you. The only difference is I'm not afraid to admit it.

William: Well, you just think you got it all figured out now, don't you?

Me: Oh, I know I do, and if you were in front of me, I'd prove it to you. But you're too scared to do that, aren't you? Too scared to have me prove you wrong.

Pocketing my phone, I pay for the beers before bringing them back over to the guys. We've moved from the pool tables over to a regular table. Glancing around, I realize we're nearly the only ones in here. I check my phone a few times, but as I figured, there's no response. If I had to guess, he'll probably ignore the message all night, pretending I didn't say all of that because he's afraid to face it. I get it; the fact that we hooked up probably isn't the most ideal, but it happened... and it was fucking great. Why deny us that? Nobody has to know. Too bad William is far too by the books for that type of fun. The fact that it even happened at all is pretty shocking, considering who he is as a person.

But he definitely kissed me back at my dad's birthday party. There's no denying that. He was an active—and enthusiastic—participant. It's only a matter of time before he cracks.

The guys and I stay at the bar for another hour or so before deciding to call it a night. We stopped drinking after that last round, and we all shared a couple of appetizers, so I feel comfortable driving home. As I get into my truck, I pull my phone out, wanting to turn some music on, when I notice a new message. From William. My skin tingles as I tap the notification, my pulse racing as I read the four words waiting for me.

William: So, come over, then.

Holy shit. I knew it. I fucking *knew it*. Sending a message back, letting him know I'll be there in five, I drop the phone on the seat beside me, and put the truck in drive as I pull away from the curb and head in the opposite direction of my house.

CHAPTER 19

COLT BISHOP

TWO YEARS AGO

Wanton, hungry lips pepper the sensitive flesh along my neck, sharp teeth scraping along my clavicle as I work his pants down to his ankles. He steps out of them as our mouths find one another again, like we're connected by some magnetic force. I quickly shimmy out of my own jeans, shoving him down onto the bed once we're both bare naked.

"Fuck, look at you," I murmur, eyes raking down his body. His thighs are slightly parted, full, round balls sitting gloriously beneath a thick, stiff cock that makes my mouth water. A cock that size would have me sore for at least a couple of days. The thought sends a fervid shiver down my spine.

"Get over here," he growls, the deep timbre of his voice sending goosebumps over every inch of flesh.

My heart is a rapid, frenzied beat, my mind reeling over the fact that this is actually happening. Climbing onto his lap, my gaze locks on his, an ocean swimming with desire and lust and a forbidden type of need. This is William Andino... my father's best friend. The man I've found attractive since I was old enough to even understand what that meant. William… the sexy, untouchable doctor who aged like fine wine. It's been *years* since I've seen him, but *goddamn*, is he even more irresistible than I remember.

Hand against his cheek, the coarse hair scratches my palm in the very best way. I lean down, bringing my lips to his, and this time as we kiss, it's softer. Slower. Like we're savoring the moment, the touch. The connection. His tongue lazily strokes against mine, flicking out, brushing against the back of my top teeth. Biting down on his bottom lip, I tug before sucking gently on the plump skin.

Everything about this moment is teasing. Like we're amping up for what's to come.

Holding on to me, William guides my hips to rock against his, the shift successfully lining us up perfectly. The friction from our cocks slipping and sliding together has my eyes rolling back. I kiss him fiercer this time, ravaging his mouth as I reach between us, wrapping a tight fist around our shared girth. It doesn't fit, not even close, but it works.

With one hand planted on the bed next to William's head, I thrust up, pumping into my fist as he does the same. Resting my forehead against his as we move together, his breath is hot against my lips, a groan rumbling from his chest as we lose ourselves to one another.

"You like that?" I ask him, voice low and deep. "Like feeling my cock rub against yours?"

"Fuck yes," he pants, fingers digging into the flesh on my hips hard enough that I know there will be marks there tomorrow.

"Did you come here tonight looking to hook up?" Sweat drenches the hair at my nape, dripping down my back, but

I don't slow down. "You wanted to fuck somebody tonight, didn't you?"

He nods, giving me a breathless, "Yes."

"Bet you didn't think it would be me you wound up naked with, did you?"

"What happened to us being strangers tonight?" he rasps.

Smirking down at him, I lift one shoulder into a shrug. "Changed my mind," I drawl. "Now, tell me, how does it feel knowing that your best friend's son is stroking your cock right now?"

William's lip curls into a snarl as a growl vibrates from his chest. He doesn't say a word, but his cock twitches against mine, which says all I need to know.

"What a dirty fucking man you are," I purr against his lips. "It turns you on, doesn't it? Knowing it's me, knowing what we're doing is wrong. You're getting off on it."

He doesn't say anything.

"Admit it," I taunt, pumping us faster in my fist. "Admit that you're dirty, and you're getting off on it."

"No."

My lips curl into a grin before I crash my mouth down on his, taking him in a kiss that's messy and hungry. "Admit. It."

A growl sounds from his throat again before he flips us in a move I don't see coming. All the air is punched from my lungs as my back hits the mattress. William brings his hand up to his face, spitting in his palm before reaching between us, and smacking my hand away, replacing it with his own as he holds us in a punishing grip.

My heart pounds harder as my mind tries to catch up with the power shift that just happened before my eyes. His eyes are wild, almost feral as they watch me, teeth bared as his hips snap against mine. Pleasure soars through my body as I lie here, unable to move or think or even breathe properly.

William leans down, bringing his lips beside my ear, and a fresh wave of goosebumps popping up all over my body. "You want me to admit it?" he rasps. "Want me to admit how much I'm fucking loving having your hot, naked body under mine? Want me to admit how turned on it makes me knowing I'm doing something wrong?"

"Yes," I gasp, getting dangerously close to the edge.

He drags my earlobe between his teeth, nipping hard enough to make me yelp. "Fine," he murmurs. "Having you writhing beneath me as our cocks slide together makes me so fucking hot. Especially when I think about who you are. You're a forbidden fruit that I shouldn't be tasting, yet here I am. Fucking consumed by you."

"Yes…" I'm so goddamn close. "Don't stop."

"You like it too, though, don't you?" His voice is a deep rumble in my ear. It vibrates through my entire being. "If I'm dirty, then what does that make you? I saw the way you watched me from across the room down there."

Oh, fuck…

"Saw the way you eye-fucked me. Felt the way your slutty ass grinded against my dick on the dance floor. If given the chance, you would've let me fuck you right there in front of all those people, wouldn't you?"

"Fuck yes," I groan, wrapping my legs around his hips, needing him closer.

"You'd have liked that, wouldn't you? You would've let me unzip your pants, pin you against the wall, as I sank my cock deep into your tight fucking ass for everybody to see. As I took your fucking hole raw. I bet you'd love it so much, your cock would even come untouched, wouldn't it?"

My hips buck up, seeking more and more and *more*. My pulse races franticly, and I can't catch my breath. The tables have turned from when we started, and I can't even lie and say I'm mad about it. Fire settles in my abdomen, pleasure swimming in my veins. My balls tighten, and I know there's no going back. No holding on any longer.

"Fuck, shit," I cry out. "I'm close. Fuck, William, don't stop. I'm going to come."

Lips dropping from my ear down to my neck, his teeth sink into the skin at the exact moment I fall over the edge. I throw my head back, moaning long and low as my release takes me by storm. Wave after wave hits me, an electrifying pleasure, and William isn't far behind. His hot, sticky cum mixes with mine on my stomach, our bodies slick with sweat, chests heaving.

I can't think straight. Eyes pinched shut, stars erupt behind my eyelids, and for a second, I swear I lose the ability to hear. As William rolls off of me onto the bed, I sit up, my head feeling light and fuzzy, almost like I'm somehow more drunk than when we came up here.

Goddamn, that was incredible. The way our bodies moved together, our chemistry, the way he kissed me. Why does this feel like the type of hookup you never get over?

CHAPTER 20

WILLIAM ANDINO

PRESENT DAY

Headlights appear at the end of the street, and I know they belong to Colt. I'm peeping out the window next to the door like a creep, with my stomach in knots and my heart working in overdrive.

What the hell am I doing? It's the question I've asked myself no less than ten times in the very short span since Colt texted me back, agreeing to come over. Why would I invite him over? What good will come from that? It's nearly midnight. Nobody comes over this late for anything innocent. When he started flirting with me through text, making comments about how he'd like to taste my kiss again or how if he were in front of me, he'd prove how much I wanted him, I should've ignored them.

I *did* ignore them for a while.

Until I couldn't anymore. It's like I lost my ability to think rationally. I lost all self-control as I was sitting on my bed, trying to read—try being the opportune word here—and the unanswered text was calling to me from where it was sitting on the nightstand. It was a siren call; something I'm clearly not strong enough to deny. And responding felt simple enough. It's over the phone, so it's easy to pretend it's not as *real*. Easy to pretend there would be no consequences from it. But now he's here, because I told him to, and I don't think there's any way I'll be able to send him away once I lay eyes on him. Colt ignites something fierce inside of me, something I have a hard time ignoring.

It's wrong, and I should be the responsible one, and put a stop to it, but why? Why shouldn't I get to be a little reckless? Why shouldn't I give in to what I want every once in a while? It's one night. My father and I went to visit my mom's gravestone earlier, and being there reminded me that life is too damn short to deny yourself what you want all the time.

His truck parks in the driveway, and I pull away from the window, resting my back against the wall as I force myself to take deep breaths. The buzzing sound of my phone vibrating in my hand is deafening in this otherwise quiet hallway. It's him, obviously. I could always ignore the message. Pretend I fell asleep after I sent the original invite. Sure, it would be a dick move, but it would ensure I didn't do something I really shouldn't tonight.

Could I do that, though? Ignore Colt, leave him outside waiting for me? No. Of course not. That's not who I am. I'm fucking polite to a fault; it comes from years as a physician. But it's not even that, is it? If I'm being honest with myself, the real reason I couldn't ignore him is because I don't want to. There's an overwhelming part of me that *wants* to see him. That *craves* the way Colt looks at me. The way he flirts with me so damn shamelessly. A part of me that has to see this through, regardless of the consequences, because the sexual tension is there between us, and I'm certain ignoring it won't make it just go away.

Blowing out a breath, I unlock my phone, finding a text from Colt telling me what I already knew; he's here. With my heart in my throat, as quietly as I can, I flick the deadbolt on the door, twisting the knob, and pulling open the door. I step out onto the porch, noting how warm it is tonight. Colt rounds the front of his truck, signature backwards hat on his head, a lopsided grin tugging at his lips, and I can't help but check him out for a moment. Sinfully tight Wranglers, a pair of boots, and a sand-colored t-shirt, the front of it tucked into his jeans showing off his belt buckle. He walks with swagger and confidence, something I really shouldn't find as attractive as I do.

"Evening, Doc," he drawls as he casually strolls up the steps. As soon as he's in front of me, I notice the toothpick hanging out of the corner of his mouth, and there's something so damn hot about that. I can't explain it. His usual citrus and leather scent envelops me as he comes to a stop in front of me, the smell intoxicating me more than the whiskey ever could.

I tip my chin. "Colt." Suddenly, everything feels awkward as a rush of uncertainty takes over my nerves. This was a mistake, inviting him here.

His smirk grows, like he knows exactly what's running through my mind. "You going to invite me in, or are we going to stand out here on your porch all night for all of your neighbors to see?"

Clenching my jaw, I step aside, letting him pass by me into the house. Like he's been here dozens of times, he toes out of his boots, setting them by the shoe rack. As I'm locking the door, I feel him come up behind me. He doesn't touch me, but his presence is blaring.

"Barefoot," he rasps. "Kind of sexy seeing you like this."

Doing my best to school my features, I turn to face him, saying nothing about his comment. "Would you like something to drink?" I offer, keeping my voice hushed to not wake my father.

Hands shoved into the pockets of his jeans, Colt watches me from beneath his lashes as he shakes his head. "Nah, I'm good, but thanks, Doc."

What are we doing?

I'm so out of my element, and I hate it. My heart is galloping and my blood is on fire, exhilarated by Colt standing in my entryway in the middle of the night. I haven't felt this way in far too long.

It's dangerous, all of this. Having him in my house. The desire burning inside of me. The heated way he's looking at me. I pride myself on being a good man, a man with morals and a clear conscience. Yet, here I am, about to do who knows what with my best friend's son. *Again.*

Colt breathes out a chuckle. "You know, as fun as it is standing here with you, maybe we could…" He gestures around. "I don't know. Go somewhere more private."

Standing tall, I mirror his stance, hands finding the pockets of my pajamas as I gaze at him head on. "Where would you like to go?"

Lips ticking up on one side, he shrugs. "Give me a tour of the house."

"You've been here before. You don't need a tour."

Colt takes a single step closer, my breath getting caught in my throat. "Yeah, but that's down here." His voice is like velvet. Like melted butter. "You haven't shown me the upstairs."

A wave of lust rolls through my veins, and my mouth goes dry. I clench my jaw, not knowing how to respond to that. What is there to even say? The insinuation is clear. This is where I'm supposed to put a stop to it. This is where I'm supposed to regain the rational side of my brain, the one that isn't being controlled by testosterone and the rasp of Colt's voice.

I know full well what I'm *supposed* to do.

Do I do that? No, of course not. That part of my brain is apparently already asleep for the night, as should the rest of me, but here I am, facing down temptation and crumbling beneath it. Without a word, I start down the hall, feet carrying me toward the staircase. I don't need to look behind me to know Colt's following me; I can feel him like a force. A force I'm not strong enough to withstand.

Each step I take up the stairs, I'm sealing my fate, digging myself deeper into trouble. By inviting Colt over tonight, I made my bed, and like hell am I getting out of this without lying in it first. Consequences be damned. It's one night.

One night to let go.

To give into my desires.

To repeat what we started two years ago.

One night couldn't hurt.

Keeping up with the charade of a *tour*, I show Colt around as we reach the top step. I don't even have to glance over my shoulder to know he's smirking, most likely wanting to call me on my bullshit.

"Here's the bathroom," I murmur, gesturing with my hand before shoving it back into my pocket. "Beside it is the guest bedroom."

For reasons I don't understand, I even go as far as turning on the light in the room, as if showing him it's real. As I flick off the light switch and exit the space, I find myself unable to look at him. Like if I make eye contact, suddenly it'll all be real.

It's absurd. Colt's here… in my house. Of course, it's real.

The half-open door to my bedroom is taunting me at the end of the hall. It's the only room left up here that I haven't shown him. It's either take him there or finally call the whole thing off and send him on his way. The latter is the smarter of the choices, the one I should lean into, but I know myself better than that. I've come this far, I'm not backing out, even if I don't quite understand what it is about him that has me saying to hell with my morals.

Something about Colt has me behaving like a teenager all over again. Reckless. Careless. Horny. And there's a part of me—the part of me I've locked away for years now in favor of building my career and making a name for myself—that relishes this. That *enjoys* this side of me that he pulls out of hibernation. A part of me who thinks that maybe I need this, this fun, wild type of energy. Maybe I've spent far too long trying to be a professional that I've lost who I really am.

So, while I may not fully understand this pull I have toward Colt, I'm choosing, in this moment, to lean into it. Not only because it feels right, but because I *want* to, and sometimes life is just too damn short to not indulge in the things you want for reasons that are purely selfish. As this resolve washes over me, I roll my shoulders back, and put one foot in front of the other as I lead Colt Bishop to my bedroom. Nothing has ever felt as wrong and forbidden and fucking good as this does, and for once in my damn life, I'm allowing myself to bask in those feelings. Embrace them.

My attraction for Colt is wrong, but I'm acting on it anyway because the fact of the matter is, we're both consenting adults, so why not?

As we enter the room, I step aside, letting Colt go in ahead of me as I shut the door. The sound of the lock clicking into place sounds an awful lot like my fate sealing. I rest my back against the tall, hardwood, my gaze locked on Colt. I expected him to look out of place in my room, like he didn't belong. But it's quite the opposite. That could be lust talking, or the fact that Colt has the ability to fit in anywhere.

"Why'd you invite me over tonight, Doc?" he asks, a smirk curling his lips.

Heat floods my system, my heart stuttering.

"I think you know why." My voice is husky, the desire evident in my tone.

Tonight, I'm going to do something I won't be able to take back, and unlike the first time, I won't have the excuse of alcohol to fall back on when the morning light shines down on me.

Tonight, I'm taking what I want, indulging in the history between us, and it's going to feel damn good doing it.

CHAPTER 21

COLT BISHOP

"*I think you know why.*"

Those five words have ignited a fire within me. I don't know what I expected when he invited me over, but I kind of figured he'd take the high road and put a stop to this long before we wound up here, in his bedroom. But I can't deny how fucking stoked I am that he hasn't.

Neither of us says anything else for a long moment, but our eye contact is heady. I'm doused in lust and need, dying to close the distance and taste him again. William reminds me of a frightened wild animal right now, though. One wrong move, and it could all be over, so I have to let him come to me. Have to let him call the shots, which admittedly, isn't easy for me. Taking what I want is something that has always come naturally. I don't beat around the bush or pussyfoot around anything, but William is in a league of his own.

If he doesn't initiate whatever is about to happen, then he'll run away like he did when I kissed him at Conrad's place. He's obnoxiously stubborn, not that it's deterred me so far.

Pushing off the door, William takes a step, then another, his gaze locked on mine the entire way. My pulse races, my heart in my throat the closer he gets. As he comes to a stop in front of me, I see it. He falters for a single moment. There's doubt in his eyes, and I know he's nervous. Thankfully, he's able to shove whatever's in his mind away because in the next moment, he's grabbing me by the back of the neck, hauling my mouth into his.

As soon as our lips lock, my hands are on him. The need to have William as close to me as humanly possible takes over, and I'm wrapping my arms around his waist while he does the same to me. It's electric, the way our lips move together. The way his tongue surges into my mouth, tasting mine. The kiss feels feral. It feels carnal; a need we both have, an itch we must scratch.

William's fingers find the hem of my shirt, and he starts lifting the material before he pauses, taking a step back. "Take this off," he growls, his ocean eyes darkened. "I want to rip it off of you, but I don't want to hurt your shoulder."

I breathe out a laugh as I do as he says. Something about the level of care he has for my shoulder hits me right in the chest in a way I didn't anticipate. He's a doctor; of course, he would be cautious of my injury, but for some reason, it feels deeper than that. Like maybe he cares for *me*. Shoving those thoughts away, I let my shirt drop to the ground as I wait on bated breath for his next instruction. As hard as it is for me to follow somebody's lead, I must admit, there's something really fucking hot about watching William boss me around.

Eyes roaming across my chest, his hands clench into fists at his side. "Fuck," he breathes out before he's on me again. His lips practically maul my mouth, and I love it. I love seeing him appear so out of control.

My greedy fingers grip the hem of his shirt next, breaking our lips apart long enough to tug it over his head. It lands next to mine as the palm of my hands caress the expanse of his chest. Our kiss gets more heated by the minute. It's messy; a clash of teeth and tongues, neither of us able to get our fill. The coarse hair that covers his chest feels amazing under my touch, and when I tweak his nipples between my fingers, he gasps into my mouth. The sound quickly morphs into a groan that settles deep in my balls.

Everything about William is all man. The way he smells, the way he feels under my touch, the way he handles me. I can't get enough.

"Why can't I stop thinking about you?" he murmurs against my lips in between kisses. "What is it about you that I can't seem to stay away from?"

I don't even think he realizes he's saying anything, but my chest swells with pride at knowing I'm on his mind as much as he's on mine. *Especially* knowing how much he tries to pretend I'm not.

"You think about me, Doc?" I smirk against his mouth as he slowly walks us backwards toward his bed.

"You know I do," he growls. "It's infuriating."

Chuckling softly, I mutter, "I would say I'm sorry, but I'm really not."

"Why is that not surprising?"

As soon as the back of my legs hit the edge of his bed, his hands come up to my chest, and he's shoving me down. His gaze is heady as he peers down at me, my heart thumping harder as I wait to see what his next move is. Stepping between my thighs, he reaches for the button on my jeans, flicking it open and sliding the zipper down in one swift motion. Next, he yanks the material down my legs, taking my briefs too, until I'm lying before him completely naked.

William rakes his hungry eyes down my body, zeroing in on my cock, and the way it's thickening more by the second. My whole being feels alight right now, every inch of flesh burning with need. After he drinks the sight of me in for a few moments, he blankets my body with his, hands coming down on either side of my head as his lips crash down on mine. If possible, this kiss feels even more supercharged than before. Even more desperate and needy. I can taste the sheer arousal on his tongue, feel it in the way he bites down on my bottom lip, tugging until I moan.

It doesn't last long, though. Before I know it, he's working his way across my jawline, nipping and sucking on the skin there, until he finds that sweet spot on my neck below my ear that sends a surge of heat down to my core. Working his way down, he peppers my chest with affection next, his movements hurried. Like he can't consume me quick enough. I prop myself up on my elbows as I watch him work his way down my abdomen, spreading my legs wider, giving him easier access.

The first and only other time we've done this, it was me in charge. It was me kissing him everywhere. Me tasting and touching and licking him. The role reversal is different, but so fucking hot. Watching him take what he wants, seeing how desperate he is for me. My blood pumps hot in my veins, the organ in my chest nearly busting out of my ribs, the lower he sinks, the closer he gets to where I need him.

But because this is William, and I swear he enjoys making me suffer, he doesn't put me out of my misery so quickly. His lips press down everywhere *but* where I want him, and I'm going out of my mind. My dick is rock hard and leaking, aching for attention. Sitting back on his haunches, William caresses my thighs with his rough, warm palms while he peers at me. His lips tug into a smirk, clearly very aware of what he's doing to me. A quick, shameless glance down the front of him reveals how turned on he is.

"Touch me," I beg, my voice coming out like a whine, but I can't help it. It feels like I'm going to explode with my need for him.

"Your patience could use some work," he throws back as he gropes himself over his pajama pants. The sight does nothing to tamp down the desire coursing through me.

"Well, you got me all worked up, Doc," I rasp, reaching down with the intent of stroking myself, but he slaps my hand away before I have the chance.

"No touching," he growls.

"Why the fuck not?" I ask, gawking at him.

Fingers dancing along the sensitive flesh of my inner thigh, his gaze drags up my body until it locks on mine. "Because," he starts, a ravenous glint in his eyes, "while we're in here, this"—I shiver as his index finger brushes along the underside of my shaft in a featherlight touch—"is mine, and you don't get to touch what's mine. Am I making myself clear?"

Holy shit. I'm not going to survive this.

I can only nod, my mouth too dry to speak.

A sinister grin spreads across his face. "Good boy," he purrs, and *fuck me*, I want to hear that again. I've never been known to have much of a praise kink before, but something about those two words falling from his lips has me desperate to make him proud.

"One night," he mutters. "That's all this is. We're going to have this one night, and then it's never going to happen again. It can't. Do you understand me, Colt?"

I nod, knowing full well it's a lie. In no fucking world am I about to have another taste of William, only to wake up in the morning and never do it again. I think the fuck not. But if a little white lie is what it takes for me to have his hands on me, then so be it.

"We can't keep this up," he goes on, and at this point, I'm unsure if he's talking to me... or himself. "No matter how much we want to, we can't. So, tonight."

"Tonight," I parrot, the confirmation tasting sour on my tongue. One night could never be enough with him, and whether he knows it yet or not, I'm going to make him see. William's walls are breaking down slowly; the fact that I'm naked in his bedroom right now is proof of that. A connection this strong can't be wasted on one fucking night. He'll come to his senses soon enough.

CHAPTER 22

WILLIAM ANDINO

One night.

O I can do this. I'm a strong man with self-control. I can enjoy the time we have tonight, and surely move on with my life starting tomorrow. This is simply an itch. Something we need to work out of our systems... again. And doing that tonight will scratch it.

I can do this.

Colt looks mesmerizing lying before me. Completely nude on my bed, his stiff cock waiting for my touch. Dripping for me. His body is a work of art. Despite his inability to work out because of his injury, his body is still taut and tone. Lean muscles, sharp lines, and beautiful tan skin. Colt's a tall man; not nearly as tall as I am, but his limbs are long and lean. Bull riding has done his body well. He's a sight for sore eyes, that's for sure.

Being here with him, I'm overwhelmed in the very best way. He's laid out, not so patiently waiting for my next move, but that's the thing... I don't even know where to start. There's so much of him I want to consume, and knowing we only have tonight puts the pressure on me. And I'm stuck between wanting to drown myself in him as quickly as possible and wanting to take my time and savor him, make it last all goddamn night.

"You're killing me, Doc," Colt whines, his brows pinched together as he rolls his hips up, silently begging me to touch him.

Smirking, I ask, "What did I say about patience?"

"It's running *real* fucking thin," he huffs with a small laugh, and a thrill shoots down my spine at how needy he is right now. I'm honestly surprised he's even listening to me or letting me call the shots.

Unable to go another second without touching him, I lean down, pressing my lips to his hot, smooth chest. Colt exhales a shaky breath as he watches me cover the area. I work my way down once again, not leaving a single inch untouched. I want all of him. I want my every sense to be muddled by Colt. The lower I get, the shallower his breath becomes. It's so quiet in my room you could hear a pin drop.

I drag my tongue down the strip of hair under his navel that leads to his groin, reveling in the way his body trembles. Nipping at the sensitive skin on his thighs, I work my way all around his cock, saving it for last. He's so damn hard, the tip glistening with his arousal, and my mouth waters to taste it. To lap it up and let the flavor simmer on my tastebuds. I bet it'll be fucking divine. Peering up at him from beneath my lashes, I lick a hot, wet stripe up the center of his nut sack, feeling them tighten under my tongue as he groans, the sound low and throaty, his hips rocking up, chasing more.

Colt's natural musk, mixed with the faint scent of his sweat, makes for an intoxicating concoction that shouldn't be as addicting as it is. My cock twitches behind my pants as I drag in a whiff of him, memorizing the scent. Propped up on his elbows, Colt peers down at me, his lip tucked between his teeth, eyes glassy and hooded. He looks like the embodiment of sex as he watches me. Gazing up at him, it's no wonder I was unable to resist him. He looks like an angel with the mouth of a devil.

I finally allow myself to take him in my hand. Hot, hard flesh fills my fist, velvety to the touch, a glistening bead shimmering in the light on the slit. Colt's cock, like the rest of him, is a work of art. Not too long, maybe six inches or so, but it's got some impressive girth. The tip is flared and red, shaft pale pink with a prominent vein running along the length of the underside. A vein that I fully intend to trace with my tongue here in a minute.

Colt's breath comes out in harsh pants through his nose as I pump my fist up and down, slowly stroking him as I maintain eye contact. His cheeks are flushed, nipples taut, and he's clenching his hands into fists. It's killing him to stay still, and that lights me up inside—having Colt at my mercy.

Wetting my lips with my tongue, my stomach dips as I watch Colt track the movement with his hungry eyes. I lean in, lapping up the seeping pre-cum spilling down his length, a groan rumbling inside my chest at his delicious flavor. Colt gasps as my lips close around the tip, tongue flicking the flared head before I sink farther down, taking more of him. It's been a *long* time since I've sucked a dick, and my gag reflex kicks in embarrassingly fast.

"*Fuuuuuck,*" Colt groans, hips rocking up so gently I'm not even sure he's aware he's doing it. "I wish you could see how fucking sexy you look taking my cock in your mouth, Doc."

Locking my eyes on his, my head bobbing up and down, I drink in the lust-drunk sight of him. It's something I wish I could photograph, to look back on night after night.

Every time I sink a little lower, his moans get a little more desperate. Colt's a vocal man in bed; it's one thing I remember *vividly.* There's something so attractive about a man who voices what he likes. When you can tell he's into what you're doing. Some men, be it toxic masculinity or just plain insecurity, are damn near silent the entire time. Not Colt. Reaching down, I roll his balls in my palm as I continue to suck him. He's practically writhing beneath me before he gasps, hand flying out to my shoulder as he roughly shoves me off and scoots back.

"I don't want to come yet," he husks when I narrow my eyes at him, my spit-slick lips tugged into a smirk. "Get over here. It's my turn to play with you, Doc."

A shiver rolls down my spine at the authority in his tone, and the way he grabs my arms, flipping us so it's my back against the mattress now. Wasting no time, not waiting for any response from me, he drags my pajama pants down my legs, my stiff erection jutting out.

He bites his lip with a groan. "Fuck, it's as beautiful as I remember," he mutters, wrapping a steady hand around the base, stroking up with a flick of his wrist. My chest quakes with a moan as I watch him lean down and take my whole length into his mouth in one go. Doesn't give himself any time to adjust, doesn't go slow. He swallows me like a starved man, and my body seizes up when I feel his throat muscles constrict around the head.

Colt sucks dick like it's a prize. It's sloppy and slick, the sound of him deep throating me lewd and erotic. His hand fondles my balls, tugging on them gently, and as his finger brushes along my taint in a featherlight touch, I swear I see stars. Colt peers up at me, eyes wet and bloodshot, as I touch the back of his throat. Cheeks hollow, he sucks me hard all the way back up before swirling his tongue around the tip.

I'm not going to last much longer if he keeps up like this. Colt must sense this because after another moment, he backs off. "Where's your lube?" he asks, sitting back, fisting his cock. The sight is something out of my hottest dreams. I could watch him stroke himself for hours.

I gesture toward the nightstand. "In there."

He climbs off the bed and pulls the drawer open, grabbing the clear bottle from inside. Eyes flicking to mine, he says, "I'm tested regularly. The last time was right before my accident, and I haven't been with anybody since. It was negative."

The insinuation is loud and clear. He wants me to fuck him without a condom. I don't ever do that, but the idea of any sort of barrier between Colt and me tonight doesn't sit right with me. If we only have one night, I want to feel all of him.

Nodding, I tell him, "Got one at my last physical; it was negative too. Also haven't been with anybody since."

Like my response pleases him, he grins, then wastes no time flicking the cap open, pouring a glob of the clear gel onto his fingers, and I spend the next minute watching in rapt silence as he preps himself for me. His eyes never leave mine, and as soon as he's done, he climbs onto my lap, lining the tip of my cock up with his tight hole.

As he sinks down, inch by inch, his gaze holds mine, bright green eyes nearly black with lust. The air in the room is thick, and it feels like my lungs can't drag in oxygen fast enough. His lips part, and he lets out a deep groan once I'm fully seated inside of him. His hot channel sucks me in, squeezing me tight enough that my eyelids fight to stay open.

Hands moving to his hips, I grip him as he starts sliding up and down my shaft. "Christ, Colt," I gasp, the feel of him unreal. "You feel… so… fucking good."

He smirks. "You like my tight hole taking your thick cock?"

"God, yes," I growl, throwing my head back as he fucks himself faster on top of me. His dick is hard, the skin shiny from being pulled taut, and he's leaking all over my stomach. I love seeing how turned on he is, but I'm going out of my mind. Tightening my grip on his hips, I flip us quickly, before he has a chance to stop me. With Colt flat on his back, I grab onto the headboard, and drill into his sweet little ass, his legs automatically wrapping around my hips.

Sweat lines the back of my neck as my heart pounds. Colt reaches between us, pumping his fist up and down his length as I fuck him harder and deeper. Neither of us says a word, nothing but our heavy breathing and garbled moans filling the air, but the way we're looking at one another, gazes locked, it's overwhelming. Unlike anything I've experienced. Somehow this feels more intimate, like Colt can see right into my soul as I bring us closer to the edge.

Every inch of my skin is on fire, this passion burning straight into my core. I can't catch my breath, and this moment seems way larger than me. Larger than both of us. My chest feels cracked open, frayed. It's too much.

Does he feel it too?

"I'm close," he moans, and it's like those two words are enough to set me off.

I nod, my balls tightening up to my body. "Me too."

His jaw drops open, a moan falling off his lips. "Fill me up, Doc," he growls. "Come in my ass. Mark me. Make me come."

"You'd like that, wouldn't you?" I tease, my voice foreign to my own ears. "You want to go home tonight and feel me leaking out of you?"

His eyes somehow manage to darken even more as he nods. "Fuck yes. Do it."

"Maybe you'll wake up in the middle of the night, your cock throbbing, and you'll slip a finger or two inside your used hole, desperate to feel as full as I make you feel."

"Fuck," he gasps, head thrown back as the long column of his throat is exposed to me. "Yes, yes, yes. Please, fill me with your come."

Colt cries out as his cock erupts, spilling thick, white ropes all over his stomach, and that's all it takes for me to get there too. Pounding into him once, twice, three more times, my balls throb as I empty myself deep inside of him. It goes on forever, and by the time I'm finished, my body feels boneless.

I pull out of Colt, and collapse on the bed beside him, chest heaving as I fight to catch my breath. Colt immediately rolls onto his side, placing his hands underneath his cheek on the pillow, looking sleepy and sated.

"That was fucking amazing," he blurts out, making me choke out a laugh.

"It was," I agree, this moment still feeling way too intense.

We watch each other for a moment, silently, a dozen things being said without words. Reaching over, I brush a strand of hair out of Colt's face before wrapping my hand around the back of his neck. I lean in, brushing his lips with mine gently. The kiss is soft, but it's easy to get lost in, especially after what we just did. My tongue caresses along his, tasting him, and feeling like once will never be enough with him. It's a thought that stops me in my tracks and has me pulling back. Reality sets in, and I'm fighting the urge to panic. My cum is still fresh inside of his body and his taste still slick on my lips, and I'm already berating myself for not being able to resist him.

What was I fucking thinking?

Colt's body stiffens. He must sense my unease because he clears his throat before sitting up. "Well, as fun as this has been, I don't really want to be here when your dad wakes up and catches us."

It's right there on the tip of my tongue to stop him, tell him to stay, but what for? What good will come from him staying any longer? Will we cuddle? Fall asleep in each other's arms? That can't happen, nor would he even want to do that, I'm sure. It's best to end this now before we get in any deeper. No matter how much it stings watching him get dressed. Eventually, I tug on my clothes too, and we walk toward the door, and then down the hall before quietly taking the steps as softly as I can to not make them squeak.

My pulse is deafening in my ears as we reach the front door, and everything in me is screaming to not let this end like this. But no words come out. It's like that nightmare you have as a kid, where you try to scream but no sound escapes.

What is going through Colt's mind right now?

He turns and meets my gaze, reaching out to slap a hand down on my bicep. "Thanks for the dick, Doc," he mutters. "Catch you later."

And just like that, he's gone. Clearly not as messed up about what all this means as I am. Huffing out a breath, I lock the deadbolt before grabbing a glass of water from the kitchen. I'm an idiot for letting this happen, and an even bigger idiot for feeling like shit about him leaving right now.

Why do I care?

It was only one night.

CHAPTER 23

COLT BISHOP

Unbelievable. I huff, sitting in one of the folding chairs at the check-in table at the free clinic. I've checked everybody in, and it'll be time to go home soon. William just came out of one of the make-shift rooms, and like he's done all day long, he does anything in his power to look anywhere *but at me*. It's driving me fucking nuts.

It's been two whole weeks since William and I hooked up at his place. Two fucking weeks, and damn near radio silence. It's driving me insane. I'm not exactly one to hook up and then expect a call the next day, but damn, *something* would've been nice. I didn't expect his silence to sting so much. The morning after, we had to be here, but it was so busy that day, we really didn't have a chance to talk to each other. Then after we were finished, he hightailed out of here so fast you would've thought his ass was on fire. I've considered texting him a number of times, demanding he face what we've done and talk to me… and to be honest, I don't really know why I haven't. It's not like I'm one to shy away from confrontation, but I don't know.

Everything with William is never how it usually goes for me, and this is no different.

Shaking these clingy thoughts from my head, I turn around, annoyance at myself flaring inside of me. What the hell is it with this guy? I'm Colt fucking Bishop, a world championship bull rider. I've had men and women flocking to me for years. I don't chase, I don't overthink, yet this one man has me all twisted up in knots. And for what? Some dick? I mean, yeah, it was *fan-fucking-tastic* dick, but it's not like I've never had great sex before. Even when I did, I didn't behave like this. I didn't obsess over the person. I promptly forgot about them by the next night.

Luckily, the last couple of weeks have been busy, so it's not like I've been sitting around, pouting about it all the time.

In fact, I've barely noticed. Okay, that's a lie, but I really *have* been busy.

Last weekend, I finally moved back into my house. Honestly, I probably could've come back a while ago—when I got my sling off—but I was kind of enjoying having my mom cook dinner every night, so I dragged my feet a little bit. And I know she didn't mind having me around to feed and look after. However, now that I'm settled in my own place again, I'll admit, it's nice. The bed at my house is much comfier than the one at my parents' place, and having more privacy than just a bedroom is also a plus.

On top of that, I'm finally able to hit the gym again—albeit very carefully. So, between that, physical therapy, and getting back into my normal routine, I've been pretty busy, but I'm about sick of this silence. William doesn't just get to fuck me as good as he did, and then act like it never happened. That's normally *my* move. Checking my watch, I note that we'll be leaving soon, and I'm determined to not let him run out of here like he did last time. Whether he likes it or not, he'll be talking to me today.

"What's wrong with you?" Meg asks, pulling out the chair beside me and dropping down into it.

My brows pinch together. "Nothing? I'm fine."

She snorts. "Yeah, right. You've been in a mood all day."

"Have not." *I totally have.*

"Did something happen with Dr. Andino?"

My pulse kicks up as I turn my head to meet her gaze. "What? No. Why would you think that?"

"Well, you've been glaring at him all day," she explains with a shrug. "And he's been rather snippy, so I figured maybe he snapped at you or something."

Hmm… snippy, huh? Wonder what that's about.

"Nah, I'm good, just an off day."

"Want to talk about it?" she asks, pulling her phone out from her scrubs.

I shake my head. "Nothing to talk about."

It's obnoxious how much this shit with William is getting to me, but I can't say that to Meg. Driving over to his house after the bar that night, I knew whatever was going to happen, he would flip out and act all weird, but it's still fucking annoying. The sex was damn good, and I *know* he enjoyed himself. He needs to get out of his head and roll with it. Forget all the reasons we shouldn't and embrace the chemistry we have. Why is that so hard?

Meg stands up, pocketing her phone. "Alright, well, I'm going to help Dr. Braylon clean up his area and load up his car. You got Dr. Andino?"

This is how Meg and I have done things since the first free

clinic; she always assists Dr. Braylon with cleanup, and I always help William, so I know what she means, but the question makes me chuckle to myself anyway. "Yeah, I got him."

"Alrighty, see you at Whiskey Creek, right?"

"Wouldn't miss it." A grin tugs at my lips as I wink at her. Smiling back at me, she nods before waving and heading toward Dr. Braylon's station. Tomorrow is her birthday, so to celebrate, the four of us are going to the bar in town to have a few rounds and hang out. Should make for an interesting afternoon, considering my current state of silence with William. Can't say I'm not looking forward to it, though.

Standing up, I fold the two chairs up before doing the same with the table, setting them off to the side like we do every weekend we're here, then I go find William. He's in one of the makeshift rooms, breaking down the hospital bed. Taking advantage of the fact that he hasn't noticed me yet, I allow myself a moment to admire him. His hair is mussed up, like he's been running his fingers through it. It's sexy in a just-fucked kind of way. The short sleeves of his black scrub top are rolled up once, showing off his thick, corded arms, and the pants are doing absolute fucking wonders at accentuating his round ass. I clench my jaw, swallowing a groan while I imagine what it would be like to drop to my knees and take a bite out of one of the firm globes right now.

Glancing over at me, our eyes lock. William stands up straight, his shoulders nearly to his ears. "Colt. Hello."

My lip tips up into a grin. "Hey, Doc."

Scanning the area, presumably seeing if we're alone, he asks, "What are you doing?"

"Coming to see if you need any help, but it looks like you're mostly finished?"

He nods. "The bed in the room beside this one needs to be broken down, but other than that, I'm pretty much done."

"I'll take care of it," I call out as I start toward that area.

William grunts a quick 'thank you' under his breath, but nothing else is said. He's so damn tense; it's a real shame he doesn't let me take care of that for him. I could have him relaxed in *no* time. By the time we're all finished, the tension between us is stifling. I bring the last bed out to his car, thankful that I can finally help with shit like this, and I find him standing awkwardly by the hood of the vehicle.

"That's the last of 'em," I say as I shove it in the back. It's nice that they're able to do this twice a month, but it's shitty that they have to tote all of these supplies back and forth from the office to do so. "Wanna ride together to the bar?"

William glances up, brows pinched together, lips pressed into a thin line. "I don't think that's such a good idea."

Huffing out a laugh, I approach him. "Why not?" I ask with a raised brow. "Scared I might talk you into fucking me on the side of the road?"

"Colt," he grits out, his nostrils flaring on a harsh exhale.

"William," I toss back, the smirk on my lips growing. "It's just a car ride together. I'll even promise to keep my hands to myself inside the vehicle."

Studying me for a moment, not saying anything, I'm convinced he's going to tell me to fuck off. But then he finally blows out a breath and nods his head. "Yeah, okay. Fine."

"Cool, but first, can you follow me to my house so I can drop my car off, and then we can go?"

"Colt."

I hold up my hands innocently. "My house is right around the corner, Doc. I don't want to leave it parked at the arena."

"Your house is no less than ten minutes from here," he drawls. "I wouldn't exactly say that's right around the corner."

"That's my parents' house," I explain. "I'm back in my own house, which *is* right around the corner." Taking a step closer, his rich mahogany scent fills my senses. "Maybe you could've asked me that if you hadn't spent the last two weeks ignoring me."

His jaw flexes as he meets my gaze. "I haven't been ignoring you."

My lips tip up as I pat beneath his shoulder with my hand. "Sure, you haven't. Now, follow me to my house, *Doc*."

It's a damn miracle when he finally climbs into his car as I'm starting mine. About ten minutes later, we're pulling into a parking spot in front of the bar. The parking lot isn't very full, but that's not surprising, even for a Saturday afternoon. Meg and Dr. Braylon—I guess maybe I should call him *Doug* outside of the free clinic—are already here, as is Scott, Meg's boyfriend.

William and I draw closer to the table they're sitting at, and he's still stiff as ever. Meg smiles when she sees us. "Yay, you're here!"

"A round of shots for the birthday girl?" I ask, hiking my thumb over my shoulder toward the counter.

Her eyes widen with excitement. "Yes, let's!"

William groans beside me, but it's quiet enough that I'm sure only I heard him. I chuckle to myself as I head to the bar and order a round of tequila shots. By the time I bring them back to the table, William has found himself a seat beside Doug, and much to my pleasure, the only other open one is right next to him. Setting down the tray of shots, I sidle up beside William before passing the tequila out.

"To Meg," I announce, holding my glass up. "May this be the best twenty-first year of your life."

She snorts. "I'm twenty-seven, dork."

"Yeah, says who? Drink up, birthday girl."

We all toss the liquid back; some of us better than others. Meg's boyfriend almost pukes as he downs the liquor. *Wimp.*

"Are you doing anything with your family for your birthday?" William asks.

Meg nods. "Yeah, we're going to Cheyenne next weekend for a little trip. It should be fun."

"How long have you two love birds been together?" I ask, indicating between Meg and Wimp Boy.

Glancing at him, there're practically hearts in her eyes. She smiles before glancing back to me. "It'll be three years next month."

As casually as I can, I lean back in my chair, letting my leg inch over, right up against William's. My ankle rubs his, and I have to bite the inside of my cheek to keep from grinning at the way his body stiffens beside me.

"How'd you meet?" I ask.

Meg dives into a semi-interesting story about how she and Gags McGee were set up on a blind date through mutual friends over the holidays. There was ice skating and hot chocolate and mistletoe involved. But I'm finding it rather impossible to listen when the pressure of William's calf is brushing against my own. When I can see out of my periphery the way the vein in his neck is throbbing, and the way his Adam's apple rolls in his throat when he swallows harshly. When I can see the way his chest rises and falls a little quicker as his breathing gets more rapid. There's something so... alluring, so intoxicating, about knowing I have the ability to affect a man of his caliber the way that I do. The way a single brush of my foot sends him into a panic. The way I'm willing to bet a year's worth of rodeo winnings that if I were to reach over right now and cup him through his pants, I know I'd find him hard for me. And that little tidbit of information has my cock thickening in my jeans as the time goes on.

We end up ordering some nachos and mozzarella sticks for the table, along with a pitcher of beer. The conversation flows easily, and even William seems to be relaxing a bit. And what a perfect time to fuck with him some more. Sitting back in my chair, I kick my legs wide, the side of my thigh now pressing against his. He visibly stiffens immediately, but he doesn't pull his leg away. A quick glance around the area tells me that nobody is watching us, so I stealthily bring my hand under the table, running my palm across the top of his thigh. The muscles tense beneath my touch, and I hear William exhaling roughly. Poor guy's probably ready to explode.

Maybe I should stop...

Who the fuck am I kidding? I'm not doing that.

"Doug," I murmur, my gaze finding him across the table. "How're Heather and the kids?"

"Oh, they're good." He smiles in that faraway way that somebody does when they start talking about their spouse and children. "My youngest started karate last week."

As he pulls out his phone to show the table all the pictures, I squeeze William's thigh before inching a little farther in. My palm rubs up and down as we all listen to Doug explain his kid's first class and how it went. With my free hand, I grab my beer, bringing the chilled glass up to my lips as I take a sip. When I set it back down on the table, I glance quickly at William, finding him stock still, jaw clenched as he watches Doug, pretending to be paying attention when I know for a fact his mind is everywhere but this conversation.

Before I have a chance to move my hand any closer to

where I really want to go, he reaches under the table, placing his hand on top of mine, squeezing. His hand is warm and soft against mine, and I allow myself a moment to relish the feel of it before I turn my hand over, linking our fingers together. A bolt of electricity and arousal settles through my veins as I hold his hand in mine, like it's the most natural thing in the world for us to do.

Yes, I'm mostly doing it because I know this isn't what he was intending when he grabbed me, and I'm sure it's annoying him. But also… I'm kind of taken aback by how much I like it. How much I don't want to let go. Surprisingly, he doesn't pull away right away. Doug finishes gushing about his family, all while, the soft heat from his palm radiates into mine. And when he does finally withdraw, I find myself missing the touch almost immediately.

I don't care how I do it, but I will have William underneath me again by the end of the night, whether he knows it or not.

I need him on a visceral level. Need to be touched by him. Kissed by him. *Held* by him… What would that be like? I'm not a cuddler, but something about his big, strong arms has me wondering what it would feel like to try.

I'm in trouble, but I can't find it in me to care. This can never go anywhere, so I may as well enjoy it for what it is while I can—some hot, low-down fun.

CHAPTER 24

WILLIAM ANDINO

It's nearly five o'clock by the time we leave the bar, and my body is so damn keyed up I can hardly think straight, let alone get in my car and properly operate the vehicle. I've been on edge since the minute Colt sat down beside me. I'm surprised I was able to tame my stiff fucking erection before it was time to get up.

That would've been fun to try to explain to my colleagues.

"That was fun," Colt quips from the passenger seat. I clench my jaw, my grip tightening on the steering wheel. *Fun.* Sure. Right. A whole hell of a lot of fun being fondled under the table while my business partner told us about his karate kicking toddler. *A fucking blast.*

I don't bother responding. He's either delusional or he's trying to get under my skin. My guess goes to the latter, so gracing him with any sort of a response is just fueling his fire. A fire I don't need raging between us. All I have to do is drop him off at his house, then leave, and I'll be fine. It's that simple.

I can do that. I'm a strong-willed man. A fucking doctor,

for Christ's sake.

So, then why are my palms sweating and my heart racing?

The radio is turned off, so there's nothing to occupy my mind during this drive that seems to be taking forever. Colt must notice the absence of music because after a moment he starts humming. It takes me a moment to place the tune, and then it clicks...

"Is that *Dust on the Bottle?*" I ask him before I can stop myself.

Flashing me with a crooked grin, Colt nods. "Sure is."

Good God. That's one of my favorite songs.

"Do you always drive with no music on?" he asks when I don't say anything back. "Reminds me of Whit."

"Whit doesn't listen to music?"

"He does, just not when he drives. It's bizarre."

Arching a brow, I glance at him out of the corner of my eye. "Why is that bizarre?"

Colt scoffs like he can't believe I'd ask such an idiotic question. "Because Doc," he starts, shifting in his seat so his body is facing me. His hands move animatedly as he speaks, something I've noticed he does a lot when he's really into what he's talking about. "There's nothing better than driving down a back road with the windows rolled down and the music cranked way up loud. It's... freeing," he adds. "And exhilarating."

Typically, I do enjoy a good tune as I'm driving, and truth be told, I'm not entirely sure why the radio is turned off right now. I think it's just that my thoughts are loud enough to occupy me.

"What's your favorite song to listen to while you drive?" I ask him, although I'm not sure why. Conversing with Colt about anything personal is about the last thing I should be doing.

"Shoot, that's an impossible question." Making the mistake

of flitting my gaze over to him, he's wearing a bright smile that makes his green eyes glimmer. It's a breathtaking sight. I tighten my fist around the steering wheel as I return my attention to the road while Colt continues. "There's no way I could pick. What about you?"

I pause for a moment. Not because I don't have an answer, but I'm unsure if it's wise to share it with Colt. Even if it's just a song, it's like letting him get to know me outside of the bedroom is a disaster waiting to happen. "Well, the song you were humming is a great one, but there's only one right answer, especially if it's a warm summer evening."

"Yeah? And what song is that?"

"*Sweet Home Alabama.*"

Colt whistles. "Lynyrd Skynyrd, can't go wrong there." Then he pulls out his phone before reaching for the dash.

"What are you doing?"

"Gimme a second," he offers, that damn smirk still on his face. A moment later, a familiar guitar intro reaches my ears, and I can't help the grin that tugs on my lips. "Roll your window down," he orders as he turns the volume up and rolls his own down.

"No," I grunt, now biting the inside of my cheek to hide the smile.

Colt reaches over, smacking my thigh with his palm. "Just do what I say, Doc," he shouts. The smile weaves between his words, and it's enough to make me crack. Glancing over at him, putting on my best bored expression, I press my finger down on the button that rolls my window down. His smile widens. "There we go!"

Turning the volume up even louder, Colt plays the air drums—perfectly, might I add—as he sings along to the lyrics like nobody is watching. I'm finding it hard to keep my eyes on the road because the urge to watch him is much stronger. Luckily, it's not long before I'm turning into his driveway. As soon as I put the car in park in front of his house, I shift in my seat, taking in the carefree man in my passenger seat.

The one who very much shouldn't be there.

The one I shouldn't be enamored with.

The one with the backwards hat and the crystalline eyes and the warm, bubbly personality that you can't help but bask in like a cat lying in the afternoon sun on the back porch.

Colt is a ray of sunshine. A tight hug. He's Saturday morning coffee, and a Sunday afternoon nap. He's all of those things, and I feel it true right in the center of my chest. The dull ache that I want to gnaw at with my knuckle because this isn't how it should go. It's not how it should be. In no world should I be looking at the son of my best friend the way that I am. In no universe should I gaze at him and feel warmth settle in my bones.

I shouldn't want to sit right here and watch him for hours.

Shouldn't want to pull him into me and crash my mouth against his. Taste his desire. Shouldn't have a burning ache for him the way that I do.

Something so wrong has never felt so damn good.

The song comes to an end, and it's like all of the oxygen has been sucked out of the vehicle at the same time. The air is thick, and sweat lines the back of my neck. My pulse soars as his gaze lands on mine. Humor leaves his eyes, replaced with something dark and carnal. Like everything I was just thinking, he's thinking too.

My throat tightens.

Mouth runs dry.

Colt's tongue pokes out, pink and glistening, as he wets his lips. A movement I somehow feel everywhere.

"Come inside with me, Doc." He says it so simply. Effortlessly. A barely-there smirk... not a taunt. A request. A plea.

I want to. I'd be a bold-faced liar if I claimed I didn't.

Drop him off, then leave. It's the fucking plan.

Clearing my throat, eyes dropping to the center console, I say softly, "I can't do that."

Without missing a beat, Colt replies, "Yeah? And why is that?"

Again, there's no taunting in his tone.

I can't respond as my gaze flickers up, meeting his, a rush of heat flooding my veins at seeing the way he's biting down on his bottom lip. The smirk. The air of confidence that surrounds him. The sex appeal that comes so naturally to him.

Every. Little. Thing.

"You think you couldn't keep your hands to yourself if we were behind closed doors?" he asks, voice huskier than before.

Turning my head, I look straight ahead, breathing harshly through my nose. In a move I don't see coming, Colt hooks his index finger under my chin, forcing my head back in his direction until I'm looking him in the eye.

"Answer the question, Doc."

Goosebumps bloom all over my body. "I know I couldn't," I admit quietly. Cowardly. And it's true; even one more minute alone with Colt, and I know I'd be all over him.

Brow raised, Colt cocks his head. "And why exactly would that be such a bad thing?"

"You know why," I growl.

His hand drops from my chin. "No, actually, I don't." Lifting his hat off his head, he brushes his fingers through his hair before putting it back in place. "The way I see it," he goes on, "is that you want me, and I want you. It doesn't get much clearer than that. Not everything needs to be a fucking existential crisis. Sometimes it's okay to give in to your desires, no questions asked."

I huff out a breath through my nose before gritting out, "Not when you're you and I'm me. Do you not see how fucked up this is, you and me? I'm your dad's—"

"Best friend," he finishes for me, rolling his eyes. "Yeah, I fucking get it, William. Trust me, I get it. Get off your fucking high horse." Nearly choking on my own spit, I cough, clearing my throat. "The line has been crossed, Doc. Hell, the line's been obliterated. You're constantly saying one thing and doing another. You invite me over in the middle of the night, fuck me damn good, and then act like there's nothing going on between us. Get over yourself. Live a little and do something you want for a fucking change. He doesn't have to know. I can keep a secret."

Something red-hot surges inside of me. I want to say it's anger, but I don't think it is. It's something deeper, something more... lecherous. Something akin to yearning. I grit my teeth, holding my breath as Colt leans forward, bringing his face so close to mine I catch a whiff of his aftershave.

"I'm giving you two options. Either do what you really want and come inside with me, or I'm climbing in your lap, right here and now, for all my neighbors to witness." Sitting back, looking too fucking pleased with himself, he adds, "Your pick."

An angel and a *very* insatiable devil sit on either shoulder, both shouting at me, one becoming significantly louder than the other as the seconds pass.

But you know what... Colt's right. The line has been crossed, so why not cross it again?

To hell with the fucking plan.

The devil wins.

Eyes never leaving his, I turn off the ignition and pocket my keys. The faintest of smirks crosses his face as we both get out without another word exchanged. The energy between us pulsates as I follow him along the pathway toward his front door. Colt retrieves his house keys from his jeans pocket, and as he slides it into the deadbolt, I can't help but sweep my gaze around the area, the paranoid part of myself needing to know that nobody is watching us.

The second he gets the door unlocked, we barrel through, bodies colliding and lips crashing. Shoving the door shut with my foot, we blindly walk farther into the house, but we don't get far before Colt rips his mouth from mine. Heated eyes on me, he reaches behind himself, tugging the shirt over his head. I do the same. As soon as the material hits the floor, it's like a mad dash to see who can get naked the fastest. Kicking out of our shoes, Colt flicks the buttons on his Wrangler jeans while I untie the strings to my scrub pants, and we both push them down like they're on fire.

Once we're free of any clothes, Colt rakes his gaze appreciatively down my body as I do the same, but it's short-lived as we're on each other like glue in the very next moment. Hands come up to my chest, shoving me until I connect with the back of the couch. Movements hurried and needy, his lips meet mine, tongue pressing into my mouth like he can't get his fill fast enough. My hands find his hips as our bodies align, becoming flush with one another. I'm already hard, and so is he, and the feel of his rigid length brushing against mine has a moan pulling from my throat.

Colt kisses me fiercely, and I give it back to him just as hard. Everything about this moment feels animalistic. Carnal.

Like neither of us could've gone a single second longer without indulging in each other. This need I have for him burns like molten lava. It wraps around my bones, squeezing. It's a force not to be reckoned with. There's no denying this connection between us. This hunger.

Breaking the kiss, Colt spits into his palm, reaching between our bodies to take us both in his wide, tight fist. The first touch is like an electric shock; I feel it from my head all the way down to my toes. It energizes me. Awakens something inside of me. Pumping us steadily, Colt's mouth seeks mine out once more, only gentler this time. Tongue caressing mine, teeth nipping at my lip, he kisses me like we have all the time in the world. He kisses me like he's cataloging it to memory.

My hands grip the back of the couch as my head drops back, Colt's lips working a hot, wet path along my jaw and down to my throat, his hand never faltering. My body is on fire, every nerve ending lit up with this need for him.

"Fuck, Colt," I gasp as he drags my earlobe between his teeth.

"Like that, Doc?" His voice is like warm honey dripping down my chest.

"Yes," I grit out. "But I need more."

"You wanna fuck my tight little hole again?"

He's going to be the death of me. "Yes."

Suddenly, his hands and lips are gone, and before I can complain, he's rounding the couch, opening the drawer in the side table, and he pulls out a bottle of lube.

Brow raised, I ask, "You keep lube in your side table?"

His lips tip up on one side. "Never know when it'll come in handy." Handing it to me, he adds, "Clearly."

The vision of him doing this very same thing with somebody else in this very spot flashes through my mind, souring the back of my throat, but I push it away. I can't think about that right now, nor should I care.

Colt faces the couch, planting his hands on the back as I position myself behind him. Glancing over his shoulder, he smirks as he arches his back beautifully for me. "Prep me for your fat cock, Doc."

My length twitches as a rush of heat shoots down my spine. Without thinking, I drop to my knees behind him, the lube falling to the ground as I spread him with my hands. Running the flat of my tongue along his crease, his flavor explodes on my tastebuds, and it has me drunk on him instantly. With a groan, he pushes back onto my face until I'm happily suffocating on all of him. My tongue lashes out against his puckered hole as I reach between his legs, grabbing his stiff cock, stroking it as I get his entrance nice and softened. As he relaxes, I lean back, grab the lube, and coat my fingers.

There's no finesse to this next part. Easing a finger into his tight ass, I thrust in and out before adding a second digit to the mix. Continuing to pump his cock in my hand, I take a bite out of his round, pert cheek, my dick twitching and leaking at the sounds coming out of him. Working a third finger in, I stretch him as quickly and as thoroughly as I can, not wanting to hurt him, but needing to be inside of him as soon as possible. Once I'm sure he's good and prepped, I stand up, coat my cock in a generous amount of lube, and line myself up.

Colt glances at me from behind, my hand gripping his shoulder as my other holds myself at the base. His gaze connects with mine as I slowly sink into him inch by inch. Jaw slack, eyes glassy, he lets out the sexiest moan as I fully seat myself inside his tight, hot, velvety channel.

"Fuck…" My eyes roll back as I give us both a moment to

adjust. "You feel like fucking heaven, baby."

He hums, throwing me a look over his shoulder, a glint in his eyes. "Then what are you waiting for?" he asks, mischief dancing in his big, round orbs. "Fuck me like you own me."

Huffing out a laugh, I tighten my grip on his shoulder, my other hand finding his hips. "Careful what you wish for," I mutter, pulling all the way out to the tip before slamming back into him roughly.

Colt gasps, the sound quickly morphing into one of pleasure as my hips find a steady rhythm against his ass. Nails biting into the flesh of his hip, I grit my teeth as I let myself get lost in Colt once again.

"Is this what you wanted?" I growl.

"Fuck! You know it is."

"Tell me... have you been fantasizing about me fucking this tight, slutty ass since you first saw me this morning?"

"Yes!" he pants while he white knuckles the back of the couch, his head dropped between his shoulders.

"So. Fucking. Needy." Each word is accentuated with a brutal slap of my hips against his body. "Taunting me and teasing me at the bar. You love that, don't you?"

Pushing back, meeting me thrust for thrust, he grunts out, "So do you, Doc. *Fuck.* Don't act like you haven't made yourself come to the memory of you fucking me last time."

"You'd like to think that, wouldn't you?"

"I'm. Right," he growls, arching deeper, pushing back harder.

Sweat drips down my back, my heart pounding as he fucks himself just as hard as I'm fucking him. "You're so desperate for my cock, aren't you, boy?"

"I fucking love it." Colt's voice is hoarse, drenched in lust and arousal. "But so do you. Fucking admit it."

"No."

"You're not fooling anybody, Doc." A long, low moan escapes him as I prop my knee up on the couch beside him, hitting him from a different angle. His hand flies to my leg, the blunt tips of his nails biting into my skin.

We're so lost in the moment, deaf to the world, as the sound of our bodies crashing and writhing together fills the air. Nothing matters outside of what we're doing right this second. It's how we both manage to miss the front door opening until it's too late.

"Oh, fuck!" someone behind me blurts out with a chuckle.

Colt and I both freeze, our heads snapping to the voice, and my heart plummets as my eyes land on Shooter Graham, standing in the entryway of Colt's house, the front door still wide open. His gaze darts between me and Colt before he walks backward out the front door, shutting it after him. Just as I'm about to pull out of Colt, he reaches behind himself, grabbing onto me.

"Don't fucking stop," he growls.

"Colt, we can't keep going. Your friend just walked in on us." I say this while making no effort whatsoever to leave his body.

"Don't mind me!" Shooter calls out, words muffled by the door. "I'll wait right here. You two finish whatever the hell that was."

Colt's body shakes with laughter as I hang my head, sighing. *Fucking hell.*

"This is not funny, Colt."

"Yes, the fuck, it is."

"One question before I let you guys get back to doing the nasty," Shooter hollers out again. "Why the fuck didn't I know you were getting dicked down by our doctor, Colt? I thought we were buddies!"

"Oh, for fuck's sake," I mutter as I pull my softening cock out of Colt and reach for my pants. This cannot be happening.

CHAPTER 25
COLT BISHOP

Shooter couldn't have shittier timing, I swear to God. William and I get dressed in complete and utter silence, as he's most likely panicking. He won't even look at me. Shit. Buckling my jeans, I grab my hat where it fell off earlier, placing it on my head as I glance over at William. He's tying the strings to his pants, his jaw tight and his brows set in a hard line.

"You good?" I ask.

Eyes drifting up to meet mine, they narrow as he scoffs at me. "No, Colt, I am not *good*. Your friend, who, may I say, clearly has no boundaries and should learn to knock—"

"Hey, I heard that!" Shoot chimes in through the door, and I have to bite the inside of my cheek to keep from laughing. William finds nothing about this funny.

"As I was saying," William grits out, running a hand through his hair. "Your friend just walked in on us having *sex*." He says the word like he's a little boy trying to hide his porn stash from his parents. "There's nothing *good* about that."

Scrubbing a hand over my mouth to hide my grin because he's sexy as fuck when he gets all huffy, I clear my throat. "I just meant, are you decent enough for me to let Shooter in?"

His jaw clenches as he stands up straight, brushing a hand down his abdomen as his nostrils flare on a heavy exhale. He looks from me to the door, then back at me. "Yes, that's fine."

I cross the room in a few long strides as William reaches for his shoes. Pulling the door open, Shooter's already waiting for me, a shit-eating grin on his face. "You guys could've finished," he drawls as he steps past me into the house. Internally, I groan, knowing whatever is about to come out of my friend's mouth isn't going to bode well with William and his current state of fight-or-flight.

"What're you doing here, man?"

"Uh, what do you mean?" he asks, looking positively offended. "We had plans."

Staring at him, befuddled for a moment, it clicks. "Oh, shit, you're right. We did."

I completely forgot that Shooter and I made dinner plans tonight to check out this sushi place they just opened right outside of town. His boyfriend, Sterling, doesn't like sushi, and he asked if I'd go with him. How the fuck did I space that?

Shooter snorts as if he can read my mind. "Given the way Dr. Andino just had you pinned to the couch with his cock in your—"

"Alright, okay," William growls. "That's about enough from you. I will be leaving now."

"You don't have to go," I murmur, even though I know it's futile. He's practically one foot out the door already.

"Yes, I do." He still won't look at me, but he has no problem looking Shooter right in the eye as he points a finger at him. "I trust you to keep this to yourself?"

My God, he's so serious. The vein in his forehead is about to burst.

Shooter, looking like a kid who just got caught with his hand in the cookie jar, pinches his lips together as he nods. "Yes, sir."

I don't think I've ever seen him look so shocked.

Finally, William's gaze flits to mine, but only for a moment. "Very well."

Then he leaves. *Very well?* The man gets caught balls deep in somebody, and he turns into an eighty-year-old professor? Shooter and I don't say anything for a moment. The sound of William's car door shutting and the engine starting reaches my ears, and I finally glance over at Shooter, who's already watching me. Laughter bubbles up his throat as I shake my head, a rogue smile splitting my face.

"This is bad," I curse, bounding down the hallway toward my room, needing to change before we leave. Although, now I don't even want to go. If I'm being honest, I'd rather follow William. Yes, to finish what we started—because that was insanely fucking hot—but also to smooth things over. He was already on edge and not wanting to take things there with me, but *now* that he knows somebody knows, he'll never want to touch me again.

And oddly enough, that makes my stomach clench in a way that's foreign to me. I don't like it.

It's no surprise to me when I hear Shooter's footsteps following behind me. "I'm going to need a little fucking clarification here," he drawls.

"What you need," I call out, "is to learn to knock, my friend."

He scoffs. "Not you too."

"Well." I laugh as I rip my shirt over my head, tossing it in the hamper as I pull a new one out of the closet. "I knock when I come over to your house. People do that, you know. It's called common courtesy."

Flopping onto my bed, Shooter rests his hands under his head. "Oh, fuck off." He huffs out a chuckle. "You're just mad that I scared your fuck buddy away."

"He's not my fuck buddy, and I'm not mad. Get your fucking shoes off my bed, you animal."

Flipping on the light in the bathroom, I hear the sound of his boots hitting the floor as I reach for the stick of deodorant.

"So, how long has that been going on?" he asks.

"I don't know, not long."

"Well, what I saw definitely looked far too comfortable for a first time, so how long? A few weeks? Months?"

I chuckle to myself, knowing it's driving Shooter nuts, not knowing. "We made out at my dad's birthday party."

He's quiet, most likely doing the math in his head. "That wasn't all that long ago."

"Yeah... and there was that time when I was twenty-one..."

Wait for it...

"What the fuck?" Chuckling, I turn my head, watching as Shooter sits up, eyes trained on me. "This has been going on for multiple years, and I'm just now finding out about it?"

"No, dipshit. Let's go. I'll explain on the drive."

Locking up the house, we opt to take his truck. As soon as we hit the road, I give Shooter the CliffsNotes version of the history between William and I, starting with our very memorable one-night stand in Seattle.

"Well, I'll be damned," he mutters when I finish. "You sneaky bastard. Does your dad know?"

Turning my head and staring at him, deadpan, I ask, "What the hell do you think? It was never meant to happen more than the one time, but it just… kind of did."

Shooter laughs, pulling into the parking lot of the restaurant. "This is blowing my mind, Bishop. But hey, good for you, my friend. That is one fine-ass doctor, and by the looks of it, he damn well knew what he was doing to you."

Despite myself, I feel my cheeks flame. I don't even know why; it's not like Shooter and I have never talked sex before. We've known each other since we were kids, so it's definitely a topic that's come up a few dozen times over the years. But something about sex *with William* feels different. Personal. Sacred almost. That's fucking dumb to think.

Clearing my throat, I glance over at Shooter, flash him a sardonic smirk, and say, "Yeah, well, thank to you, it's probably the last time we'll be doing that."

"Oh, I doubt that," he chuffs.

"He couldn't even look at me before he left. There's no way he'll want a repeat." William has always been a little flighty, but he seemed pretty agitated when he left, which makes me think he won't brush it off as easily as I'd like him to. I try to ignore the way that leaves a bad taste on the back of my tongue.

Shooter takes the keys out of the ignition, but doesn't make any move to get out of the car yet. Turning my head, I find him watching me, an expression on his face I can't read. It's unnerving.

"What?"

"You…" His smirk grows as he shifts in his seat, his body facing me. "You have feelings for this guy."

"What?" I scoff, looking away. "I do not. We're having sex. That's all."

He snorts. "Right, because I believe that."

"Well, it's the truth, so…"

"You forget that I, too, was very much in denial about my feelings not that long ago, and I sounded an awful lot like you do right now."

Scrubbing a hand over my face, I heave a sigh, reaching for the door handle. "We going to go inside to eat or what?"

Chuckling, Shooter follows my lead, exiting the truck. "Fine, we'll drop it. For now."

Spoiler alert: we didn't drop it. But the sushi was good, so there's that. Shooter brought me back home about a twenty minutes ago. As soon as I got through the door, I sent a text message to William, and haven't heard back yet. Granted, he could just not be near his phone or he could be busy, but I think the more likely conclusion is that he's ignoring me. Or avoiding the message altogether.

And I don't like that. Don't like it one bit.

Which is why I'm currently in my truck, driving over to his place like a lunatic who has lost his ever-loving mind. After seeing the look on William's face when he left earlier, I haven't been able to shake this feeling that I have to *fix* this. But why, though? It's the million-dollar question I haven't been able to figure out. I'm no stranger to a hookup, but never have they felt like this. This need to get to know William. The need to be near him. To breathe the same air. To make him laugh, make him loosen up a little bit.

Earlier in his car, the way he watched me as I sang along to that song like an idiot… it warmed me, made me feel a way I wasn't used to. The smile on his face and the way it made the creases on the outside of his eyes deepen. It lit up his whole face, and it was directed at me. I want to make him smile like that more. That thought makes me uneasy, though, because I've never wanted something like that. And not even for any good reason. I've just always been so focused on rodeo and going pro, that anything else that could've potentially stolen my attention, I shut out. It didn't seem worth it to me. Relationships and feelings and all that shit weren't even on my radar. So why are they now? Why can't I shake this fucking feeling I get deep in my chest when I think about William? Why can't I accept his silence and move on?

What the fuck is it about him?

Pulling into his driveway, I turn my truck off and get out, not giving myself a moment to talk myself out of this. As I glance down at the watch on my wrist, I note it's a quarter to eight. Bringing my fist up, I knock on the door and wait. And wait. Finally, after about a minute, I hear rustling on the other side before the door is opened. Roger appears in the doorway, dressed in matching pants and shirt wiener dog pajamas.

Okay, that's fucking cute.

"Well, hi, Colt," he greets, stepping to the side to let me through. "What brings you here?"

"Is William home?" I ask, feeling like an idiot for being here at all. What good, appropriate reason would I have for showing up unannounced this late at night?

If Roger finds it weird that I'm here, though, he doesn't show it. "He's taking Winnie potty. They should be back inside in a minute." Ushering me farther into the house, he adds, "Come, come. Would you like anything to drink?"

"Oh, I'm fine. Thank you, though."

"Will told me about the birthday celebration you guys had for Meg. Sounded like a lot of fun."

For some reason, I think it's so sweet knowing that William talks to his father about his day. "It was. What about you? Did you do anything fun today?"

"Oh, Winn and I took a nice, long walk on the trail earlier. That's pretty much it."

"It was sure nice out. Sounds like a great way to spend the day to me."

"How's the shoulder treating you, son?"

"Eh, it's still not one hundred percent yet, but it's getting there."

The back sliding glass door opens before Roger can respond, and my head turns, gaze colliding with a startled pair of ocean blues. My heart clenches, not knowing how William's going to respond to me being here.

"Colt," he says lowly before clearing his throat, gaze flitting to his dad for a second before returning to me. "What are you doing here?"

Roger heaves a sigh, our attention turning to him. "I guess I'll be off to bed now." Patting his thigh, he says, "Come on, Winnie girl." That's all it takes for her to scurry after him, her tail wagging behind her. They're halfway down the hall before he turns around and adds, "Now, I hope you two are a bit quieter tonight than you were the last time you were here."

With a wink and a Cheshire cat grin, Roger turns and disappears into his room without another word, leaving William and I to sit with that bomb he just dropped on us.

Jesus fucking Christ. First Shooter, and now this. He's going to toss me on my ass before I even get a chance to say a word at this rate. Chancing a look at him, I find him as expected: jaw clenched, lips pinched, and his hardened gaze staring at the area his father was a moment ago. The air feels thicker.

Goosebumps are raised on my arms, and not the good kind.

Deciding it would be best to just cut to the chase, I say, "Can we talk?"

Gaze flitting to mine, my body heats up from the one look, the memory of what we were doing just hours ago coming back to the forefront of my mind. How good it felt to have his hands on me and his cock in me. The way his filthy words washed over me like the most potent of drugs. Experiencing William in that way—feral, hungry, and so goddamn free—is a high unlike anything I've ever experienced. He's breathtaking when he lets go.

Nodding tersely, brows set in a hard line, William mutters, "Let's go on the patio."

Well, I guess this is better than kicking me out.

Sitting in one of the spacious patio chairs, William drops into the one beside me. There's a tense silence that passes between us, and I don't like it. It's uncomfortable.

Fuck, may as well get this over with. "Shooter's not going to say anything," I blurt out. When his eyes lift, meeting mine, I add, "If that's what you're worried about."

Sighing heavily, William brushes his fingers through his hair. "I'm worried about a lot of things, and Shooter gossiping about what he saw isn't high on the list."

My brows pinch with confusion. "It's not?"

"Not necessarily, no," he mutters.

"Then why did you run out of my house earlier in such a hurry?"

"Colt..." The way he says my name, like it pains him, has my throat tightening. "Where do I even start? Aside from the obvious, that even being with you in an intimate way is a betrayal to my friendship with your father, how about the fact that you're half my age?"

Annoyance flares in my chest. "Those are fucking coward excuses, and you know it."

His eyes flash to mine, narrowing. "Excuse me?"

"It's not a betrayal to your friendship," I start, my pulse racing. "Do you have some romantic history between you two that I'm not aware of?"

"Oh, for Pete's sake, Colt," he scoffs. If I wasn't so irritated, I'd laugh. "Of course not. Don't be ridiculous."

"Okay, didn't think so. It's not a betrayal." Sitting forward, I press my elbows into my knees, my hands clasped in front of me. "Sure, he'd probably be kind of pissed if he found out, but it wouldn't be the end of the world. And who fucking cares if I'm half your age. I'm an adult, you're an adult. Everything we're doing is consensual, so why does it fucking matter?"

"Kind of pissed?" he balks. "Colt, have you met your father? He'd be more than *kind of pissed*. This is so much bigger than you and I being consenting adults, why can't you see that? I've known you since you were a baby! You don't see anything wrong with that?"

I huff. "Not really, no. It's not like this started when I was a child, and you moved away when I was a teenager, William! It had been years since I last saw you before that night in Seattle."

"You really think people would believe that?" he scoffs.

"Who fucking cares what people think!"

"Colt, I am a doctor!" he shouts before lowering his voice. "I am a goddamn professional, a respected member of this community. My reputation matters. I can't *not* care what people think. Quit being so fucking ignorant. You may be able to live however you want, do whatever you want, and not give a fuck about how the world perceives you, but I don't have that same luxury."

"Excuse me?" Blood roars in my ears as my pulse races, my body boiling.

"You're behaving like a child, throwing a temper tantrum when he doesn't get his way."

A child? "Fuck you," I spit out, standing up. "You want to talk about throwing a temper tantrum? Look in the fucking mirror, *Doc*."

William raises, grabbing my arm as I try to pass by. It takes me by surprise, my body reacting like I've been shocked. My head snaps to the side, gaze crashing with his, and for a moment neither of us says anything. It happens so fast, I don't even see it coming. One minute, his hand is wrapped around my forearm, and the next, it's hauling me into him by the back of my neck. Our mouths collide brutally and messily. There's nothing sweet or soft about this kiss, and it's over before it even has a chance to begin because as soon as my brain catches up, I shove him away with a hand to his chest.

Fuck that. He wants to act like an asshole and call me a child, he doesn't get to kiss me like nothing happened. "Don't touch me," I grit out, my head spinning from the metaphorical whiplash William is giving me. But also, maybe a little from the kiss.

Clenching his jaw, he takes a step back, putting some much-needed distance between us. "You should probably go," he murmurs.

"You think?" I huff out a laugh. "It's probably past my bedtime anyway, since, you know, I'm a child."

As I blow through the backdoor, I don't hear him following me. It's probably for the best. The entire drive home is spent in silence, my mind reeling over what the fuck happened today. It's not until I park my truck in front of my house and turn off the ignition that I realize how fucking gutted I feel. There's an ache deep in my chest that refuses to go away, and I don't understand it.

William is just a man I was fooling around with. Nothing more.

So, why does it feel like so much more than that? Why does it feel like I've lost something?

CHAPTER 26
WILLIAM ANDINO

"You want cream and sugar?" Conrad asks.

"Please."

It's been almost two weeks since everything went down with Colt, and it's been weighing heavy on my mind every day. I can't stop thinking about what I said to him. How hurt he looked, and the way he tried to hide it under his anger. I need to get all of this off my chest, maybe get some advice, and since telling Max is currently out of the question, the next best person is Conrad. Although, now that I'm here, about to do just that, my palms are sweaty. I don't think he would ever judge me, nor do I think he would go and tell Max, but this is the first time I'm admitting what's been going on to anybody. Even after my father all but announced that he knew about us, I've done my very best to avoid the topic. I'm just not ready to go there with him, or really anyone. But after he just about bit my head off this morning for the piss poor mood I've been in—his words—I can't keep it bottled in any longer.

"Here you go." Conrad hands me a coffee mug with the

Powder Ridge Arena logo on it. "Let's take these out on the porch."

Following him, I mentally prepare myself to divulge this massive secret to my friend. Truthfully, I didn't expect to be as nervous as I am. I can only imagine how it'll be when I actually tell Max.

It's not until we sit down that I realize I just mentally said *when* I tell Max, not *if*.

"You alright over there?" Conrad asks, and when I glance over at him, he's watching me warily.

I get it. I texted him this morning asking if I could stop by, gave him no reason, and I've been in my head since I got here. I'd probably be wary too if the roles were reversed. Finally, I drag in a deep breath, take a sip from my coffee, and decide to just go for it. It's not going to get any easier the longer I wait. "Listen, there's something I wanted to talk to you about," I blurt out, louder than intended.

Conrad's brows pinch with confusion. "Okay. What's up?"

"I don't know how to say this without it sounding awful, so I'm just going to spit it out." My heart pounds ferociously. "I've been… sleeping with somebody for a little while who I know I probably shouldn't. It started as a one-night stand a couple years ago, one I never thought would happen again, but then it did. Happen again, that is."

I lift my eyes, meeting his gaze, taken aback when I find them narrowed on me and his jaw clenched. He looks *pissed*. "Will, you're my friend and I love you, but so help me god, if you're about to tell me that you've been sleeping with my ex-husband, I will murder you with my bare hands and bury you on this property where nobody will ever find you."

Rearing back like I've been slapped, I shake my head.

"What?" I hiss. "What the hell are you talking about? Why would I be sleeping with Whit?"

The scowl doesn't leave his face. "Maybe because you're acting fucking weird, and you just vaguely told me how you've been sleeping with somebody you shouldn't. Who else would have you this stiff and nervous about telling me?"

"Will you relax," I mutter. "It's not Whit. It's..." Scanning the yard like I'm about to find Max watching us and overhearing everything, I lower my voice and say, "It's Colt."

Conrad's brows shoot all the way up his forehead before he lets out a deep, gruff chuckle.

"This is funny to you?" I ask incredulously.

Rubbing a hand over his mouth, he manages to pull himself together enough to say, "Could've seen that comin' a mile away."

"What the hell is that supposed to mean?"

What is happening? Are we in the twilight zone?

Conrad levels me with a look. "I didn't miss the way you two kept eyeing each other at Max's birthday party. Or the way you two came out of the house at the same time."

I'm confused before it hits me... that's the night we kissed in the bathroom. *Fuck.* "Why didn't you say anything?"

He shrugs. "Figured if you wanted to talk about it, you'd bring it up. Not my place to butt into your business where I don't belong."

This is why Conrad is one of my closest friends, and always has been. He's the most no-nonsense man and low-maintenance friend. He's there when you need him without expectations. Growing up, he was always the most level-headed one out of the three of us, and I think it's that same level-headedness I need right now.

"Well, I do," I murmur, feeling nervous all over again. "Want to talk about it."

"When did it start?" he asks before taking a drink from his water.

"The one-night stand happened about two years ago at a bar in Seattle, but it started back up again at Max's party."

Face stoic and unreadable, Conrad nods once. "I take it Max doesn't know?"

"Absolutely not. You think you wouldn't have heard it from him if he knew." I chuckle, even though it's not funny.

He nods, the ghost of a smirk on his face. "So what happened that made you want to tell me now?"

After taking a drink of my coffee, I set it on the table between us before saying, "Shooter walked in on us having sex almost two weeks ago."

Conrad's brows raise. "Damn."

Huffing out a breath, I say, "Yeah, and then I panicked and stormed out of Colt's house. He came over later that night, and we got into a pretty explosive fight where I said some shitty things."

"Like what?"

"That he was ignorant and that my reputation in the community matters, so I can't just be with whomever I want, regardless of what people think."

"Ouch. Little harsh, don't you think, Will?"

I rub a hand along my jaw, breathing out a sigh. "Yeah, I know. We haven't talked to each other since, and it's eating away at me."

My words hang in the air for a moment, Conrad thoughtfully quiet before asking, "Do you have feelings for him?"

I take my time answering the question. Not because I'm unsure, but because the answer makes me uneasy—or I should say, speaking it out loud makes me uneasy. Eventually, I nod. "Yeah, I think so. I tried to ignore it, tried to shove it down, like if I pretended it didn't exist, I could make myself stop. Tried to tell myself it was just sex, and nothing more."

Arching a brow, he asks, "Take it that didn't work?"

Breathing out a laugh, I say, "It did not. The longer we go not talking, the more my skin crawls. But I also can't ignore the concerns I have—the concerns I've always had."

"Which are what?"

If anybody is going to understand this, it's Conrad. Exhaling a heavy breath, I glance over at him. "He's twenty-three, and I'm in my mid-forties, but more than that, I've known him since he was a baby, Conrad."

Not an ounce of judgement on his face, he asks, "What did Colt say when you brought this up to him? Assuming you did."

"I did," I confirm. "He is convinced it doesn't matter because we're both adults now, and nothing started before he was twenty-one."

"What do you need from me?" There must be a puzzled look on my face because he adds, "Do you need me to simply listen and let you get this off your chest, or do you want my opinion?"

I sit up straighter, maybe subconsciously preparing for him to tell me what an idiot I am. "I'd like your opinion."

Conrad shrugs. "He's not wrong."

"But still, you don't think it's… I don't know, *wrong* that I've known him his entire life?"

"Do *you* think it's wrong?" he asks, flipping it on me. "And not what you think should be considered societally wrong, but in your heart of hearts, do you think the way you feel about Colt is wrong?"

The question makes me pause, mostly because I've never

asked myself from that angle. "No," I reply, and realize with absolute certainty that it's the truth.

"Then fuck what anybody else has to say," he grunts. "There will always be people who have an opinion on what you do, but they don't matter. You know how many people had something negative to say when Whit and I got together? Yeah, our age difference isn't as large as the one between you and Colt, but Whit wasn't even nineteen yet when we got together, and he had worked on my family's ranch since he was fifteen. A lot of people had a lot of shit to say, but in the end, none of it mattered. I knew in my heart what I felt for him, and I knew it was true and pure, and I knew there was nothing wrong with that. So fuck everybody else."

If the roles were reversed, and Conrad was coming to me for advice, I'd tell him the same damn thing. So, why is it so hard to take our own advice?

"Max deserves to know, though," Conrad goes on. "If you decide to make things right with Colt and move forward, he deserves to know. You're one of his closest friends, and if he finds out from anybody other than you, he'll be pissed. But more than that, he'll be hurt." A pang hits me right in the center of my chest at that last part. "That being said, maybe take a little time to make sure this is what you want before you let the cat out of the bag because, while I think Max will eventually get over it, I do think it'll cause a rift and take some getting used to. You should be sure of your decision before you go there. And maybe apologize to Colt for being a dick."

I can't help but chuckle.

"You're not going to tell me how selfish or idiotic I'm being?" I ask.

His brow quirks. "Do you want me to?"

"No." I shake my head. "I just assumed it was coming."

"Didn't you hear me when I said I was thirty-three when I fell in love with an eighteen-year-old Whit. Who the hell am I to judge your romantic choices?"

Huffing out a laugh, I say, "Well, when you put it like that."

"You're a responsible, good man, Will," Conrad murmurs. "I know you wouldn't do anything maliciously or without thinking it through. Besides, take it from me, you don't get a say in who the heart wants."

A moment passes before either of us says anything, and I can't help but laugh. "I can't believe you thought I was talking about Whit."

Conrad shakes his head, chest rumbling with a chuckle. "Well, you were practically sweating while trying to spit it out. What was I supposed to think?"

By the time I leave Conrad's, I know I need to talk to Colt. I need to apologize, but I also need to come clean about how I feel. About how this isn't just about sex for me anymore.

Hell, maybe it never was.

CHAPTER 27

COLT BISHOP

The top button of his shirt is undone, revealing a sneak peek of the salt and pepper smattering of hair I know is underneath it all. Just a little bit, though. A *tease*. Left hand shoved into the pocket of his Chinos, his right is holding a rocks glass filled with just about three fingers of my father's favorite whiskey.

Clenching my jaw, I bring the glass up to my lips, letting the amber liquid flood my mouth. It's smooth as it heats a path down my throat, my gaze locked on the man across the room who I haven't been able to take my eyes off since he walked through the front door fifteen minutes ago. He looks casual tonight. Relaxed. A smile stretches his cheeks as he chuckles at whatever my father is telling him, but every once in a while I'll catch his eyes flitting in my direction. Only for a split second, though.

It's been a couple of weeks since I stormed out of his house, and we haven't spoken since. I want to say I'm dealing with it, and that it's not driving me nuts, but that would be a lie. William is on my mind all the fucking time, and it's irritating.

He won't leave. And what's even more annoying is the fact that I'm probably not even on his mind at all. William's probably living his life like nothing ever happened, if that carefree grin on his face as he chats it up with my father is any indication.

It was *so* fucking easy for him to put a stop to this, like it meant nothing to him. He was constantly trying to fight against it; I should've known. What a fucking idiot I was for chasing him like some pathetic puppy. Maybe he was right, after all. Maybe I am too young. Maybe we have nothing in common. And besides that, my job takes me away for a chunk of the year—assuming I'll make it onto the circuit again—so maybe we never would've worked.

Maybe I was fooling myself.

But then a larger part of me says maybe I wasn't. Maybe we could've been good together if William was able to get over his own shit. Not that I'll ever know now.

Scoffing to myself, I rip my eyes away from him and head into the kitchen, where my mother is slicing potatoes. She informed me earlier this week that she'd like to start having weekly family dinners on Sundays now that I'm back in my own place again. I love the idea because one, I could eat my mom's cooking all day, every day and never get sick of it, and two, I knew they'd invite William, and call me a glutton for punishment, but I wanted to be around him. See if being near me affected him. See if maybe I could fuck with him a little.

But now that I'm here, and it seems like he's doing just fucking fine, I'm regretting my entire plan. I should've just stayed home. Or better yet, gone over to Shooter's house and got drunk watching football.

"Hi, honey," my mom says softly.

"Need any help?" Reaching over her, I grab a small glob of

shredded cheddar cheese, tossing it in my mouth. She's making scalloped potatoes, my favorite.

"I think I got it, but thank you." Brushing her hair out of her face with the back of her hand, she smiles up at me. "Could you maybe just check on the ham for me?"

"Sure."

Opening the oven, the heat and aroma from the honey glazed meat wafts over to me. It smells incredible. I add a little more water to the pan before shutting the door. "It smells good, Mom."

She wipes her hands on her apron, grinning. "Thank you, baby. You doing okay?"

My brows knit together. "Yeah, I'm fine. Why?"

"You seem a little off today. A little quieter than normal. Just wanted to make sure." Closing the distance between us, she brings her hand up to my arm, squeezing. "I'm always here if you need to talk. I know I'm just your mom, and you may think I don't understand what you're going through, but I was there for your father when he was injured, and I know how hard it can be mentally. But I'm here for you."

"I know, thanks, Mom."

What does it say about me that riding is the furthest thing from my mind lately? That I've been so wrapped up in this shit with William to even be upset about my injury. I can't tell if that's a good or bad thing, but it's true.

"And for what it's worth," she adds. "You seem to be healing very nicely. I have no doubt that you'll be able to compete next season if you keep it up."

I smile, knowing it probably looks as forced as it feels. "Let's hope so."

"I love you, Colt, and I'm so proud of everything you've

accomplished. You're a good man."

Swallowing around the lump forming in my throat, I say, "I love you too."

I've never been an overly emotional, in touch with my feelings type of guy, but the last few months I have been, and I don't get it. Nor do I like it. I'm blaming it on my injury and the fact that I've had a lot more downtime to think about things. Feelings are *not* all they're cracked up to be, especially when I'm standing in the kitchen with my mom feeling my nose tingle and my throat tighten, like her telling me she is proud of me may actually make me fucking cry or something.

Fuck that.

"Hey, I'll be right back. I'm heading up to my room for a minute. Think I left something in there when I moved back into my place."

Suddenly, I feel so overwhelmed. Like the weight of the fucking world is sitting right on my chest, making me feel like I can't drag in any air. *What is going on with me?* That's not the first time my mother has told me she loves me or that she's proud of me, so why is it hitting me so fucking hard? Blowing past my dad and William, I bound up the stairs, taking them two at a time before I make it down the hall to my old bedroom. Once the door is shut, I let out the breath I'd been holding, resting my back against the hard wood.

You're a good man.

Am I, though? Would she still think I was a good man if she knew what I'd done with the man downstairs? Would she still think I was a good man if she knew how much I wanted to do it again and again? Is William right? Is what we were doing wrong? Crossing the space, I sit on the edge of my bed, elbows rested on my knees as my head hangs between my shoulders.

I shouldn't have come today. Should've told my mom I was sick, and that I'd make it to the next Sunday dinner. Based on the way that William was in my every waking—and sleeping—thought, I had a feeling I was in way deeper than I'd originally intended. Clearly, I've developed feelings for the guy, just like Shooter had said. God, I fucking hate when that cocky bastard is right.

When the hell did that happen?

And how the hell did it happen?

This is *not* me. I don't crush on people. Don't get caught up in my feelings for them. Hell, I don't do feelings at all when it comes to sex. Sex has always been about fun for me. For release.

My head snaps up as the door creaks open. William walks in, a solemn look on his face as he closes it behind him. Standing up, I cross my arms over my chest. "What the hell are you doing in here?" There's a bite to my words that takes me by surprise. "You don't think it'll be a little suspicious when my dad comes looking for you and finds you in here?"

"Your mom sent him to the store for some milk and a few other things. Apparently, she didn't have enough to make the sauce."

My heart clenches as he steps farther into the room. He stops before he's too close to me. Maybe an arm's length away. "Okay, and where exactly does my mom think you are?"

"The bathroom. I asked if she needed any help, and she shooed me out of the kitchen."

"What are you doing in here?"

William's close enough that I catch a whiff of his rich mahogany scent, and it makes my head fuzzy. His ocean eyes gaze at me imploringly before he utters, "I'm sorry, Colt."

The apology takes me by surprise, and for a moment, I

don't know what to say. "What? Sorry for what?"

Taking another step closer, my breath hitches at his new proximity. His eyes dip down to my mouth before coming back up. "For everything I said at my house the last time you were there. I was freaked out over getting caught by your friend, and I lashed out. I didn't mean any of it."

I let his words wash over me as my breaths come a little quicker. I want to take comfort in them, lean into them, but something makes anger flare in my gut. "If you're so sorry and you didn't mean it, then why the hell didn't you reach out to me? It's been radio silence from you since I left that night."

William sighs. "I want to say it was because I was trying to give you space. You made it clear that night that you were upset—and rightfully so—but I think if I'm being honest with myself—and you—it's probably because I'm still very nervous about all of this."

"Yeah, you made that perfectly clear before."

"I know," he murmurs. "But I'm having a hard time with the way I feel about you lately, and the guilt that comes from knowing I'm keeping something from Max. I pride myself on being an honest man and a good friend, and I feel like I'm not being either of those things right now."

Biting down on my molars, I breathe out harshly through my nostrils. "Well, then I guess it's a good thing that whatever this was between us is over."

Something like disappointment passes through William's eyes, but that can't be right. Why would he be disappointed when he was the one to put a stop to this. But that's confirmed when he places his hand on my hip and steps even closer. My breath hitches.

"That's the thing... I don't want it to be over."

What?

My heart pounds so powerfully, I'm certain William can hear it with how close he is to me. I don't say anything; I don't think I could even if I wanted to. My throat is tight, mouth dry as I gape at him.

"I made a mistake, Colt," he goes on. "I let my fear get the best of me, but I miss you."

I miss you… Those three words nearly stop my heart.

I square my shoulders, biting down on my tongue hard enough to make it bleed. "Well, that's too bad. You were right when you ended it. It's for the best." The words are like chalk in my mouth. I don't mean them, but my pride won't let me back down. He hurt me that night, even if I refuse to admit it, and I don't take kindly to being hurt, especially when it's not that easy to get under my skin. Not much gets to me. The same way William prides himself on being an honest man, I pride myself on being easygoing and generally happy.

The grip he has on my hip tightens, sending a layer of goosebumps all over my body, and the way he's looking at me—intense and desperate—has me wanting to look away. But I don't. I can't. It's like William's got me under some sort of spell.

"You don't mean that," he grits out.

"Yes. I do." The words sound weak even to my own ears. How is it possible that he can read me so damn well? What is happening to me?

His brows dip inward. "Colt, please."

It feels like thick, wet concrete is coating my throat as I swallow. The backs of my eyes sting, and I grit my teeth before muttering, "We can't."

William works his jaw, his gaze hardening. "Like hell we

can't," he growls, the gruff sound of his voice startling me and exciting me all at the same time. The hand holding my hip snakes around my back, hauling my body into his as his other hand comes up, cupping the back of my neck. His mouth is on mine before my mind even has a chance to catch up. Lips harsh and unforgiving, his tongue surges into my mouth, wholly owning mine, kissing me like his life depends on it. My head is dizzy, heart thrashing behind my ribs as my hands come up, fingers gripping the front of his shirt. I'm not even sure if I'm trying to hold him to me or push him away, not that I have much of a choice with the way he's holding on to me. I'm trapped in his grip, and in this moment, I don't even fucking care.

Eventually, my body relaxes and melts into his touch, and I tilt my head, letting him take the kiss deeper. His tongue glides against mine, and his taste explodes in my mouth. The whiskey he was drinking, and the sheer hunger he has for me, are potent and intoxicating all at once. Heat sears down my spine, pooling in my groin, and before long, my cock is rock hard and aching behind my pants. I'm desperate for more, and like William can read my mind, he rips his mouth from mine as he drops to his knees before me.

Holy shit.

My gaze darts over to the door behind him, noting that he somehow managed to lock it when he came in here without me noticing. *That dirty fucking man.* Shit, that's hot. His movements are hurried as he gets the button and zipper down on my jeans, wasting no time pulling my stiff length out. Something about the way he doesn't even bother sliding my pants down just really fucking does it for me.

Peering up at me from beneath his lashes, he fists my shaft as he takes the tip of my cock into his mouth. His wet heat wraps around me, feeling like heaven as his tongue swirls around.

"Fuck, you look damn good on your knees for me, D." My voice is guttural, a groan vibrating from my chest as he sinks down further, taking more of me, not stopping until I'm seated in his throat. He swallows around the head, the tightness making my eyes roll back. There's no easing into this, no taking his time. William sucks me down like it would kill him to go another second not consuming me. He takes me deep and sucks me hard, like he's making up for lost time. Like he's making sure I know how sorry he is.

William moans, his mouth stuffed full, and the sound sends vibrations through my whole body. I thread my fingers through his thick, styled hair, gripping the strands but letting him control the pace. He looks so fucking sexy, taking me in his mouth like that. Wet, red-rimmed eyes, flushed cheeks, swollen lips stretched wide.

"Pull yourself out," I rasp. "Let me see how you stroke your fat cock while you swallow mine down."

As if he was waiting for permission, he hurries up and opens his pants, stuffing a hand inside to pull himself out, and just as I figured, he's already hard and ready to go. My mouth waters at the sight, even more so when he wraps a tight fist around the shaft, pumping his hand up and down as he continues to throat me.

"That's it," I moan, taking in the sight. "You like sucking my cock, don't you?"

He nods, humming around my length.

"It gets you off, doesn't it?"

Another nod.

I cluck my tongue at him, smirking as I gaze at him down

my nose. "Choking on the cock of your best friend's son. What a filthy fucking man you are."

William moans, his eyelids fluttering closed. The entire length of my body is one long strip of live wire. My skin tingles, my chest is tight, and flames swim through my veins. Everything about this moment has my head dizzy, like I'm floating.

My muscles tighten, and I know I'm not going to last much longer. Not with the view I'm graced with.

"You wanna swallow my cum, Doc?" Another moan as he nods. His fist is flying up and down his cock now, and I'm desperate to see him let go. Watch him explode. "Eyes up here," I growl, and his gaze immediately finds mine. "Look me in the fucking eyes as I come. God, your mouth feels so good. That's it, *mmm*... fuck, that's good."

My release hits me like a hurricane, taking hold of my body as I empty myself down his throat. I cry out, unable to care about how loud I'm being. Wave after wave crashes into me as my orgasm feels never ending. I swear I even black out for a moment. William pulls off my mouth, standing up as he shoves me onto my knees. My lips part, tongue sticking out as I peer up at him. His fist is steady, working his cock over, and I know he's near the edge. He's falling apart, and it's a beautiful fucking sight.

"You drive me crazy," he growls, eyes swimming with lust as they bore into me. The tip of his cock brushes along my tongue as he strokes himself, the salty flavor of his arousal spilling onto it. It floods my senses, and I'm dying for more. For it all. "I can't get enough of you. Even when I know I should stay away, I can't. I don't want to. Fuck, I'm coming." He groans, deep and throaty, as his release coats my tongue, spurt after spurt of hot liquid flooding my mouth. Once he's finished, he drags the underside of his cock along the mess he made, gazing down at me with a sated look in his eyes. "Swallow." The single word is a deep growl that sends a shiver down my spine, and I gladly oblige, drinking him down like I've wanted to for weeks.

William's chest heaves as he fights to catch his breath, and after a moment, I stand up, tucking myself back into my jeans, and zipping them up. He does the same before running a hand through his now-mussed up hair. Movement catches out the window, and I notice my father pulling back into the driveway. I chuckle to myself. *Perfect timing.* Now that the reality of what just happened sets in, I can't help but wonder if William meant what he said or if he was simply looking for a quick nut. The air around us turns tense, and I wonder if he feels it too. Suddenly, I'm too nervous to look at him. So, I don't. Instead, I walk to the other side of the room, checking myself in the mirror above the dresser to make sure I look put together. We're clearly going to have to go back downstairs in a minute, and I can't exactly look like I just had my mind—and cock—blown.

"Colt," William murmurs softly. "Can you look at me, please?"

Steeling my spine, I turn around and, reluctantly, meet his gaze. I expect to see regret in his expression, but I don't. Not at all. In fact, it's quite the opposite. If anything, the look he's giving me is full of warmth and adoration. It takes me aback, especially when he closes the distance between us and takes my hand in his.

"Eventually, we will have to tell him," he says, not needing to elaborate. I know who *him* is. "There's no way around it, especially because I clearly can't stay away."

Swallowing thickly, I nod.

"But not yet. I want to enjoy and explore whatever this is with you before he puts in his two cents. Is that okay?"

My pulse races, hearing him admit to wanting to explore this more. Hearing I've been on his mind as much as he's been on mine.

"William, I've never once pushed you to tell my dad. All I've wanted is for you to let go of this notion that we shouldn't be doing this. So, yes, that's okay with me."

"Hey, William?" The muffled sound of my father's voice downstairs filters up, and we both stiffen at the same time.

"Shit," William mutters under his breath. "What do we do?"

A flash of something passes through William's eyes, and just like that, I'm second guessing if he'll actually be able to go through with this. If I mean enough to him to be honest with my dad. It's a punch to the gut.

He must see my doubt written all over my face, because his brows pinch together as he slips his hand into mine, tugging me closer. "Hey, don't go there," he says softly, like he can read every thought in my mind. "I mean it, I want to do this with you, and I want to tell him about us, but right now is not the right time. That doesn't mean I don't want this. We will tell him, I promise."

Leaning in, William captures my lips in a sweet, gentle kiss that makes my chest squeeze and somehow makes me feel that much better.

"You go downstairs first," I tell him. "I'll be down in a minute."

"How do I explain being up here?"

"Aren't you supposed to be the smarty pants doctor here?"

He stares at me, deadpan, making me chuckle. "Colt. Be serious, please."

"Just tell him you were using the bathroom up here because you didn't want to blow up the main one downstairs."

Pinching the bridge of his nose, he sighs. "Colt, I'm not

going to tell him that. That's ridiculous."

"Fine." I shrug. "Then tell him you were on your knees, gagging on his son's cock. Because that's definitely less ridiculous."

"I'm leaving now," he grumbles, rolling his eyes at me.

Before he can pull away, I tighten my grip on his hand, pulling him into me. Pressing another quick kiss against his lips, I whisper, "Thanks for the head, Doc."

A smile forms, brightening his face, and it makes my chest tighten. "Come downstairs in a few minutes," is all he says before he leaves.

I watch him go. *Wow.* That was not how I envisioned today going. Time to go have dinner with my parents while pretending my dick wasn't just in their friend's mouth. Should be easy enough, right?

CHAPTER 28

WILLIAM ANDINO

Colt: **I want to see you today.**

Smiling down at my phone, I climb into my car, setting my briefcase on the passenger seat. It's a little after four, and I'm just leaving the office. It's been a hectic day, and this is the first time I'm getting to look at my phone since earlier this morning. The timestamp on the message shows Colt sent that about three hours ago. Starting my car, I decide against texting him back in favor of calling. Call me old-fashioned, but I much prefer hearing his voice through the line than reading a text.

It only rings a couple of times before connecting.

"Well, hello, Doc," Colt drawls through the line, a sultry lilt to his tone that sends a zip of heat down my spine.

"Hey, I just got your text. Sorry it's taken me so long to get back to you."

"It's all good," he mutters, sounding out of breath. "I know you're a busy man."

"How was your day? What are you up to?"

"It's been a pretty great day," he replies, and I can hear the smile through the phone. "I'm at the arena, getting a little training in. Want to come by here? I should be done soon."

"Right now?" My stomach flutters as a smile spreads across my face. "Is it okay if I'm there?"

"Yeah, right now, and of course, it's okay." He breathes out a chuckle. "If you don't have anything going on."

Putting my car in reverse, I back out of my spot before heading down Main Street. "I'll be right over."

We hang up, and I spend the entire drive with my skin tingling and my heart pounding. To be honest, I kind of always thought you outgrew this nervous, jittery feeling. It was something I experienced with my ex-wife when we first started dating, but I was so young back then, and it hasn't happened since, so surely, it's something you outgrow after a certain age. But I'm coming to realize that isn't the case at all. Apparently, with the right person, those nervous, jittery tingles will hit you no matter the age. Early twenties or mid-forties, they don't discriminate. Can't say that I hate it either.

I pull up outside the arena, and he's already outside the front doors waiting for me. His signature backwards hat is replaced with a cowboy hat pulled low on his head, and he's wearing a plain white t-shirt, snug light-wash Wranglers, and a pair of cowboy boots that match the color of his hat. He's got his shoulder rested against one of the wooden beams, arms crossed over his chest, and a warm smile spread across his face. My heart kicks up as I get out of the car and approach him, mouth watering as I drink him in.

He's in his element, and it shows. The confidence, the swagger. It's sexy.

"Hey, Doc." His smile grows the closer I get.

"Hey, baby." My pulse races as soon as I say the pet name, worried he'll hate it or think it's dumb, but the opposite happens. Instead, he bites down on his bottom lip as he snakes a hand out, grabbing ahold of my shirt to tug me into him. I have to fight the way my body wants to freeze and freak out, having him grab me like this in public, but I know the parking lot is empty.

"Baby, huh?" he murmurs before pressing his mouth to mine for a slow, sweet kiss. His tongue slips past my parted lips, lazily stroking mine. "The only time you've ever said that was when you were railing me. Kinda like it both ways."

I lift a brow. "Yeah?"

"Mhm. C'mon, let's get inside before I give the passersby a show they didn't ask for."

Once we're inside, Colt leads me down the hall toward the arena. I'm familiar with the layout, thanks to the free clinic, but I haven't been in here for anything else in well over a decade. I used to come here when I was in med school to watch Max compete. It's changed a lot since then.

"You can sit on the bleachers over there." Colt points across the way. "I should be finished shortly."

Leaving me to do just that, Colt jogs into the center of the arena, where a mechanical bull waits for him. I proceed to watch as he climbs on, slipping his right hand underneath the handle, using his left hand to pull the rope tight. He wraps the loose end of the tail around his hand before scooching up and getting situated. After a few long moments, he raises his left arm, glancing straight ahead, as he nods, presumably to somebody out of sight. After a beat, the bull begins moving, slowly at first. Forward and backward, and Colt follows, body swaying rhythmically as the mechanical bull picks up speed.

This continues until the eight-second buzzer goes off. Colt hops off the bull and jogs over to the direction he nodded toward the first time, where a guy I don't recognize appears. They converse for a few moments before he mounts the mechanical bull and does it all over again. He does this several times, the speed of the bull getting faster each time, and the entire time I'm mesmerized. It's not the real deal, but I can only imagine how he'd look on the back of a live bull.

Admittedly, I've never seen him ride. Of course, I've seen photos of him during rodeo events, but never videos.

I know his injury really messed with his head, and he has doubts about whether he'll make it back out there this coming season, but I truly believe he will. Colt is ambitious and hardworking and goal oriented, just like his father was, and if anybody could recover from something like this and make it back out in less than a year, it's him.

Eventually, Colt climbs off, grabs a white towel, and wipes his forehead off as he makes his way over to where I'm sitting. His eyes meet mine, and he smiles, wide and bright in a way that makes my stomach dip and my heart race.

"Like what you see?" he drawls as he drops down on the bleachers beside me.

"I do." I nod, turning my head to look at him. "Can't wait to see the real deal."

An adorable, boyish grin slides onto his face. "You going to come see me compete, Doc?"

"I wouldn't miss it," I reply honestly.

Colt watches me with an expression I can't quite place before leaning over and placing a quick kiss on my lips.

"How was your day?" he asks.

"It was good," I say. "Work was busy with Doug on vacation,

but all in all, it wasn't a half bad day."

Peeking up at me, a smirk slides on his face. "The idea of you helping patients all day, being the only doctor there, manning the fort, really does something for me, Doc."

I huff a laugh. "Is that right? Got a doctor kink?"

"I got a William kink," he throws back with a shrug. "Everything you do does it for me, I think."

"Good to know." Crystalline eyes shimmer as they gaze into mine, warmth spreading from my chest out to the rest of my body. "What about you, what else did you do today?"

"Had physical therapy this morning, then came here."

"Yeah? How do you feel it's going?"

He grumbles a bit. "Slow as fuck."

That makes me chuckle. "Give yourself some grace, Colt. You had actual surgery on your shoulder; it's not going to go back to normal overnight."

"I know that, but we're six months from the start of the season, and I don't know what I'll do if I can't compete."

"Six months is a long time to work on physical therapy, training, and getting your strength up. I think you'll be surprised in yourself." Rubbing my hand gently up and down the side of him, I add, "And if for some reason you're not able to compete when the season starts, you'll stick with it and make sure you're ready for the next one."

Colt's quiet for a moment. Letting out a deep exhale, he says, "I know you're right, and logically speaking, my recovery is going as well as can be expected and I *am* on track to competing on the circuit, but I can't help this small, negative part of my brain that's telling me my career is slipping away from me the longer I have to wait."

"That is not true, Colt," I tell him, even though I know he

knows that. I'm well aware of how sneaky self-doubt is, and I know he's scared to follow in his father's footsteps, but these situations are just not the same. Not even close. "You're so young. Your career has just begun. You'll get back out there when your body is ready, and you'll kick some ass when you do."

Watching me for a moment, he chews on the inside of his cheek. "If I do go back on the circuit in the spring, what's that mean for us?"

The question takes me by surprise, almost as much as the uncertainty written on Colt's face. Truth be told, it's a question I've asked myself a lot lately, especially when I realized I was feeling a lot more than lust toward Colt.

"What do you want it to mean for us?" I ask, nerves taking hold of my chest.

Breathing out a nervous laugh, he looks down at his hands. "I don't know. I know it's a lot to ask from somebody. Dating a rodeo cowboy isn't easy, I'm sure."

"Dating, huh?" I lean in, nudging him with my shoulder, all the while loving how that sounds. "Are you saying I'm your boyfriend?"

Shoving back playfully, he smiles and nods. "Yeah, well, I mean... what would you call us?"

I grin, unable to bite it back. "I like the sound of boyfriend, actually."

"Yeah?" He raises a brow, biting the inside of his cheek.

"Yeah. And I don't see why you leaving would have to change anything for us," I reply softly, feeling oddly vulnerable. "If you don't want it to, that is."

"I don't," he hurries and says. "Want it to change, I mean. I know you've got work and your dad and a life of your own, but it would mean a lot to me if you came to see me on the road, maybe." Colt's cheeks darken to a deep shade of pink, and I have to bite the inside of mine to keep from smiling at how adorable he is. "I mean, I know we've got months to go, and who knows what's going to happen with us, but—"

Placing a hand on his thigh, I cut him off with a brush of my lips against his. I kiss him slowly, but deeply, making sure he can *feel* how much I mean this. Pulling back, I murmur against his lips, "I would love that, Colt."

A grin splits his face. "Yeah?"

"One hundred percent."

"Okay, cool."

I have no clue what's going to happen in the future, but I can't deny that in this moment, being here with Colt feels more right than anything I've done in a really long time.

CHAPTER 29

COLT BISHOP

"I cannot believe I let you talk me into this," William grumbles beside me as he adjusts the scarf around his neck for the tenth time in the last seven minutes. "It's freezing out here."

Chuckling, I nudge him with my elbow. "Oh, would you relax, you big grump."

"I can't relax when my body is enduring such freezing temperatures."

William's dramatics make me laugh because he's normally such a put-together man. Apparently, frigid weather is his breaking point. "Well, if you quit your bitchin', we can hurry up and find a tree, then get some hot cocoa when we're done."

Christmas is coming up in a few weeks, and it's my favorite holiday. Every year, I make it a point to fully decorate my house, both inside and out, and this year will be no exception. With some convincing, a whole lot of puppy dog eyes, and some pretty damn impressive road head—if I do say so myself—I talked William into coming with me to pick out my Christmas tree. I purposely picked one outside of Copper Lake to avoid the chance of running into anybody who may tattle on us to my parents, which is more than a little inconvenient, but neither of us is ready to take that step yet.

It's been about a month since William and I made up at my parents' house, and I think I speak for both of us when I say we've been enjoying this little bubble we're in. Not that I think telling my parents will change anything, but I do know it'll put a damper on things, and I'm just not ready for that yet. I've been really busy lately with physical therapy and training, and I've been helping out down at the arena where I can. Helping the team get ready for upcoming events or assisting with fundraisers, mentoring a high school rodeo kid; really anything to keep me busy and feel like I'm being productive, so we've only been seeing each other a few times a week. But I look forward to every moment I get to spend with him.

It's how I envision dating like it's supposed to be... something I have no prior experience with considering everybody in my past has been one, maybe two, nights before I never see them again. Something I didn't expect myself to enjoy so much. I'd be lying if I said the fact of telling my dad doesn't hang over my head like a dark cloud, though. When William and I first started fooling around, the idea of my dad finding out didn't bother me. I don't know if it's because I didn't really see this going anywhere, so telling him seemed like a far-off thing that would never happen, but lately, it's on my mind constantly. My mom's words from that day in her kitchen come back to me daily... *'you're a good man.'* Will she still think I'm a good man when all of this comes out? Am I going to disappoint her? Hurt my dad? The thought guts me, but I try to push it out of my mind because at the end of the day, like I told William, we're two consenting adults. Hopefully, that's enough. It has to be, because the more time I spend with William, the more I find myself falling for him.

Like right now, for example, when William and I are walking around the tree farm, his heavily gloved hand in mine—another thing I didn't expect to like so much—as we search for one that I like. Coupley things that seemed so cheesy and mundane to me before, now feel swoony and comforting.

After a while, we find a winner. Actually, we find two winners—one for both of our houses. Unlike *National Lampoons Christmas Vacation,* we do not chop down our own trees here, the staff handles it all for us. After informing us that they'll have the trees for us up at the front, William and I head toward the area that's heavily lit with Christmas lights, music playing, and heaters blasting all around.

"Oh, they have apple cinnamon donuts," I say with much more enthusiasm than I mean to, reading the sign while we wait in line. "You want a couple of those to go with the hot cocoa?"

That seems to perk him up. "Yeah, that sounds great."

"Why don't you go find us a seat near the heaters while I order."

Reaching for his pocket, he nods. "Okay, let me give you some cash."

"Put your money away, Frosty." I chuckle. "This was my idea tonight, so it's my treat."

He gives me the same annoyed expression he's given me every time I offer to pay. I'm coming to realize William is very old-fashioned in that sense, and while it's endearing, I make more than enough to foot the bill.

Luckily, the line moves pretty quick, and before long, I have our drinks and a white paper bag full of fresh donuts that smell way too damn good. By the time I reach William, I've already convinced myself that I'll need to order a dozen more before we leave to eat at home.

"You gonna help me decorate my house, Doc?" I ask, passing him his drink and a donut, along with a napkin. Taking a giant bite out of the cinnamon sugary pastry, I groan because it tastes even better than it smells.

"Do you want me to?" His brow raises.

"Obviously." I chuckle. "Do you think your dad will like the tree we got for your place?"

Finishing chewing first, he nods and says, "The holidays are hard on my dad since my mom died, but I think he's going to love it."

"That makes sense." My heart aches for Roger. I can't imagine being with somebody as long as he was with William's mom, celebrating each holiday every single year, and then one year, they're gone. It has to feel empty. "Maybe he can come over with you to help decorate my house, and then we can all go to yours to decorate over there. We can play some Christmas music, have some spiked eggnog, and lift his spirits."

His eyes glisten as he watches me for a moment, a smile spreading across his lips. Leaning in, he runs his tongue along my bottom lip, surprising me. "Had a little sugar," he explains with a sexy grin before pressing his mouth to mine for a sugary-sweet kiss. "Didn't take you as the Christmas spirit type," he says as he pulls back.

"Oh, I'm very serious about it," I reply in a stern voice that makes William chuckle.

"When do you leave for Vegas?"

"Next Monday," I reply before bringing the Styrofoam cup up to my mouth and taking a sip of the rich hot cocoa. Next week marks the start of National Finals Rodeo, and while I clearly won't be competing in finals this year, several of my buddies will, and I want to be there for them, so I'll be flying to Las Vegas, where the event is held.

"How are you feeling about all of that?" William asks.

"I'm excited," I say, meaning it. "Part of me wondered if I would dread the entire trip because, in all honesty, and not to sound conceited—"

"You, conceited? Never."

"Ha ha, Doc. You're so funny."

He smirks, looking pretty pleased with himself. "I know."

"As I was saying," I mutter, feigning exasperation. "Had I not been injured, I'm willing to bet my left nut that I would've made it to finals, so I worried I would maybe resent my friends for making it. Which, I know sounds shitty, but that isn't the case at all. I'm pumped to go to Vegas with a handful of my closest friends to celebrate their success. I'm genuinely so happy for them."

Nodding, he says, "I think it's natural to worry about that given your situation, Colt, but I'm glad you're able to go and be there for your friends. I'm sure they'll appreciate having you there."

Once we're finished eating, we make our way toward the front to pay for the trees. William scoffs again when I refuse to let him pay for either of them. It doesn't take long for the two of us to strap 'em both into the bed of my truck, but by the time we get into the cab, and I turn it on, William is scowling at me all over again because he's cold.

"You're kind of a baby when it comes to the cold," I muse as I pull out of the parking lot. "Has anybody ever told you that?" Shooting daggers at me, he says nothing. Laughing, I ask, "How the hell did you live your entire life in Copper Lake up until you moved away, and you're this bad at handling winter?"

"I simply don't like it," he deadpans, rubbing his hands together in front of himself so vigorously I wouldn't be surprised if he started a fire.

"Don't worry," I drawl, peering over at him before focusing on the road. "I'll warm you right up once we get back to my house."

Something like a growl sounds in the back of his throat, and he slides his hand over to my thigh, squeezing as I try to focus on driving. Having to go out of town for this damn tree really sucks when all I want to do is get home and devour William. About thirty *long* minutes later, I pull into my driveway, and I'm wound up tight. He's done nothing but tease me the whole drive. Putting the truck in park, I leave it on as I take off my seatbelt and slide onto William's lap.

He breathes out a laugh, hands finding purchase on my ass as my lips crash down on his. I kiss William with fervor, my blood on fire, doused in my need for him, and he kisses me back just as fiercely. I love how he always seems to want me just as much as I want him, and he's not afraid to show it.

Making out like a couple of horny teenagers who are out past curfew for a while, we finally break apart, breathless, lips slick and swollen, and I need him more than ever. "Let's get this tree inside so we can finish what we just started," I whisper against his mouth before begrudgingly climbing off his lap.

Once inside, we get my tree set up, but agree to wait until tomorrow when he can come back over with his dad to do the decorating.

The air between us is practically sizzling as we work as fast as we can to get it set up. Electricity shoots between us, our eyes dancing over to one another every few moments, and it's like my skin is on fire already, the anticipation of what's about to come almost too much. Once I'm satisfied the tree won't tip over in our absence, I take a step back, keeping my eyes trained on William as I toe out of my shoes and begin shedding off the many layers of clothing I'm wearing. First, my beanie, then my scarf, letting both drop to the floor while the weight of William's gaze washes over my body like a physical force. Next, I unzip my jacket, shrugging out of that before reaching behind my head and tugging off my shirt. The only thing left are my pants and my briefs, which I slowly work down my legs while William then begins undressing in a similar fashion.

The lights are off and the room is silent, only the sounds of our breathing and the clothes hitting the floor, which somehow amplifies the tension between us. We haven't even touched each other yet, and I already feel so keyed up. My heart races, blood pumping hot through my veins, as it feels like my skin is on fire. I need him something fierce, and every single second spent watching him strip for me is agonizing and thrilling all at once. Once he's fully undressed, we both take a step, then another, meeting in the middle of the room. I couldn't even say who made the first move, our bodies colliding in a mess of limbs and lips and tongues.

Despite us being out in the cold not that long ago, his body is burning up against mine, sending all the blood in my body down south. I'm hard and throbbing in no time, and we've barely begun. Standing in the middle of the living room, bodies flush, lips locked, we lose ourselves to one another for a while before I begrudgingly pull away and take his hand, leading him back to my bedroom.

The moonlight spills in through the crack in the curtains, covering us in an ethereal glow while our hands and mouths find each other once more as we fall onto the bed. Lying in the center, I spread my legs, making room for William to blanket my body with his. He kisses me slowly, sensually. His tongue caressing mine as his large, warm hand trails down my body with featherlight touches. Fingers brushing against my sensitive, taut nipple, a tremble rolls down my spine as a groan builds in my throat.

William's lips leave mine, trailing a path along my jawline, down to my neck. Peppering his kisses along the area, he works his way down, leaving nothing untouched. His tongue flicks across the hardened bud, sending a shock wave of pleasure through my body before he continues his descent. As he gets farther down my abdomen, I prop myself up on my elbows, glancing down at him with a heavy gaze.

Peering up at me through his thick, dark lashes, William smirks before sinking all the way down, and running the flat of his tongue along the *very* hard length of my cock. I gasp as his lips wrap around the swollen tip, sucking hard as he lowers down, taking more of me in his mouth. By the time I'm seated in his throat, it's an effort to not let my eyelids flutter closed. The heat, the wetness, the suction, the sight of my cock in William's mouth… it's all so fucking good.

Head bobbing up and down with skilled precision, his hand cups my balls, rolling them around in his palm, tugging on them gently.

"Fuck, Doc, that feels amazing," I moan, letting my head fall back for a moment as he deep throats me, the sounds coming out of him only intensifying the pleasure.

A whimper falls past my lips when he removes his mouth and hands, but then I watch as he reaches for the nightstand, grabbing the bottle of lube from the drawer, and my heart pounds in my chest with giddy anticipation. William takes his time prepping me, making sure I'm stretched enough to welcome his thick girth. By the time he's finished, my body is flushed, burning up, and sweat coats every inch of my body. I'm so fucking ready for him to fill me up.

Coating his length in the cool gel, he peers up at me as he pumps his cock a few times. His ocean blues are nearly black with desire, glossed over, and his jaw is slack. He's as gone as I am, and I fucking love it. "I can't wait to sink into this tight fucking hole. *My* hole," he growls, lining himself up.

The possessiveness in his tone ignites something feral deep inside of me, and I can't help myself. I reach down, wrapping a tight fist around my aching length as I feel the blunt tip press against my entrance. His eyes never leaving mine, William pushes past the tight muscle, easing in inch by inch. The pressure and the burn are intense, quickly morphing into a white-hot pleasure that I can feel down in my toes. Once he's fully sheathed, we groan in unison as he gives my body a moment to adjust.

William pushes my thighs forward, gaze dipping down to take in where our bodies meet. A growl rumbles in his chest. "I don't think I'll ever get over how perfect you look taking my cock." Using his thumb, he traces my hole lazily. "So fucking tight, and all mine, isn't it?"

Heat spreads through my veins as he glances up at me beneath his lashes, a sexy smirk tugged on his lips. I can do nothing more than nod.

"That's right," he purrs. "This ass is mine." Reaching up, he swats my hand away, replacing it with his own. "This beautiful cock is mine." The pads of his fingers dance up my abdomen and throat before he pushes two digits past my parted lips. My tongue immediately spears between them, lips closing around them and sucking. "And this mouth," he growls, pulling his cock out to the tip before sinking back in to the hilt. "All. Fucking. Mine."

My eyes roll back from how full I feel, from the pleasure soaring through my body. William pulls his fingers out of my mouth, wrapping his hand around the back of my neck as he lowers his body onto mine. His hips rock into me with long, deep, rough strokes, and the way his body blankets mine creates the perfect amount of friction against my throbbing length. His mouth is a hairsbreadth away, his hot breath fanning my face while his thick, delicious cock splits me open. Every sense is drenched in William, and I can't get enough.

"That feel good, baby?"

I nod, lips parting. "Yes... *fuck* yes."

"That's it," he coos, the grin on his face making my stomach flutter. "Let me hear how I make you feel, boy. I fucking love it when you're loud."

Adjusting his position in the slightest, his cock now brushes over my prostate with each stroke. My body is lit up like a strip of live wire. "Oh, fuck, like that," I gasp. "Don't stop, please don't stop."

Using his thumb to my chin, he turns my head, bringing his mouth to my ear. "I wouldn't dream of stopping," he rasps, teeth nipping at my lobe. The pain mixes with the pleasure, making for an intoxicating concoction. "If I could live here, inside of you like this, I would. You're *everything*, Colt. Fucking everything."

Hands grappling at his sweat-glistened back, I turn my head, lips colliding with his. His tongue thrusts into my mouth, flicking against mine as he fucks me in slow, deep strokes. The air around us shifts, and suddenly, this feels different. It feels *more*. I can't explain it. The way he's worshipping my mouth, giving me everything I need with his cock. This moment is heady, it's suffocating in the very best way.

My throat tightens as I give myself over to William fully. He's owning every single part of me, and I wouldn't have it any other way. His tongue lashes into my mouth, tasting me, savoring me. His teeth nip my bottom lip. His cock sets my body ablaze. And the friction from his body rubbing along my dick is enough to send me over the edge.

Heart racing, my chest heaves with ragged breaths. My body is overheated and sensitive. Pressure builds low in my abdomen, pleasure amplifying, every nerve ending on fire. "William... fuck," I gasp into his mouth. "I'm going to come."

His kiss turns ravenous as he fucks me impossibly deeper, and I simply can't hold on any longer. My muscles are coiled tight, balls full and drawn up to my body, and like a hair trigger, I detonate. With my head thrown back, I cry out as my cock pulses, spilling cum all over us while wave after wave of pleasure rocks me to my core, tingles spreading through my limbs. William's mouth finds my throat, and I feel his teeth sink into the flesh as his body stills, his own release taking hold of him.

Time stands still as we remain wrapped up in one another, both of us trying to calm down our erratic breathing. My sticky release covers both of us, and his spent cock stays inside of me, neither of us seeming to want to move. I turn my head again, lips finding his as I throw my all into this one kiss. It's deep, sensual, and sends goosebumps all over my body. I don't know how it's possible to feel so much from a single kiss, but it's like that all the time with William.

After a while, he finally rolls off of me, heading into the bathroom. He comes back out with a warm washcloth, and he cleans my stomach up before cleaning himself up. After he tosses it in the hamper, he climbs back into bed, pulling me into his chest. I have no clue how long we lie here, but it's long enough for us to doze off.

Everything about today has been utter perfection. I never want it to end.

CHAPTER 30
WILLIAM ANDINO

"Anybody need another beer?" I ask, standing from the card table, eyes scanning the three men opposite me. Everyone glances up at me, nodding as they continue their conversation. Walking into the house from the garage where my dad, Max, Conrad, and I are playing a round of poker, I pull open the fridge and grab four bottles of Bud Light.

Back in the garage, I drop down into my folding chair, passing the bottles out to everybody. Max has a cigar hanging out of the corner of his mouth, and I can't help but chuckle at how ridiculous he looks.

"Hope you guys are ready to lose your fucking money," he drawls, cracking open the bottle and downing a swallow.

Nobody is competitive like Max. I think it's what made him such a damn fine bull rider back in the day. The overpowering need to beat everybody else took over. Tonight's poker night was his idea, and I gotta say, it was a good one. We've been talking about getting together for a good old-fashioned guys' night since I moved back to Copper Lake, but it just hadn't happened yet.

"Do you guys remember playing poker when we were teenager during our senior year?" I ask. Chuckling at the memory, I glance at my dad, knowing he has no clue what the hell I'm talking about.

"God, those were the days," Max murmurs, huffing out a laugh.

"I don't think my parents ever did find out that we'd take over the barn at the ranch nearly every weekend," Conrad adds, as he brings the bottle up to his lips for a sip.

"Did you ever catch on to the fact that I would sneak your beer from the fridge?" I ask my dad.

He laughs. "Of course, I did. I wasn't an idiot, son, and you weren't exactly slick."

I don't know why, but that's surprising to me. My dad wasn't exactly overly strict, but did have rules, and he had no problem reaming my ass for not following them. "Why'd you never say anything?"

Shrugging, he shuffles the deck. "I was young once," he replies simply. "I knew where you were, who you were with, and I knew you boys were good kids. Couple beers wasn't going to hurt you." Then he shifts his gaze to Conrad before adding with a smirk, "And your parents absolutely knew what you were doing because I told them. Yours too, Max."

We all laugh, the nostalgia from back then hitting me hard.

"You boys thought you were so sneaky, but little did you know, we were always two steps ahead of you."

"I guess that's how it is, huh?" Max asks, a glint in his eyes. "As a parent now, I can relate." He chuckles deeply, as if thinking back on a specific memory. "Colt thought he was slick too. Always running off with Cope and Shooter, getting into who knows what up at the ranch."

At the mention of Colt's name, my blood heats at the same time guilt racks my nerves. We're still lying to Max, and it makes me feel like shit. Colt's been in Vegas for a few days now, and we haven't spoken much today because he's been busy with his friends. The phone in my pocket is practically yelling at me to pull it out and see if he's texted me. I'm like a damn fiend for him, which is a little inconvenient considering I'm sitting around a poker table with his father.

"I wonder if my great, great, great grandparents knew when they purchased that land that it would become the regular hang-out spot for high school teenagers to drink and fuck around." Conrad breathes out a laugh as my dad deals the cards.

"It really is a great spot for that type of thing," I add.

We play for a while, the game getting pretty heated, before my father decides to call it a night. I grab the rest of us another beer as we sit around the table, shooting the shit like we used to. There's something so special about being in my mid-forties and having the same two friends that I've had since I was little. Not many people can say that nowadays.

So, Christmas is right around the corner," Max murmurs. "Conrad, I know you're coming over, but Will, you and your dad should come too. I know it's your first Christmas back home."

"I'll talk to my dad, but that should work."

"Trish has already hounded me more than once to make sure you and Roger come." He laughs. "She tried to get him to come last Christmas, but he wasn't having it."

"Stubborn old man," I muse.

"Conrad, what's new with you lately up at the ranch?" Max asks, eyeing him from across the table.

Blowing out a breath, Conrad replies, "Not a whole lot, really. Things have been pretty steady for a while. My nana is coming to visit in a couple months, though."

My brows raise. "The one that lives in Norway?"

"The one and only."

"Well, that'll be nice, right? She hasn't been back to the states since, what, your parents' funeral?"

He nods, sighing. "Yup, it's been a while."

"Why don't you look excited?"

Conrad has always had an incredible relationship with his nana. When we were kids, she lived in Copper Lake, but once Conrad's papa died several years back, she moved to Norway, where she was originally from. Something about a long-lost sister she never knew she had who was still there. Either way, she doesn't make it back very often, especially now that she's getting older.

"She doesn't know Whit and I aren't together anymore," he murmurs, brows furrowed.

I nearly choke on my beer. "Excuse me? How is that possible? You guys have been divorced for years."

Conrad grumbles, the expression on his face telling me he's over this conversation already. Any time Whit gets brought up, it's like he can't get off the topic fast enough. He's always been a private, closed-off man, but it's even more so when it comes to Whit and their relationship, or lack thereof now.

"She loves Whit, and I didn't have the heart to tell her about the split so soon after my parents died," he explains grimly.

"And it just never came up?" Max asks.

"We don't talk on the phone all that often, and when we do, I lie and say Whit's at work but that he sends his love."

I can't help it, I throw my head back and laugh at the

predicament he's put himself in. "Conrad, what the hell are you going to do when she gets here, and you live very much alone? Whit has a boyfriend, doesn't he?"

His scowl deepens as he looks across the table at me. "Yes, he does. And I don't know what I'm going to do. Haven't figured it out yet."

"Oh, man. I don't envy you, my friend."

Finally giving in to the itch, I reach into my pocket and grab my phone, pulling it out. My chest tightens and my stomach flutters when the screen lights up and I see I have a new text message.

Colt: Howdy, Doc. How's poker going? About to head to the arena with Whit and Xander.

A picture is attached, and my mouth waters at the sight. Instead of his signature backwards hat, Colt's wearing a cream-colored cowboy hat, a royal blue patterned pearl-snap shirt, a pair of deliciously form fitting Wranglers, and his boots. Whit's in the picture with him, an awkward smile on his face as Colt flips the camera off, his tongue sticking out of his mouth. He looks sexy.

Me: Remember... mine. ;)

Checking the time stamp of his message, it was sent about a half hour ago, so he probably won't see my response for a while if he's already at the arena. I feast my eyes on the picture again, taking in every detail.

"Who's got you smiling like that?"

My head snaps up, gaze colliding with Max's smiling face. He looks amused, and my stomach drops as I quickly lock my phone and shove it back into my pocket.

"Oh, no one," I say. *Real fucking smooth, Will.*

He chuckles. "You seeing someone and holding out on us?"

As the weeks go by, it's becoming harder to keep this from him. A large part of me wants to just tell him already and get it over with. He deserves to know. The fact that everyone at this table knows except for him doesn't help my guilty conscience either. I've found myself on more than one occasion almost reaching for Colt, or leaning into him, in front of his parents before I catch myself. It's only a matter of time before I slip up. Being around Colt feels like we're magnetically connected. The need to be touching him at all times is overwhelming.

My face heats, but before I have time to think of an answer, Conrad chimes in.

"Max, did you see the Millers bought a fancy new fishing boat?"

Max takes the bait, and they dive into a conversation about said boat, and how we'll have to go out on it with them next summer. I let out a deep breath, thankful for my friend and his ability to change the subject.

Colt and I are going to have to revisit the topic of telling him and Trish eventually, but for now, I'd prefer to tuck it away like the chicken shit I am.

CHAPTER 31
COLT BISHOP

"Knock, knock!"

My head snaps up just in time to watch William walk through my front door, looking every bit like he belongs. My lips curve into a grin as our eyes meet across the room. Wearing an adorable smile, he closes the door behind himself, kicking off his shoes beside where mine sit. He's in red and black buffalo plaid pajamas that fit him just right, and he's holding a small gift bag in his hand.

"Merry Christmas, Doc," I murmur as he approaches me.

Stopping right in front of me, he sets the bag on the bar, a hand landing on my hip as he leans in, bringing his mouth to mine. "Merry Christmas, baby."

I don't think I'll ever get tired of hearing him call me that. We kiss slowly for a moment, tongues brushing lazily, lips moving in synchrony. It's easy to get lost in William and the way he makes me feel.

Pulling apart, William glances down at the counter at what I was working on before he came over. "What're you making?"

"Homemade cinnamon rolls." I smirk when surprise takes over his eyes.

"Well, you're full of surprises, aren't you? I didn't know you could bake."

"Truthfully, I can't." I snort. "My mom came over last night and helped me make the dough, then gave me step-by-step instructions on how to bake them this morning."

"I'll be sure to thank her the next time I see her," William muses, hand still on my hip as his finger dips beneath my shirt, rubbing soothingly on my skin. Goosebumps spread from the contact. "Who does she think you're baking for?"

"I don't know." I laugh. "She didn't ask. I'm making enough to send some home with you for your dad."

He chuckles, the sound deep and delicious. "Of course, you are."

"Your father kind of loves me, you know." I can't help but huff out a laugh when he rolls his eyes, staring at me exasperatingly.

"I hadn't noticed," he deadpans. "I swear, he loves you more than he loves me."

Chuckling, I say, "Well, can you blame him?"

The smile fades from his face, and he's got a look in his eyes that sends a shiver down my spine. "No, I guess I can't."

Suddenly, my throat is tight. A giant lump blocks my airway as my heart gallops in my chest. *He doesn't mean it that way,* I chastise myself as I clear my throat and get back to assembling the cinnamon rolls. The oven beeped a few minutes ago, letting me know it's properly pre-heated.

William doesn't love me. He can't. It's way too soon.

What if he did, though? I can't deny the way that thought makes me feel... alive. Exhilarated. Happier than I thought possible.

But there's no way.

Taking a seat at the bar, William watches me roll the cinnamon-stuffed dough into pinwheels, placing them in a baking dish. We talk about this and that, and something about it feels so domesticated. So right. We're going over to my parents' house later on this afternoon for a Christmas dinner, but we wanted to spend this morning together since we won't exactly get to be *together* when we're with them.

To be honest, despite how nervous I am to tell them, I'm almost more ready than anything else. Ready to have it out in the open so we don't have to hide. I'm ready for him to park in my driveway again instead of down the block out of fear of my parents driving by and seeing his car here. As much as I love spending time together here or at his place, it would be nice to go out together in public, hold hands, watch him freely, no matter who we're around. Touch him when I want. Kiss him, even at my parents' house.

After I stick the cinnamon rolls in the oven and set the timer, William and I meander into the living room, where his gift is waiting for him. He grabs the gift bag he came in with off the bar, handing it to me before he sits on the couch beside me.

"You first," he murmurs, a smile splitting his handsome face. The sight takes my breath away.

A thick layer of nerves coats my stomach as I take the bag stuffed with light blue and white tissue paper. The idea of William putting this together sends a rush of dopamine through my veins. I can't explain it.

"It's nothing fancy," he warns. "I'm not the greatest gift giver, but I saw it and thought of you."

Plucking out the tissue paper, I place them on the coffee

table in front of us, peeking inside the bag at the baseball cap sitting inside. A smile tugs at my lips as I pull it out. It's all black except for a circle shaded like a sunset with a bull rider on the front. *Rodeo Legend* is scrawled underneath.

When I glance up at William, he's wearing a nervous grin. "I've been meaning to get a new hat, and this is perfect. Thank you."

"It's not much, but—"

"Stop." I chuckle. "It's exactly what I need, and I love it."

The idea of William shopping for me, then picking out something he likes that he also thinks I will like fills me with such pride and glee.

"I got you one other gift," he murmurs as he pulls an envelope out of his pocket, handing it to me, a boyish grin on his face.

My stomach does a somersault as I open it up, pulling out the contents inside. As I take in what it is, my eyes widen. "No way!"

William chuckles. "I checked the rodeo schedule, and it works out perfectly. The venue is only about an hour from the location you'll be in."

"This is perfect." Glancing up at him, I can't help the wide smile on my face. He got me VIP tickets to one of the biggest country music festivals around here. "I love every single artist performing here. Thank you, William."

"You're welcome."

"You're going to be able to get time off of work, right?" I ask, wanting to make sure he can come with me.

"You don't want to go with one of your friends?" he asks.

"Hell no." I snort. "You're coming with me, Doc."

He breathes out a laugh. "Then yes, I can get time off work."

Placing the hat on my head flipped around, I set the bag

and the envelope on the table, grabbing the other gift bag, and handing it to William.

"Okay, so this is technically for you, your dad, and for Winnie." I chuckle already, beyond excited for him to open this. "You may think it's dumb or silly."

Eyeing me warily, he pulls out the red tissue paper, placing it beside the others on the table. With a peek in the bag, his shoulders shake with laughter. "You're joking."

"Oh, come on. They're cute, right?" I chuckle as he pulls out the pajamas I got for all three of them with sweet Winnie's face all over. "You guys will all match!"

"Oh, just what I've always wanted," he says, while trying to hide a bright smile.

"Your dad gave me your sizes."

"Of course, he did."

"Grady can take family photos," I suggest, which wins me a scowl. Rising off the couch, I pad down the hall, opening the closet, pulling out one last wrapped gift. "Okay, I got you one more thing. This one's just for you."

William's gaze dips to the large, wrapped square in my hand, his eyes lifting to meet mine, an unreadable expression floating between them. I hand it to him, sitting down beside him as I watch as he tears the paper bit by bit, almost reluctantly, before revealing the twenty by twenty-four inch frame. His jaw tightens as his eyes get glossy, his gaze jumping to mine.

"Where did you get this?" His voice is hoarse.

My lips quirk. "Guess."

Breathing out a laugh, he deadpans, "My father."

I nod. "I noticed you don't have any family pictures around your house, and he showed me this one of the three of you after your graduation from med school. I asked if I could borrow it to blow it up for you."

"Colt..." His throat rolls on a swallow. "This is... I don't even know what to say. I didn't even know this picture existed. Thank you."

My nose stings, a lump forming in my throat. "You're welcome."

Gently resting the picture frame against the table, he wraps a hand around the back of my neck, pulling me into him, his soft lips crushing mine. So much is poured into this one bruising kiss. Like he's trying to convey to me without words how much this means to him. How much *I* mean to him. This kiss gives me goosebumps. It has my heart pitter-pattering. My skin tingling. It's a kiss I'll feel for the rest of my life. A kiss they make movies about.

By the time we pull apart, we're both a little breathless and a lot turned on, but we don't take it any further. This morning isn't about that. It's about so much more. William's hand stays anchored around the back of my neck as his eyes meet mine, a smile curling his swollen lips.

The timer goes off, signaling the cinnamon rolls are done, and it's not until right then that I realize how incredible the house smells. I've been so caught up with William that everything else was muted. I grab them out of the oven, then the homemade icing out of the fridge. While I work on frosting them, William whips us up some hot cocoa... the real fancy kind—from a packet. He even tops them with miniature marshmallows and drizzles some caramel on top.

Both of us at the dining room table, that I literally never use, we dig in.

William groans sexily as he takes his first bite. "Christ, Colt. These are amazing."

"They really are," I say, kind of surprised by myself. I mean, I know my mom made the dough, but I didn't burn them or anything. "Maybe if I can't make it back out on the circuit, I can moonlight as a baker."

Once we finish, William helps me clean up the kitchen. It all has me wondering what it would be like to do this on a regular basis with him... like every day. Six months ago, an idea like that would've probably freaked me out. But now? It sounds pretty fucking incredible.

"As much as I don't want to, I should get home," he murmurs with a sigh while drying his hands on a dish towel. "I have to pick my dad up before we go to your parents' house, and we probably shouldn't show up together anyway."

Joking, I say, "Maybe we tell 'em today. Merry Christmas, Mom and Dad! Meet my new boyfriend."

"Oh yeah, that'll go over well." William chuckles. "Maybe let's not tell them on Christmas."

"That's probably smart. Can't have my dad losing his cool over the honey-glazed ham," I tease.

"After the new year?"

"You're sure?" I ask. "What if he doesn't forgive us?"

Something in William's features softens. "He will. First of all, he's your dad, and I don't think there's anything you could do that would be unforgivable in his eyes and, secondly, we've been friends for nearly as long as I've been on this earth. It may take some getting used to, but I can't see this being the one thing that breaks a nearly four-decade-long friendship. I'm more than sure about you, Colt."

That one sentence settles so much inside of me. *I'm more than sure about you, Colt.*

With one last long kiss, William leaves. Grabbing a towel

from the closet, I hop in the shower and get ready, taking my time since I still have a couple of hours until I have to leave. I decide to wear the hat he got me, smirking to myself, knowing that it'll be our little secret tonight.

I get to my parents' place around two, and I'm the first one there. Conrad, William, and Roger should be the only other people coming over. Conrad spends every Christmas with us, and he has for years. Helping my mom in the kitchen to kill some time, I prep the ham for her before sticking it in the oven, then peel a ridiculous amount of potatoes while she gets the sauce ready for her famous scalloped potatoes. By the time we're finished, I've worked up a sweat.

"Thanks for your help, honey." My mom smiles wide at me, and I return it.

"Anytime, Mom."

With a beer in hand, I head out to the living room where I can hear everyone has arrived. My gaze connects with William's right away, and we share a small smirk before I say hi to everybody. My family always does a white elephant gift exchange, and this year is no different. The afternoon passes quickly; lots of laughter and joking, drinking beer, and watching the game until it's time to eat.

At the table, William and I sit directly across from each other, and this time, it's his foot that finds mine under the table. *Oh, how the tables have turned.* I wonder how next Christmas will go. Will we still be together? Is William right? Will my dad learn to accept it whenever we tell him? I sure as hell hope so. I don't think I'd forgive myself if their friendship was ruined, even if I'm starting to think my feelings for William go much deeper than just *like.* As I'm watching him from across the table, eat his food and mingle, I have a gnawing suspicion that I might, in fact, be in love with him. Despite telling myself just this morning that that's impossible. That it's too early.

It may be, but that doesn't make it any less true.

After dinner, I spot William coming out of the bathroom, and I smirk as I approach him. My dad's in the kitchen, doing the dishes, and my mom and everybody else are outside. She wanted to show them her new garden that she and dad are going to plant after winter is over. So, it's just him and me in this hallway.

"Fancy running into you here, Doc," I drawl, loving the smile on his face.

"Seems we have a tendency of meeting outside of bathrooms in houses we really shouldn't be."

Our first kiss comes back to me. Well, our first kiss after he moved home. I can't even hide my grin as I glance up, pointing innocently at the mistletoe hanging in the hallway. My mom has always been a sucker for mistletoe. She hangs it all around the house every year.

William breathes out a laugh. "You're going to get us in trouble, aren't you?"

Holding up my hands innocently, I say, "I don't have a clue what you mean, but it is bad luck to not kiss somebody when you're under the mistletoe."

"It is not bad luck."

"Yeah? You willing to risk that?"

Shaking his head at me, grin plastered on his face, William snakes an arm around my waist, hauling me into him as he presses his lips ever-so gently to mine. It's a kiss that's over before it even really begins, but my insides light up from it anyway.

"Merry Christmas, Doc," I murmur against his lips before we pull apart.

Passing by me, William leans and whispers into my ear, "Merry Christmas, baby."

CHAPTER 32

WILLIAM ANDINO

New Year's has always been something I enjoy. It's not everyone's favorite, but it's one of mine. Getting to look back and reflect on the last 365 days and make little goals or wishes for the upcoming year just resonates with me and calms something inside of myself. This past year has had more changes, both big and small, than I've experienced in several years. Making the decision to move back to Copper Lake when my dad retired, I truly didn't know what to expect. Being gone so long, I got used to living one way. I was... comfortable, for lack of a better word, with the way my life was, but knew in my heart that it was the right thing to do to move back and take over my family's practice.

That didn't mean I wasn't nervous, or I wasn't worried that it would be something I'd grow to regret. After all, I left Copper Lake for a reason. However, as I stand around this bonfire with members of this community, my family, and my closest friends, I can't help but think everything may have worked out just the way it was supposed to. A beer in hand, I glance over the roaring flames, gaze locking right on a pair of shimmering green eyes that are already watching me. Even looking at him has my heart skipping a beat.

If I had never made the decision to come back, I never would've gotten this chance with Colt. Sure, that first night we hooked up in Seattle, I woke up feeling like it was a huge mistake. I berated myself for going there with him, but the reality is, Colt is so much more than just my best friend's son. For the first time in almost twenty years, I feel alive. I feel relaxed and carefree. He brings out a side of me I thought I'd lost. Something I thought maybe died from all the years of being by myself.

It's New Year's Eve, and it's nearly midnight. We're all at Conrad's ranch for a huge barbecue, and all I want is to the end the year with my lips on Colt's and my arms wrapped around him, but that's nearly impossible with all of these people around, Max and Trish especially. Eyes scanning the area, I find them sitting off to the side, chatting with the Grahams. With one last look at Colt, my face hopefully saying what I want it to say, I step away from the fire, walking with long strides toward the side of the barn. A quick look at my watch tells me we only have a few minutes until midnight.

Luckily, Colt seems to have caught my drift because a moment later, he's rounding the corner, a boyish grin plastered on his face like he's the cat that got the canary. Stalking closer to me, he backs me up against the side of the barn, his hands planting beside my head. The scent of his cologne and the beer on his breath washes over me, settling in my bones.

"Sneaking away to make out with me, Doc?" he drawls, voice raspy and rough. "What a naughty man you are."

"You love it."

He huffs out a chuckle. "Damn right, I do."

I place my hands on his hips, pulling his body closer to mine. "Having fun tonight?"

"Yeah." He nods. "Shooter's pretty drunk, and it's funny. He keeps talking about how he and Sterling should start having babies. Actually, what he said is…" He clears his throat. 'We should have a couple tiny little rugrats with your precious honey eyes and my good looks.'"

I can't help but laugh because I can absolutely picture Shooter saying something like that. Colt's friendships remind me a lot of mine with Max and Conrad. Most of them he's known since he was little, and I think relationships like that are so special, and honestly, a little rare these days. While I can't say I've ever been all that interested in the rodeo and that lifestyle, I also can't deny how much it's brought people in this town together. It's one big family, through the good and the bad.

"What about you?" I ask.

"What about me?" His brows raise.

"Do you want little rugrats running around?"

"No way." He chuckles. "I'll be the fun uncle, but that's about it."

Something like relief washes through me hearing him say that. I love kids, but I've never wanted any of my own. The topic has never come up with us, and I didn't even think to bring it up until he mentioned them, but I would feel guilty if Colt *did* want kids because, especially at my age, that's not something I'm willing to be flexible about. So, I'm glad we're on the same page.

"Being the fun uncle is where it's at," I murmur, just as I hear everybody start to count down from ten in the distance. We both turn our head in that direction before glancing back and looking at each other. In unison, we softly join the countdown.

Five.

A smile spreads on his handsome face.

Four.

His gaze drops down to my mouth, a zing of arousal zipping down my spine at the sight.

Three.

I'm so completely gone for Colt Bishop.

Two.

I'm in love with him.

One.

"Happy New Year, William," Colt whispers a moment before his mouth crashes down on mine. Fireworks go off in the distance, but the real explosion is between us. Bringing his hands to my face, he tilts my head, tongue slipping past my parted lips as it brushes against mine. My head swims as I taste him, feel him. Colt presses his body into mine, hard and hot, pinning me to the side of the barn, and everything around us vanishes.

In this moment, the fireworks, the cheering, all of it falls on deaf ears. It's me and Colt, reveling in one another, and nothing—and I mean, *nothing*—has ever felt this right. It takes no time at all for the kiss to turn heated and messy, like around Colt I become insatiable. I don't know how long we stand here, but before long, I hear a voice cut through, and it turns my blood ice cold.

"What the fuck is going on here?"

At the same time, Colt and I freeze. Our eyes pop open, and there's a brief moment where they lock before we turn our heads, gazes landing on a very pissed-off looking Max.

Shit.

Trish is running up behind him, a look of dread on her

face. "Max, knock it off," she calls out as she comes up to his side, placing a hand on his arm like she knows he's about to come unglued.

"What the hell is going on?" he repeats, his voice low and palpably angry. His eyes are narrowed into slits on us, face turning a bright shade of red.

"Dad, stop." Colt steps forward, placing his body slightly in front of mine.

Max's eyes slice over to his son. "I catch my best friend and my son making out, and you tell *me* to stop?" His chilling gaze darts to me, and my heart pounds harder in my chest. "What the fuck is happening, Will?"

Stepping forward, beside Colt, I hold out a hand and say, "We planned to tell you soon. This isn't how we wanted you to find out."

Trish's hand comes up to cover her mouth. Our gazes meet for a moment, and for some reason, she doesn't seem quite as surprised as her husband.

"You planned to tell me what, exactly?" Max grits out.

"Max, honey," Trish cuts in. "Let's go home, and we can all talk about this tomorrow when you haven't been drinking."

"No, Trish, I want to talk about it now," he says roughly. "Planned to tell me what, Will?"

I drag in a deep breath, knowing whatever I say isn't going to go well with him. "Colt and I have been seeing each other for—"

"Are you fucking kidding me, Will?" Max spits out, his face flushed red. "My fucking son? I thought we were friends?"

"We are friends."

"It has nothing to do with you, Dad," Colt blurts out, and my eyes fall closed as I bite down on my molars. *Shut up, Colt.*

Max scoffs, looking from his son to me. "He's half your fucking age," he bites out, then takes a step toward us. "Half your fucking age. You have known him since he was a fucking baby. What the fuck is wrong with you, Will? I trusted you."

With each sentence, he steps closer until he's right in front of us. Hands clenched into fists at his sides, I know whatever's about to happen won't be good.

"It's not like that," I say calmly, trying like hell to diffuse the situation.

"Whoa, hey!" Turning our heads, we all watch as Shooter jogs up to us, a drunk grin on his face, eyes bouncing between the three of us. "What's going on here?"

"Not now, Shooter," Max growls, his furious eyes never leaving mine. "What, did you think you could just fuck around with my son, and I'd be okay with it?"

Annoyance flares inside of me at the flippant way he says that. Like Colt's nothing more than a notch on my belt. This isn't how I wanted Max and Trish to find out, but in this single moment, I'm realizing that maybe this is okay. I'm sick of hiding Colt. Sick of hiding how much I care about him. "It's not like that," I grit out again, harsher this time. "If you'd fucking calm down and let me explain, maybe you'd understand."

"I don't need to understand anything because it's fucking clear what's going on. I thought you were a better fucking man than this, Will."

Everything that happens next happens in a flash. One minute, Max is glaring down his nose at me, the next he's got my shirt fisted in his hand as he rears back his other, landing a hit I don't see coming right in my jaw. A round of collective gasps sounds around us, and all hell breaks loose. Max's hold on my shirt drops as Colt steps between us, shoving his dad back with enough force that Max nearly falls over.

"What the fuck is wrong with you?" Colt growls. "You're acting like a fucking idiot. William and I are both adults!"

Rubbing a hand along my jaw, knowing it's probably going to bruise, I stand to my full height, wanting to make sure Colt doesn't do anything he'll regret, like deck his father back in my honor. That's about the last damn thing we need.

"Max, let's go home," Trish barks behind him, clearly worried about the same thing.

Just then, Shooter steps in between us. "Let's all take a breather, alright?" he says coolly. "William and Colt make each other happy, why does it matter?"

Stepping back, I pinch the bridge of my nose. Between Colt's big mouth and Shooter's, this isn't going to end well. I can see Max getting madder by the minute.

"Max, please," I try to plead with him. "Let's call it a night like Trish said, and talk about this in the morning."

"How long has this been going on?" he asks, ignoring everything I said.

"It's... complicated."

"How is it complicated? When the fuck did it start?"

Oh, for fuck's sake. "Technically, two years ago."

His eyes widen. "Excuse me?"

"Oh dear," I hear Trish murmur. Then she steps up, wrapping a hand around his forearm, tugging him back. "That's enough, Max," she says sternly. "It's time to go. You've had too much to drink, and now isn't the time to talk about this. We can talk about it when you've had a chance to cool off."

"Trish, knock it off."

"No, you knock it off!" I'm taken aback by her tone. Trish is many things, but feisty isn't one of them. "You're acting like a caveman right now, and it's embarrassing. Get in the damn car with me before I make Conrad put you over his shoulder and carry you there."

Shooter snorts. "Please do that."

Colt snickers beside me.

"You know he will," Trish threatens. "Now, let's go, Max."

Gaze dragging from Colt to me, I see the moment he decides to drop it. His shoulders relax, chest a little less puffed out. "Fine."

They walk away, and I let out a breath I'd been holding.

Shooter laughs, turning around. "Well, that was fun."

My eyes narrow as my pulse races. "You're both idiots," I blurt out.

"Hey, what did I do?" Colt asks with a chuckle.

"You don't know when to keep your mouth shut, that's what."

"Oh, come on. My dad was being ridiculous. He *hit* you!"

Leveling Colt with a look, I say, "He just walked over and caught his best friend and his son making out. What exactly did you expect him to do? His reaction was pretty normal, all things considered."

"He's drunk," Colt counters. "And acting like a hothead."

Blowing out a breath, I run a hand through my hair. "It's late," I say. "I'm going to head home. I want to make sure Winnie isn't too freaked out from the fireworks."

"I'll go with you," Colt offers, grabbing my hand.

"You don't have to do that." Although, I would love it. "You're here with your friends."

"Yeah, but the night's nearly over. I want to go home with you." Then Colt shifts, his face twisting up. "I mean, only if you want me to."

Uncertainty looks adorable on him. "Of course, I do. I'm

just saying, you don't have to if you aren't ready to go."

"I am," he insists, and it warms my chest.

"Holy shit," Shooter blurts out. "Colt is a kept man." He laughs. "Never thought I'd see the fucking day. Bye, you two. I'm off to find my own man." Taking a few steps, he stops and looks over his shoulder to add, "You're welcome, by the way."

My brows pinch together. "For what?"

"For stopping Max from kicking your ass."

Shooter doesn't wait for a response. He smirks before disappearing into the night.

"He wouldn't have kicked my ass," I grumble as Colt and I walk to my car.

"Sure, he wouldn't have," Colt teases.

I can't deny how much better I feel knowing we're at least out in the open now. Sure, my friend is pissed and hurt, rightfully so, and he may never forgive me—although, I hope he will—but at least we don't have to hide anymore, and that's still a win in my book.

The rest we can worry about later.

CHAPTER 33

COLT BISHOP

Rolling over in bed, I peel my eyes open, the morning light peeking in through the crack in the curtain. I grab my phone off the nightstand and check the time. It's just after eight. It's been four days since the blowup with my dad on New Year's Eve. The next morning, I called my mom, and she suggested giving my dad a little more space, as he was still pretty pissed. But I'm ready to hash this shit out already.

I roll out of bed, going to the bathroom to take a quick leak before padding down the stairs. The savory, slightly sweet scent of bacon fills my nostrils, making my stomach grumble as I walk down the hall, finding William standing shirtless with a pair of flannel pajamas slung low on his hips with his feet bare in his kitchen in front of the stove.

"Morning," I rasp, dragging a hand through my sleepy, mussed up hair.

Glancing over his shoulder, a smile curves his beautiful, full lips. "Good morning. How'd you sleep?"

"Great. Your bed is comfier than mine. I think I need to

buy a new mattress."

William chuckles. "There's coffee." He nods toward the pot in the corner. "And breakfast is almost done."

Walking up behind him, I wrap my arms around his large form, cheek pressed against the warmth of his back. Covering my hands with one of his own, he squeezes while he continues flipping the bacon or stirring the eggs or whatever it is he's doing that I can't see. Since New Year's, we've spent every night together. We've both been busy—him with work, me with training—but it's like neither of us wants to sleep without the other. We spent a couple of nights at my place before coming here. There's something so enjoyable about starting my day eating breakfast with William and Roger.

"Want any help?" I murmur, not wanting to let him go.

"Nah, I got it." His chest rumbles with his deep voice. "My dad and Winnie are outside on the back porch if you want to go out there. I'll bring everything out on a tray when it's done."

"Okay."

Turning around, he leans down, pressing his lips to mine for a quick kiss. "I'll never get over how good you look in my house in the morning."

My cheeks heat as I turn and leave the kitchen, padding through the house toward the back door. It's a chilly but nice morning. The sun is shining bright, the grass frosted over from how cold it got overnight. Roger's sitting in one of the recliners out there, wrapped in a huge robe and fuzzy socks, a portable heater blasting in his direction.

Eyes lifting from the phone in his hand, most likely reading the news, he smiles when he spots me. "Good morning, Colt."

"Morning." Wrapping a blanket around my shoulders, I take a seat in the chair next to him, Winnie jumping in my lap right away. I've really come to care for Roger. I've always liked him; he was my doctor for most of my life, but since getting to know him a bit more personally, he's a really cool guy.

"You guys going over to your folks' today?" he asks, gaze flitting over to me.

"Yeah, after breakfast, I think we're going over there." Nerves line my stomach. "We'll see how it goes."

"He'll come around, son."

"What if he doesn't?" It's a question that leaves me feeling vulnerable. If I'm being honest with myself, it's a genuine concern of mine. *What if my dad doesn't come around?* I care deeply for William—hell, I think I'm in love with him—and nothing will make me walk away from him, but it would sting to know my dad wouldn't approve.

My whole life, I've looked up to my father. Wanted to be just like him. Make him proud. I know he's proud of me and the life I've fought for, but I need him to accept my feelings for William. I can't imagine not getting to share that part of me with one of the most important people in my life. My dad is my hero, my original role model. Even as a grown adult, I crave his acceptance and pride. I think anybody would.

"Colt, I've known your dad his entire life. "He can be stubborn and a whole lot hotheaded, but you're his son. He loves you more than life itself. He may be mad, probably a little blindsided, but he'll come around. That much I know."

Chewing on the inside of my cheek, I think about what he said. "Can I ask you a question?"

"Of course, you can."

"You seem to be okay with me and your son," I say. "I could be wrong, but you haven't even seemed to bat an eye since you found out. Why not?"

Roger smiles, the wrinkles around his eyes creasing. Bringing his coffee mug up to his mouth, he takes a sip while he seems to ponder my question. "I've spent many years wishing my son would find his person," he murmurs, setting the mug back on the coaster on the table between us. "He spent many, many years alone all the way in Seattle, and I just knew there was someone out there for him. Someone to bring him joy, make him feel young again. That person, son, is you."

My throat tightens, chest squeezing. "How did you know that, though?"

He chuckles. "I saw it from the very moment I met you. The way Will looked at you. The way you challenged him and got under his skin. I saw the fire you ignited in his soul. You sparked something in him that I haven't seen in years from my son. How could I possibly be anything but ecstatic about that?" He arches a brow before adding, "It probably helps that you're not my lifelong friend. Give your dad a little grace. I'm sure it's a lot to take in, given the relationship he and Will have shared their whole life."

Not long after, William comes out, a tray of delicious smelling goodies in hand, and we all dish up. William's the better cook between the two of us, but I'm more than okay with that. After we finish eating, I help him tidy the kitchen before we run upstairs to get dirty in the shower before cleaning each other up. Getting ready side by side, I can tell we're both feeling nervous about what's to come today. The mood is a little sullen, and we're both quiet, but I feel better that we're going into this together. A united front as we try to make my father understand.

"Ready?" he asks as I'm finishing buckling my belt.

"Yeah, let's go."

Stopping me with a hand around my waist before we can walk out of the bedroom, William looks me in my eye and says, "Whatever happens today with your dad, it doesn't change anything for me."

I didn't realize how much I needed to hear that. It's like a weight is lifted off my shoulders, and I can breathe easier. "It doesn't change anything for me either."

There's a moment when we just hold eye contact, not a single word spoken between us, yet so much is said. Loud and clear. Then I lean forward, pressing my lips to his, and allow myself this one kiss before we go face my dad, and hope for the best.

We take William's car, and on the way over, I send my mom a text, letting her know we're on our way. By the time we're pulling into the driveway, my stomach is in knots. How does *this* feel more nerve-wracking than I've ever felt sitting in the bucking chute, getting ready to ride a literal bull? William turns off the car, and we both glance at each other, a moment for reassurance, before we get out.

Rounding the front of the car, William takes my hand in his as we make our way up the walkway. Right about now, I'm ready to turn back around and head home. I have no clue how this is going to go. At the New Year's party, when my dad had William's shirt fisted in his hand, he looked like he was ten seconds from decking him. Bringing his hand up, William knocks on the door.

"Fuck, I'm nervous," I breathe out with a laugh.

Chuckling softly, William says, "Me too. It'll be fine."

The door opens, my mom appearing before us. She looks from William to me, a hesitant smile on her face. "Hi, Will. Hi, honey. Come on in."

Giving us both a hug, she closes the door behind us.

"Where's Dad?"

"Getting dressed," she murmurs as she walks past us toward the chair. "He just got out of the shower."

"Does he know we're coming?"

Wincing, my mom shakes her head. "No."

"Lovely." I huff out a laugh.

The floorboards creak as my dad bounds down the stairs, three sets of eyes darting in that direction. As soon as he reaches the bottom step, he turns, looking from William to me, then to my mom, his jaw clenching. "I guess we're doing this today?" he drawls.

"Honey, they came over to talk to us," my mom says softly, like the absolute saint that she is. "Can you please come sit down?"

Heaving a sigh, he takes a seat in the other recliner, his brows set in a hard line to match his jaw.

Glancing at William, I nod, letting him know I want to start. "Mom, Dad," I murmur, nerves tight in my throat. "I'm sorry—we're sorry—that you found out about us the way that you did. We had every intention of telling you, but we wanted time to explore what this was first, and then it didn't feel right to drop the bomb on you around the holidays, so we decided to wait. And well, that blew up in our faces."

My mom's quiet while my dad huffs, rubbing a hand over his mouth. "I had my suspicions," he mutters, not looking at anyone in particular. "The way you two behaved around each other whenever you were here. On Christmas, for example. But I brushed it off because I thought, surely, there'd be no way my best friend would be sleeping with my son." He laughs dryly. "I mean, who would do that?"

William winces beside me.

"Then when I saw you"—he glances at William, gaze hard—"walk away from the fire at Conrad's right before midnight, followed by Colt, I knew my gut had been right all along."

"It's not what you think," William says.

"Yeah? Then tell what it is then, because I'm having a real fucking hard time wrapping my head around how you could do something like this, Will. You've been my friend since we were kids. You held my son when he was born, goddamnit! What the hell am I supposed to think, huh?"

Sitting forward, William rests his elbows on his knees, gaze pointed directly at my dad. "I understand you're mad," he goes on. "You have every right to be. We should've told you sooner, and that's on us. And I get this is unconventional and probably even a little uncomfortable for you—both of you." He glances toward my mom for a moment before looking back at my dad. "But I think I speak for both of us when I say that we didn't mean for this to happen. I don't think either of us expected us to wind up here, for this to have gone as far as it has. But it did, and Max, I'm in love with your son, and I won't apologize about that."

My heart stutters, my body freezing. Time stands still as I take in what William just admitted. There was zero hesitation in his tone. I can't wrap my head around it, my mind spinning. He... *loves* me.

"Wait," I cut him off from whatever he was saying. All eyes flit to me, but it's the deep ocean eyes beside me that I'm looking at. "You do?"

His gaze softens as the smallest of smiles lifts his lips. "I thought it was obvious," he murmurs with a light laugh, his cheeks turning pink.

"You never said anything."

I'm overly aware of the fact that both of my parents are watching us right now, but I can't find it in me to pay either of them any mind. Not when it feels like I'm floating.

William loves me.

Taking my hand, eyes never leaving mine, William says, "I love you, Colt. I've fallen so unexpectantly hard for you, and I can't imagine my life without you. You're stubborn, sometimes a little too cocky for your own good." We both laugh, the backs of my eyes stinging. "You drive me crazy most days, but I can't imagine living without your type of crazy."

"I..." Swallowing around the lump in my throat, I squeeze his hand. "I love you too, Doc."

William leans in, pressing his lips to mine, seemingly unbothered by our audience. The kiss doesn't last long before my father clears his throat. "Alright, that's enough."

"Max!" my mom scolds, emotion thick in her voice. Glancing over at her, her eyes are red rimmed, and her cheeks are wet.

"No, Trish," he growls. "I'm not going to sit here and pretend like I'm okay with this. This has been going on for God knows how long under our noses. Why did nobody think to tell me? Don't you think, as your friend, I deserved to know?"

"Maybe because it wasn't about you, Dad," I bark. William sighs beside me, and I know I should probably shut my mouth but, fuck, I can't. "Yes, of course, we wanted you to know, but we wanted the time and privacy to figure out what exactly this was before telling people. And have you ever considered that maybe we were nervous to tell you because we knew you'd act exactly like you are now? Not everything is about you. Neither of us started this with the intent of hurting you or making you mad. Like William said, we didn't expect any of this, but it happened. I love you, Dad, and I understand where you're coming from, I really do, but I'm an adult. I'm more than capable of thinking for myself, and I know this is weird for you, and for that, I am sorry, but I can't help how I feel no more than you can help how you feel about mom."

My dad's nostrils flare with harsh breaths, but he says nothing. So, I continue.

"I'm not going to get into details, but William and I ran into each other one night two years ago when I was visiting Seattle. It was unplanned, but there was an instant connection. I didn't think anything would come of it, and it didn't for two years, but when he moved back to Copper Lake, it became abundantly clear the connection from that night was still there. None of this was done to hurt you."

"You're his doctor," my father grits out, gaze shifting to William. "Never mind the fact that you've known Colt his entire life, you're his physician."

"No, I'm not," William replies. "I transferred him to Doug after that first visit after his accident."

A heavy silence falls upon us, and when I glance over at my mom again, her eyes are still red, but she smiles at me.

Finally, after a few tense moments, my dad sits forward, heaving a sigh. "I don't know what to do here, but I need some time. This is... a lot. I can't do this right now. I'm sorry."

Standing up, he leaves the room, taking the stairs two at a time without another word. Nobody speaks for a moment. If I had to guess, I'd say we're all kind of at a loss for words. On the one hand, it could've gone worse. At least he didn't punch William. But on the other hand, it would've been nice to work through this today.

"Give him time, you two," my mom says, her kind eyes

looking into mine and then William's. "He'll come around."

That's exactly what Roger said, but will he?

"Thanks, Trish," William says, voice strong yet quiet.

Feeling defeated, I stand up. "I guess we'll get out of here."

"Honey, you don't have to go."

"I know, but it's probably for the best. I'll call you?" I don't know why I phrase it like a question, but she nods anyway.

With that, William and I leave my parents' house, and all I can do is keep repeating the same two sentences over and over.

It could've been worse. He'll come around.

Maybe if I say it enough, I'll believe it.

CHAPTER 34
WILLIAM ANDINO

ONE MONTH LATER

"You *made* these?" My eyes lift, lips twitching with amusement. Colt's standing before me in *my* pair of Winnie pajama pants that he got me for Christmas, no shirt, an apron tied around his neck with eggplants and peaches all over it, and a black headband on his head, holding back his messy, dark brown strands that have gotten so much longer in the last month than I've ever seen them. "Like, homemade?"

He nods, proud, a crooked smile on his face. "Cope gave me the recipe, but he didn't help me this time. Made the sausage gravy myself too."

Lately, Colt's been taking an interest in baking. Specifically, bread. He even brought over a giant mason jar filled with a sourdough starter that he named Bertha. Whatever the hell that means. He has one at his house too. In between training at the arena, he's been trying out various recipes that he gets from his mom or the internet. Some have been an epic failure, but some—like I think this one might be—are delicious. And it's cute watching him focus and try to get it just right.

The sound of the front door closing reaches us in the kitchen, and a moment later, my dad walks in, Winnie following closely behind him. "What smells so dang good?" he asks.

"Colt made homemade biscuits and gravy for breakfast."

My dad's gaze slides over to Colt, a huge grin spreading on his face. "You did? Well, ain't that something."

"Hungry?" Colt asks him, brow quirked.

"You know I am."

If there's one thing about Roger Andino, it's that he's always down to eat. Even with age, that hasn't lessened.

Dad and I set the table while Colt finishes what he's doing in the kitchen. Once it's all done, we dish up and sit around the table, scarfing down the—very delicious—biscuits and gravy.

"Colt, these are incredible," I tell him in between bites. "This may be your best creation yet."

"I'm with Will," my dad adds.

"You guys can just call me Berry Crocker." He snorts, clearly pleased with himself, and I can't help but chuckle.

"Your appointment is this week, right?" I ask him.

He nods, chewing on the inside of his cheek. "Yes, and I'm hoping to get cleared finally."

Colt's been working his ass off, trying to get back to where he was pre-injury. I'm proud of how far he's come, and how responsible he's been about it. Aside from that one time right after the accident where he was working out when he shouldn't have, he's been taking it slow and following doctor's orders for everything.

"I've got a good feeling about it," I tell him, trying to reassure him because I know he's anxious. "You've come so far, and you're doing so well."

The last month has been nothing short of amazing. Getting to be out in the open with him and my feelings for him, getting to hold his hand in public. Kiss him while we're out and about. Max and I still aren't on the best of terms, but we're getting there. I think it'll be a slow process, but it's one I'm willing to be patient about. His relationship with Colt is probably going to take a little more time, mostly due to how stubborn Colt is. He would never admit it, but I think he's hurt, more than anything, and that hurt is causing him to want to turn the other cheek and not even try to mend the relationship.

Which, of course, is every bit his right, and he's entitled to his own feelings, but I think if he put the stubborn hat to the side, took his own feelings out of it, he'd see where Max is coming from. It doesn't help that Max is equally stubborn as his son.

Sunday dinners are still paused for the time being, but I think with time, things will be okay. Trish has come over to Colt's a few times, and we had her over for dinner the other night here. She seems a lot more on board with our relationship than Max does. I want to say it's surprising, but in the grand scheme of things, it's really not. She's a loving, open-minded person, and all she wants is for her son to be happy. Max does too, but it's different because of our friendship.

We finish eating, and I clean up the kitchen and the breakfast dishes while Colt heads up to my room to shower for the day. We've been spending a lot of time together, taking turns staying at each other's houses, but lately, it's been more of him at my house. I can't deny how much I love waking up with him in my bed. And even though he's never come out and said as much, I know my dad really enjoys having Colt around too. Their relationship warms my heart.

Prior to leaving Seattle, I had a feeling Dad was lonely, and had been since my mom died, but he didn't want to say anything. Being here now, seeing him with Colt and with me, I know I was right. His mood is so much brighter now than it was whenever I would video chat with him. Moving back was the right call, on so many counts. It feels like everything I have now has happened exactly as it was supposed to. Everything in life led me to this moment, and I couldn't be more thankful.

The idea of asking Colt to move in with me has been playing around in my mind, but I worry it's too soon. Then again, everything with us seems to happen quicker than I thought it would, and nothing has ever felt better. Maybe that's just how we are. And we spend nearly every night together anyway. Would it really make that much of a difference?

I don't know. I don't have to decide today, but I sure want to.

I wander out to the living room, finding my dad taking his usual late morning nap in his recliner, with Winnie passed out on his lap too. Smiling to myself, I bound up the stairs, finding Colt in nothing more than a towel in my room, water droplets clinging to his chest and shoulders.

He smirks when he sees me, and fuck, the sight takes my breath away and has my blood pumping hotter. Despite fucking him into the mattress just last night, I'm already dying for more.

"Lose the towel," I growl, stalking toward him.

The smile on his face quickly morphs into something more heated, as he does exactly as I say, unhooking the knot around his waist, letting the material fall to the ground. Biting down on his bottom lip, he peers at me from beneath his lashes as I approach. "How do you want me, Doc?"

The sultry lilt to his voice goes straight to my balls. Reaching behind my head, I yank off my shirt, letting it fall to the floor as I drop my sweats, adding them to the discarded clothes pile. I wrap a hand around the back of his neck, hauling his body to mine. Keeping my hand there, I place my other around his hip as I crash my mouth against his. His breath is minty, like he brushed his teeth as soon as he got out of the shower, and his clean, fresh body wash wafts around us, making my head dizzy.

Colt tilts his head to the side, lips parting as my tongue slips inside, rolling along his. He tastes amazing, and in no time, we're both hard and ready to go. My sexual appetite with Colt is unlike anything I've seen from myself since my twenties. I'm insatiable for him, but luckily, he always seems to be as insatiable for me.

"Hands and knees on the bed," I tell him, reaching into the nightstand and grabbing the bottle of lube I keep in there. Spread wide open for me, I allow myself a moment to take in the sight of Colt. Cock hard, balls full, they hang heavy between his legs while his tight, pink hole is on display for me. My mouth waters the longer I admire him, and before I can stop myself, I spread him impossibly wider with my hands, burying my head between his cheeks.

I drag my tongue across his taint, all the way up his crease, reveling in the way he gasps and arches his back, needy for more. Reaching between his thighs, I wrap a hand around his cock, pumping him in my fist as I eat him out. Once I feel the muscle loosen up a little, I ease my index finger inside, fucking him with it nice and slow before adding a second. He cries so beautifully when I crook my fingers and graze that sweet spot inside of him, the sound causing my cock to ache and leak.

"I need more," he gasps. "Fuck me, William. *Please.*"

He pushes back onto my fingers, tossing me a look over his

shoulders. He looks *gone*. His eyes are heavy, cheeks flushed, brows pinched together. Withdrawing my fingers, I grab the lube and lather it all over my cock, loving the way he watches as I do it. My blood is drenched with an overwhelming amount of desire, my heart catapulting in my chest. Coating his hole with a generous layer of lube, I toss the bottle to the side before climbing on the bed behind him, lining myself up.

Not giving me a chance to ease into it, Colt pushes back, spearing himself on my cock in one swift go. He throws his head back as we let out a groan in unison. The pressure and the heat surrounding my length have my eyes rolling back as my hands find purchase on his hips, nails digging into the flesh in a way I'm sure will leave a bruise later.

"You're desperate for my cock, aren't you, baby?" I ask, voice raspy and low.

"You know I am," he moans, fucking himself on me like the needy little slut he is.

"You been thinking about doing exactly this all morning?"

"Yes."

Making us breakfast in my kitchen while you imagine me stuffing you with my cock?"

Fuck," he gasps. "Yes!"

"On your stomach," I growl, pulling out of him long enough for him to oblige.

Colt closes his legs, pressing them tight as I straddle him with my legs on either side of his body. I spread him open with one hand while I guide my cock back into his channel with my other. The new position nearly makes me come on the spot.

"Fuck, Doc," Colt moans. "You feel so good."

Once I'm fully seated, I blanket his body with my own, bringing my hand around his throat as I use it to pull his head back. Bringing my lips to the shell of his ear, I nip at his earlobe. "You feel fucking perfect," I grit out, hips snapping against his tight ass. "Whose ass is this? Let me hear you."

"Yours!"

A grin splits my face. "That's right, baby. And who fucks you this good?"

"You do," he pants.

"Louder," I growl. "Who fucks you this good? Who has you sweating and crying and writhing?"

"You do!"

"You're perfect," I confess in his ear. "*God*, you're fucking perfect."

Despite being pinned to the bed underneath me, Colt still manages to arch his back, pushing back against me like he just can't help himself. "Oh, fuck, I'm close," he cries out, throat muscles tightening beneath my hand. "Don't…. stop!"

"That's it," I coo into his ear. "Come for me, baby. Let me see what I do to you. Give me that sweet fucking cum."

"Fuck, fuck, fuck." At this point, his voice is nothing more than a hoarse rasp, and I know the minute he lets go because his ass strangles my cock, clenching as he spills all over the bed.

"That's it. Such a good boy."

It's not long before I follow, groaning and panting as I release deep inside of him. We're both a sweaty mess by the time I pull out of him, but I can't help but pause and watch my cum drip down his thigh. There's something so primal and possessive about watching it spill out of him. I can't help myself… I reach out, pushing it back in with my thumb.

"So much for that shower," Colt breathes out, rolling over to glance up at me.

"Come on, let's take another." Holding out my hand, he

takes it, letting me pull him to a stand.

What a fan-fucking-tastic way to spend my Sunday morning.

CHAPTER 35

COLT BISHOP

Walking up to the booth at Lou's that my parents are sitting in, I slide in across from them, my stomach in knots. "Hey, guys."

A smile spreads across my mom's bright face. "Hi, honey. How're you doing?"

"Great, actually." Elation fills me as I glance between the two of them. "I had physical therapy this morning before coming here, and they cleared me."

My dad's brows shoot up. "Really? That's great, son."

Mom's face brightens. "Oh, baby, that's wonderful! Does that mean you can compete this season?"

"It's looking like it." I nod. Overall, my recovery has been a pretty smooth journey, but I didn't want to get my hopes up and jinx myself, so I never let myself believe I'd get to compete. Hearing this today was an incredible feeling. The season doesn't start for another couple of months, and anything could happen between now and then, but I'm finally allowing myself to think it's a real possibility. It's relieving.

"I'm so happy for you," she gushes, placing her hand over mine on the table. "And so proud of you. You've worked so hard, and I know this hasn't been easy on you, but you did it."

"Thanks." Hearing her say that lights me up inside.

Glancing awkwardly at my dad, I'm surprised to find a smiling face looking back at me. "I'm proud of you, Colt," he grunts. "I know how hard it can be to come back from an injury that takes you out of the game. You did good, and you should be proud."

My chest swells hearing him say that. Since finding out about my relationship with William, my dad and I have talked a handful of times, but never anything in depth. Things have been awkward, to say the least, and I was starting to think he may never come around until he invited me to lunch with them today. My dad's never been big on his feelings. He'll tell me he's proud of me, but he won't gush about it the way my mom does. So, hearing him say all this has my throat aching.

Our server comes, dropping off our drinks before taking our order.

"Is Will working today?" my mom asks before taking a sip from her Coke.

I nod, gaze darting subconsciously to my dad. "Doug's out with the flu, so he's busier than usual this week."

An uncomfortable, stuffy type of silence falls over us at that, and I'm more than a little shocked when it's my father who breaks it.

Fidgeting with the napkin in front of him, he clears his throat. "Listen, I know things have been tense between us, and I'm sorry about that." My eyes dart to my mom, who looks as surprised as I feel. "Finding out about you and Will was... a shock, to put it mildly. I could've handled it better, I'll admit that, but I needed some time to let it settle in. I mean, imagine if you had a kid and you found out Shooter was dating him."

That makes me snort.

"That would be weird, right?"

"Yes."

"I love you both and want nothing more than for both of you to be happy." He pauses, fidgeting with the napkin some more. He's nervous. "And if that's with each other, then I'll be supportive of that."

My heart beats harder as my mind spins. "You will?"

"Yes, I will." He nods. "But for Christ's sake, I don't want to hear about your guys' sex life ever. That's where I draw the line."

My mom and I look at each other at the same time and laugh. "That's fair," I choke out. "I wouldn't dream of discussing that with you anyway."

"Okay, great."

And that's that. Our food comes, and no more discussion of William and I comes up, but I feel lighter and... happier. I didn't realize how much I needed to hear him say that until now. We all finish eating, and once my dad pays the bill, we go our separate ways, but not before my mom invites William and me over for dinner on Sunday.

Excited and kind of beside myself, I leave the diner and head straight to William's office. I need to tell him face to face.

"Hi, Colt. Here to see William?"

I smile over at Meg on the other side of the desk as I walk in. "Please. Is he with a patient?"

"You're in luck," she says. "He just finished up with one. I'll go grab him."

My body is buzzing.

A few minutes later, my sexy white coat wearing man walks

through the door, a warm smile on his face as he takes me in. "Well, this is a surprise." Leading me into the back, we go into a patient room where he pulls me in for a kiss. "Is everything okay? How did lunch go?"

"Get this," I say before diving into what happened at the diner.

"Colt, that's amazing," he says when I finish. "I told you he'd come around."

"I know, you were right." I huff out a chuckle.

"I'm always right." He smirks, winking at me. "When are you going to learn?"

"Oh, please." I roll my eyes, not even trying to hide the smile.

"My mom invited us over for dinner on Sunday. We should bring your dad too."

"He'd like that, and so would I."

The weight of today hits me—getting cleared for competing, lunch, my feelings for William, all of it—and it's overwhelming in the very best way. "I love you," I breathe softly. "I love you so much. Thank you for believing in me, for believing in us. Thank you for believing my dad would forgive us, even when I didn't." Emotion clings to my throat. "Just… thank you so much for being everything I never knew I needed or wanted."

"Colt…" Eyes now glassy and red, he takes my hand. "Move in with me."

My heart skips a beat. "What?"

"Don't feel like you have to say yes," he replies. "I know it's a lot. And maybe you don't want to live with me and my dad, but if you do, I would love for you to move in with me. The idea of waking up with you next to me and falling asleep with you in my arms every single night, sharing that house with you, it would make me the happiest man on the planet."

"Yes," I say without needing even a single second to

consider it.

"Yes?"

"Yes, I'll move in with you."

"Are you sure? My dad isn't moving out."

Chuckling, I say, "Yes, I'm more than sure. And of course, your dad isn't moving out. I wouldn't want him to."

A smile curves his lips. "Yes?"

"One hundred percent, yes."

"I love you." He pulls me in for a kiss.

"I love you too," I gasp into his mouth.

Getting injured over the summer felt like the end of the world to me. It felt like I was losing everything that mattered most to me. Never in a million years did I expect to find something so special, so meaningful, so life changing, from a moment that I thought ruined my life. I didn't lose anything.

In fact, I've gained so much more than I ever could've imagined.

EPILOGUE
WILLIAM ANDINO

SIX MONTHS LATER

The energy in the arena is high, excitement buzzing all around. Sitting in the stands with my father to my right, Max and Trish to my left, we wait anxiously for the bull riding section of the night to begin. It's night one of Stampede Days, and the one-year anniversary of Colt's accident. He's had an amazing season so far, all things considered. It was a bit of a slow go at first, but he's gotten some great scores over the last few rodeos.

I've been able to go to almost every event he's competed in that's within driving distance. Watching him in his element has been nothing short of mesmerizing. He was so nervous about not being able to heal in time, so getting to watch him do everything I knew he'd be able to do has been rewarding. The pride I feel for him is immense.

The announcer booms over the loudspeaker, and my pulse kicks up a notch. "Here we go," I murmur, nudging Max with my elbow. He grins, meeting my gaze as the man introduces Colt. Trish claps her hands, a wide smile on her face, even though she's nervous. Despite his great season so far, I think it's natural for Trish, as his mother, to be uneasy about him competing in the same event that hurt him just last year.

Heart beating a mile a minute and my palms sweaty, I watch Colt drop onto the back of the bull behind the bucking chute. Even from all the way over here, I can see his confidence. He exudes it in waves. Getting his hand just right, and making sure the rope is tightened, he nods, raising his other hand in the air as the gate gets ripped open.

The angry bull shoots out of the gate, bucking, kicking, and spinning, all the while Colt takes every last bit of it, never faltering. He rides the motion like a wave, almost like he's expecting every single move from the beast. Just like his father, Colt is a natural. He was made to do this, and it shows. The buzzer sounds, and I'm up off the bleachers without a second thought, clapping loudly and cheering, so fucking proud of him. Beside me, his parents are on their feet, clapping joyously too, as is my father. Before he's ushered out of the arena, he looks in our direction, a proud smile bursting across his face.

After the rodeo ends, we all meet Colt behind the arena. He's still wearing all his gear, and he looks damn good in it, but no surprise, he's swapped out his cowboy hat for the baseball hat I got him for Christmas. Trish pulls him in for a hug first.

"Honey, you did so good!" she gushes, pulling back and cupping his face in her hands. "I'm so dang proud of you."

He chuckles. "Thanks, Mom."

"You really showed that bull who's boss," my dad chimes in. "You did incredible, Colt."

Colt pulls him in for a hug. "Thanks, Roger."

My chest warms every single time I see the love between them. My dad has welcomed Colt into our home with open arms, and their bond has done nothing but flourish since Colt moved in all those months ago. Sure, they gang up on me more often than not, and they're both harping on me to get a second dog for Winnie to play with, but seeing my dad so happy all the time makes my heart sing. There was always a little part of me that was worried about Colt moving in. Worried that maybe he'd get sick of living with my dad, or maybe they wouldn't always see eye to eye under the same roof, but it's been nothing like that. It's like Colt was always meant to come in and be part of our family.

"Proud of you, son," Max grunts, wrapping his arms around him in a big bear hug.

Their relationship has gotten so much better over the last six months. Same with mine and Max's. The first few months, things were awkward, and it felt almost like walking on eggshells, but I'd like to think Max has gotten used to the idea of Colt and me because it doesn't seem to bother him at all anymore. Sunday dinners are back to being a weekly thing, and Max and I even hang out by ourselves again. It's been nice, getting to have my friend but also the man I love.

Colt glances at me, lips curved up, eyes shimmering. "You kicked ass out there," I murmur, wrapping a hand around the back of his neck and hauling him into me. "So fucking proud of you."

"Thanks, Doc," he breathes before crashing his mouth into mine.

"Alright, you two," Max grumbles, and both of us choke out a laugh.

"Jeez, Dad," Colt calls out, smirking. "What a fucking cock—"

"Don't even think of finishing that sentence," Max cuts in,

and I can't help but chuckle.

Trish laughs, rubbing Max's arm. "That's enough. Come on, you guys. I baked a cake. Let's all go back to our place, and we can have some to celebrate."

Arm around Colt's shoulder, we all walk toward the parking lot. Max and Trish drove themselves, while my dad, Colt, and I took my car. The drive to their house takes about ten minutes, and the entire time I'm alternating my gaze from the road to Colt in the backseat. Whenever my father comes with us anywhere, Colt refuses to sit shotgun. He and I both know climbing in and out of the backseat is hard for my dad with his hip. The space is too small, but he'll never admit it or speak up. So instead, Colt insists he'd rather sit in the backseat.

His heart is so big and so warm, and he's so full of love. There's so much more to Colt than what meets the eye. Sure, he's cocky, sarcastic, and not afraid to say exactly what's on his mind, but he's also loyal as hell and one of the most caring people I've ever met.

If somebody would've told me when I made the decision to move back to Copper Lake that I'd end up not only dating my best friend's son, but that I would be so deeply in love with him, I would think they lost their mind. This is not at all how I envisioned my life ending up when I came back here, but I can't imagine it any other way.

Pulling into Max's driveway, I put the car in park and turn off the ignition. Climbing out, my dad tosses me a look over the hood of the car. "I'll meet you boys inside. Try to keep your clothes on." He winks at us as Colt breathes out a laugh, and then he disappears into the house.

Without a second thought, I pull Colt into my arms, his wrapping automatically around my middle. He smells like dirt and cattle and slightly like sweat, but I don't care.

"Have I told you lately how proud I am of you?"

Lips tipping up, he breathes out a contented sigh. "I could always hear it again."

Closing the distance, I press my lips to his, kissing him slowly. I slip my tongue past his parted lips, rolling against his, savoring the flavor of him. I don't think I'll ever get tired of kissing Colt Bishop.

"Look at how far you've come in the last year," I tell him, forehead resting against his. "This time last year, you were having surgery, and now you're kicking ass in the arena. I'm constantly amazed by you, Colt. I don't think you even realize how spectacular you are."

His eyes are glassy as he watches me. "Aw, getting soft on me, Doc?" he teases, but I know he's feeling just as much emotion as I am. It's written all over his face.

"I'm serious. I'm so lucky you're mine."

"Are you kidding?" he murmurs. "I'm the lucky one."

"I love you, Colt."

"And I love you, William."

The End

Turn the page for a sneak peek at Every Promise Broken, Copper Lake Book 5.

PROLOGUE

FIVE YEARS AGO

WHIT BOWMAN

Pulling up outside of my house, I put the car in park but I don't get out yet. It's been a long, grueling day, and I need a minute of silence and solitude before I go inside and face the brick wall that's been erected between me and my husband. A wall that I didn't build, nor did I want in place, but it's one I can't penetrate either way. In the matter of a few months, I've watched my once-loving husband transform into somebody I don't recognize. I've watched grief eat at him, destroy him from the inside out, and I've watched it rip us apart. Sixty-seven days ago, my sweet, heart of an angel husband lost his parents in a terrible, brutal car accident, and he hasn't been the same since.

Grief is something I'm familiar with, having lost my own mother a few years ago, but where I leaned on him through it all, he's pushed me away. He's pushed everybody away. Losing a parent is a pain unlike any I've ever experienced, and you're bound to come out of it a different person than you were before, but damnit, I miss my husband. I miss feeling his touch. His love. I miss sharing how our days were over dinner. I miss dancing in the kitchen late at night. I miss him so damn much, and the hardest part about it all is physically, he hasn't gone anywhere. When I finally work up the courage to go inside, he'll be in there, quiet and closed off. Probably on his second or third glass of whiskey of the evening.

He's here, but not really. Mentally, he's checked out.

Sometimes I don't even know if he realizes I'm there. We sleep beside each other every single night, but at some point after I've fallen asleep, he leaves. I'll wake up in the morning, and he'll be passed out on the couch downstairs, in the rocking chair on the front porch, or even clear out in the barn.

After several long minutes, I exhale a deep, exhausted sigh, turn off the ignition to my truck, and I climb out. It's time to face the music. The sad, lovesick part of me holds onto the thought that maybe tonight will be different. Maybe tonight he'll open up to me, let me in. Let me hold him. Maybe he'll finally cry on my shoulder and let me take his pain away. Maybe we'll finally connect in a way we haven't since before the accident. Maybe tonight will finally be the night that we make love again. It's been months, and I barely remember what it feels like to have his hands on my body, his hot breath on my neck.

The house is dark as I walk through the front door. Kicking off my shoes and hanging up my coat, I pad through the quiet home in search of Conrad. My guess is he's out on the back porch, a drink in his hand and a hollow look in his eyes. Either that, or the bedroom. It wasn't that long ago that I'd come home from work to dinner on the table and a kiss on the cheek. I don't bother turning on the kitchen light as I pass through toward the back door. The window sitting in front of the sink that overlooks the backyard tells me I'm right. He's out there. The bottle of whiskey is sitting, opened, on the counter, an amber mess trickled beside it where I'm guessing he spilled while pouring himself a glass.

Conrad doesn't bother looking up as I step onto the porch, nor does he glance my way when I drop down into the swing right beside him. An opened pack of Marlboro Reds sit on the table between the two chairs, a Zippo on one side of it and his nearly empty rocks glass on the other. Silence settles between us for a moment. It's tense and uncomfortable, and still so foreign to me. It never used to be like this. Things never felt this hard between him and I.

"How was your day?" I finally ask, my voice quiet, timid. Like he's a wild animal I'm trying not to spook.

That at least gets him to look at me. His once vibrant chestnut eyes now regard me with an emptiness I don't recognize. They're muted, like he's hollow inside. Like everything that once made Conrad who he is has been carved out.

"Fine," he replies. It's what he says every night when I come home and ask him that same question. Four letters. One syllable. A lie. He's not fine. He's destroyed and riddled with grief that he doesn't know how to deal with. He's numb.

"Have you eaten yet?" I ask. "I can make us something."

"I'm not hungry."

My eyes dip down to take in the glass filled with whiskey. The cigarettes he never used to smoke. The way they're taunting me. "Have you eaten at all today?"

Conrad's jaw clenches as he bites down on his molars, and I already know before he even says a word, that was the wrong question to ask. "I'm not a fucking child, Whit." There's a harshness to his words that before his parents died, he'd never taken with me. It's still jarring, even months later. "You don't need to treat me as such. Yes, I've fucking eaten today. You don't need to babysit me."

Flinching at his tone, my thumb rolls my wedding ring around on my finger over and over again as I force myself to breathe in, then out. Wanting to soothe him without pissing him off further. "I know you're not a child, Connie," I say softly. Slowly. "I'm just trying to help. I'm worried about you, and you won't let me in."

"You don't need to be worried about me," he bites out, grabbing the glass off the table so roughly it sloshes over, covering his hand. "I said I'm fine."

My heart shatters for him over how not fine he is, but it also breaks a little for me too. My husband feels like a stranger to me, and I don't know how to fix it. He won't open up to me, won't let me in. It feels like my marriage is drifting away right before my eyes, and there's nothing I can do about it.

Before I even have a chance to respond, he's out of his chair and in the house, screen door slamming behind him. Hurt pricks the back of my eyes and tears spill over before I have a chance to stop them. I don't know how long I sit on this porch, letting all the emotion expel from my body, but by the time I go back inside, Conrad is nowhere to be found. I don't bother looking for him, either. He's made it clear he doesn't want to talk, and there's only so many times I can be pushed away before my ego can't handle it anymore.

My marriage is the single most important thing in my life, and all I want is to fix it. To be there for my husband. But the more time that passes, the more I think our marriage died that night in that crash alongside his parents. I'm losing him, and

I'm terrified.

Coming November 15th.

Pre-Order Here

Acknowledgments

My daughters. They're the best little cheerleaders I could ever ask for.

My family. I'm so blessed to have such a supportive family. I'm so completely thankful for your love and support, even when writing seems to take up my entire life.

Mads. You deserve an award. Thank you so, so much for everything you've done and said throughout writing this book. You were everything I needed in an alpha reader, and your love and obsession with Colt and William means the world to me. I love you so big.

Shann. I freaking love you. Your feedback and love surrounding this book was everything to me. I can not thank you enough.

Jill and Becca. You two are beyond words amazing, and I love you both so much. You were there for me so much during this book, with everything that was going on, and I could never thank you both enough.

Ali and Ash. Incredible beta readers with the most hyped up commentary ever. I love you both, and you're forever stuck with me.

Kenzie. You're the best. Period. LOL.

My Amazing Patrons. Y'all saw every part of this story first, and your constant support means the world to me. Getting to share them with you so early was such an incredible experience. I adore you all so much!

The Author Agency. Becca and Shauna—you ladies are INCREDIBLE. I can't thank you enough for all that you do for me and my release. You're so on top of everything and so helpful. Working with you is a breeze every single time.

ARC Readers. Thank you to everybody who early read this book, everyone who reviewed and/or made gorgeous edits, and everyone who simply hyped the book up and shared teasers. I appreciate y'all so much!

Trista Boggs. Thank you for coming up with the name for Conrad's ranch—Grazing Acres. I loved getting to get suggestions from my patrons for a ranch name.

Katie with Fortuitous Designs. Thank you so much for this incredible discreet cover. Out of all 5 of the series, this is my favorite discreet.

Mel with Mel D. Designs. Thank you for bringing the gorgeous model cover to life. As always, you're an absolute pleasure to work with, and I cannot thank you enough!

Staci with Quirky Bird. Thank you for the beautiful illustrated cover! You're an absolute gem.

All my Readers. Without y'all, I wouldn't even be here. I love and appreciate each of you more than you'll ever know. You're helping make my dreams come true, and that's still so surreal to me. So, whether this is your first book by me or you've been here since the beginning... thank you.

About the Author

Ashley James is an LGBTQIA+ author who enjoys writing (and reading) the toxic, swoony, broody, filthy talking, red flag men. She is originally from Washington State—and no, not Seattle—but now resides in South Carolina with her two daughters and her Sphynx kitties, Goose and Houston.

Connect with the Author

Books by Ashley James

The Deepest Desires Series
Barred Desires (Book One)
Forsaken Desires (Book Two)
Illicit Desires (Book Three)

Hidden Affairs Series
Brazen Affairs (Book One)
Storm Clouds and Devastation (Book Two)
Insatiable Hunger (Book Three)

Copper Lake Series
Eight Seconds to Ride (Book One)
Dirt Road Secrets (Book Two)
Burning the Midnight Oil (Book Three)
The History Between Us (Book Four)
Every Promise Broken (Book Five, Pre-Order Now)

Standalones
Kismet
Wounded
Say My Name
Whiskey Nights and Neon Dreams

Made in the USA
Las Vegas, NV
19 January 2025